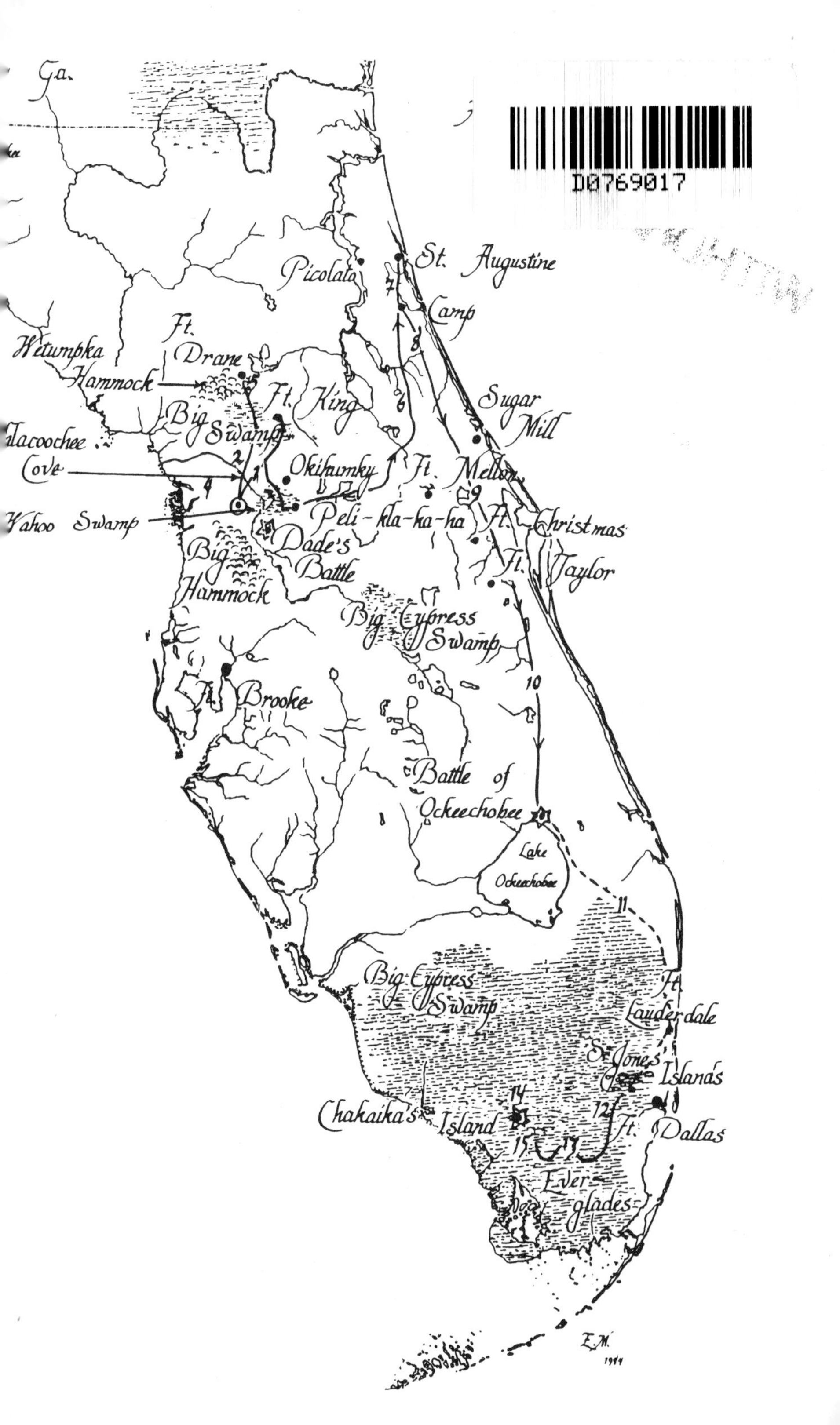
Ga.
St. Augustine
Picolata
Camp
Ft. Drane
Wetumpka
Hammock
Ft. King
Big Swamp
Sugar Mill
lacoochee
Cove
Okihumky
Ft. Mellon
Wahoo Swamp
Peli-kla-ka-ha
Ft. Christmas
Dade's Battle
Ft. Taylor
Big Hammock
Big Cypress Swamp
Ft. Brooke
Battle of Ockeechobee
Lake Ockeechobee
Big Cypress Swamp
Ft. Lauderdale
St. Jones
Islands
Chakaika's Island
Ft. Dallas
Ever-glades
E.M.
1944

Say These Names
(Remember Them)

Books by Betty Sue Cummings

Hew Against the Grain
Let a River *Be*
Now, Ameriky
Turtle
Say These Names (Remember Them)

Say These Names
(Remember Them)

Betty Sue Cummings

Pineapple Press, Englewood, Florida

Inquiries should be addressed to Pineapple Press, Inc., P.O. Box 314, Englewood, Florida 33533.

Library of Congress Cataloging in Publication Data

Cummings, Betty Sue
Say these names (remember them).

1. Mikasuki Indians — Fiction. I. Title.
PS 3553.U439S2 1984 813'.54 84-11422
ISBN 0-910923-15-9

Typography by: Creative Composition, Palmetto, Florida
Printed by: Edward Brothers, Ann Arbor, Michigan

To the women of the Miccosukee Tribe
and their true friend, Edwina Hoffman

This is a novel about the Miccosukee Indian women and children who survived the Second Seminole War in Florida. Their suffering was incredible; the fact that they survived at all was even more amazing. The children had to learn to be silent, and long after the war they were still very quiet.

Some of the characters are fictional, some real. One actual person was Apayaka, a legendary hero of the wars, a planner and thinker. A survivor. He lived in the Everglades afterward, except for a brief time at his beloved Silver Springs, and was nursed lovingly through years of senility by his people. He lived more than 100 years.

The Miccosukee women were heroic in their efforts to save their children and preserve their culture.

Contents

Say These Names
(Remember Them)

one

When See-ho-kee was a small girl, she asked her grandmother a question. "Who am I?"

Her grandmother gave her a look of alertness and sharp focus, and See-ho-kee was surprised at the length of her answer.

"You are See-ho-kee. You are Yakitisee—red person. You are Miccosukee. You are of the important Wind clan. Women of the Wind clan are called the grandmothers of the tribe. I am *everybody's* grandmother. So is your mother, and so will you be. As a member of the Wind clan, you will be allowed to take up the club against adulterers even after the club has been used up to four times."

"I don't want to do that."

"In the old days we did it," her grandmother said

sternly, "and there was not much adultery either."

She shook her head with vexation and went on with her answer. "According to the white people you are Seminole, because your people left the northern villages and came here to Florida.

"You are Hitch-e-tee. You speak Mikasuki. I used to speak Mus-ko-gee Creek as well, and now the Creeks fight against us with the white man. You are Creek from the Coo-sau and the Tal-la-poo-sa and also from the Chat-to-ho-che. We traveled those creeks and knew each other in the old times. Our warriors fought each other, some for white Americans, some against. We will be brothers and sisters again, all against the whites.

"You are your parents' daughter, part of them. You are my granddaughter. You are part of the Che-au-haus. My grandmother lived in their village."

The old woman hesitated, and her sharp look softened. Tears suddenly went down her cheeks.

"You are part of all the villages I used to know."

"What villages?" See-ho-kee asked. "Have I been there?"

"No. Those villages are dead now. No one lives there. Those people came here or went west. Or died. Still, you are part of them."

"What are the villages?" See-ho-kee persisted. Her grandmother threw her head back and sang the names so fast that See-ho-kee's ears refused to hear.

"You should remember those names," her grandmother told her.

"How can I remember them when I can't even say them?" See-ho-kee asked.

And this was the beginning of her grandmother's stomp-dance and name-song, for her grandmother was determined to have See-ho-kee learn the names of her ancestors' villages.

two

The Miccosukee babies were dying. See-ho-kee had thought about this every day since her baby sister had died thirty days ago after the big freeze. Their mother's milk had ceased to flow for want of food, and slowly, gently the baby had gone. She was sad for her mother who was old for having babies, who may not have another. The war killed the babies more surely than it killed warriors; the freeze made sure it would happen.

Now she and her family walked the trails northeast from Ouithlacoochee Cove to Fort King where the great council would be held. First in line were her father, Coosa-amathle, great warrior and micco of their clan; Eemathle, her sixteen-year-old brother, who used to be called Hopoy before he proved himself in the hunt; and Thlicklin, the second brother, already thirteen. His new name was Hitchiti-hajo, and she tried to remember it and say it out of respect for his manhood, but it came hard for her, for Thlicklin was a beloved brother and friend, and the new name was strange. Sometimes her father sent him running far ahead on the trail to watch for white soldiers, and when he ran, she thought of him as Hitchiti-hajo, but when he returned, waving and smiling, he became Thlicklin again. All the men carried guns and ammunition, and their medicine bags.

Next in the line walked her mother and herself, carrying their goods, the food and pots and blankets. Far behind was her grandmother. She looked back and loved the small, bent woman.

The walk was not wasted. Her father talked to her brothers, using the time to teach them all they had not learned about fighting, tracking, hunting. He talked in open land, not in the forest where spirits might lurk. She could tell by his proud demeanor that he was enjoying his role of teacher, making up for the years his son had been disciplined by their uncle, when he must stand aside. Never once had her father scratched the arm of a single child of his.

See-ho-kee's talking companion should be her mother, Pi-co-yee. Only last year had she heard her mother's name for the first time, for her mother (like all mothers) had given up her name when her first child came. She was "Hopoy's mother" then, and now her name had changed with his to "Eemathle's Mother." But See-ho-kee remembered the immediate pleasure she had taken in her mother's girlhood name. PI-CO-YEE. It sounded like the familiar trill of a little field bird. Pi-co-YEE! She must never say the name; it would discount her mother's importance, but often she said it to herself (Pi-co-YEE!) and thought of the little girl her mother used to be.

Her father was the one who disclosed the name to See-ho-kee. When he was smiling and joking with her mother once, the name suddenly stumbled out, and he hadn't even realized he had said it.

She wished her mother would talk too. Her mother was the same gentle, friendly person she had been before the baby died, but now she was silent. She had not overcome the weakness of spirit that struck her after the baby died.

See-ho-kee wanted to talk to her mother about the baby, but her mother's face forbade talk. Why was it Pi-co-yee could talk and laugh so much after her labors produced the baby, as if the struggle had been nothing, and yet not talk at all nor laugh nor smile for a month after she died? It was a flaw in her mother, and soon her father would become impatient over it.

Maybe her mother blamed herself. The baby had become chilled while she searched for roots for the family, and she should not blame herself for that. She couldn't blame herself for the freeze that dropped from the sky and killed their crops.

It was a flaw in her mother, this continued grief. But See-ho-kee herself could not forget the baby. She had spent many hours with the baby, watching constantly to see that she didn't cry aloud when white soldiers came near the Cove of the Ouithlacoochee. She was ready at all times to clap a hand over the tiny mouth, and she never permitted her little sister to cry.

They walked swiftly on. Coosa-amathle looked back, saw that her mother stooped under the burden. "Hitchiti-hajo," he said. He motioned to Thlicklin, gave a quick hand wave toward Pi-co-yee. Thlicklin was chagrined to take up woman's task. Baby work. See-ho-kee saw him turn from a warrior into a boy again, and she grinned. He was really no better than she was. They were, after all, nearly the same age.

Hitchiti-hajo already had killed a drunk white hunter

who galloped his horse to trample a group of young men. Hitchiti leaped, pulled the white man down under the crashing hooves.

"Hajo!" her father had said that night. "Hajo! Wild warrior!"

The white man's body was disposed of. The horse was slapped homeward. The end of it. Thlicklin became a man.

Eefe, the dog, ran the forest behind them, as he had been trained to do when there was danger ahead. He was a joyful, rough-coated dog, an Indian dog whose ancestors had walked toward the rising sun alongside her own ancestors. See-ho-kee was his special person, and she took his presence and protection for granted.

Her family loved him, would not eat him, even in time of famine, but they kept him half-wild, forced him to find his own food, took it if they needed it, cuffed him away, sent him out for more. Eefe, her friend.

More caution must be taken now, for they entered open country, not as familiar. She saw her father talk to Eemathle who then ran ahead.

They passed a graveyard. Quickly See-ho-kee opened her medicine bag and took out a bit of ginseng. She chewed it very fast and spat it out to one side, then the other. Four times she spat. Ahead of her, her father went through the same ritual. It would drive away the ghosts.

They were silent now. It was a terrible thing they had had to learn — to be silent whenever they were near white men. See-ho-kee remembered very well the sudden anguished fear in her mother's eyes at a scream of joy that got past her throat when she had caught her first fish. Her mother's hand had clapped hard across her mouth. Her mother had promised her, "When your great-uncle comes, he will punish you."

She had dreaded this. Apayaka, her great-uncle, was very dear to her; he and she laughed together and tumbled in the dirt, playing like puppies. So hated by the white man that they named him Sam-Jones-be-damned, he was loved by her, for he had never yet had to do an uncle's duty and punish her. And there were no other uncles. But Apayaka had come, and as Pi-co-yee had said, he talked to her about keeping her voice low, and he had given her three scratches on the arm with gar teeth.

She watched the blood flow down her arm and felt her tears flow, for her inner spirit hurt over the punishment. A bitter lesson quickly learned. She had never spoken in a loud voice since that day.

The freeze had touched these trees with deadly hands, making the walk from Ouithlacoochee Cove grim and sad. See-ho-kee looked at the monotony of brown grass, killed by the frost.

Other families had stayed at the cove to wait for their warriors to come home. But her father agreed to take his family to be with their cousins and to help carry back food given by the white soldiers to persuade them to attend the council. It was always like this. The white men needed to talk, and they waited till the red people were starving and said, "Come to council and we will give you food." She began to get hungry for white man's food. This time they would take home food enough so they could resist the white soldiers longer. And they would see Apayaka who told them this would be a peaceful council, for now the white soldiers understood the danger they invited when they attacked Miccosukees. Many Seminoles had already left the cove, knowing that the whites were searching for them.

They would return to their own cheke which stood a little separate from the others in a beautiful hidden place where there was water, then trees, then swamp grass, then fields of pumpkin. She knew it well, could not be lost there, and she sometimes laughed to herself thinking of the white soldiers stumbling all around it blindly.

Already she felt homesick for the cheke. Yet she felt more homesick on those occasions when Coosa-amathle, her father, left them to join other warriors and to attend council.

At home, their slaves Julius and Marcy were left to shift for themselves and to do whatever they could to improve the food supply.

King's Gifts. That was the title Julius claimed for them. See-ho-kee believed they were related to each other, though not brother and sister. The two blacks made themselves useful whenever anybody thought to ask them for help. They usually lived in the village with other blacks, but lately Negroes and Indians had drawn closer to each other for mutual protection.

Here they came to an opening in the trees, and Eemathle was not back. Her father motioned to Hitchiti-hajo to run ahead and see that all was safe for the party. Her brother went swiftly into the trail through the sawgrass, careful not to let the grass touch him and make little cuts that were hard to heal. They waited in silence at the edge of the woods, ready to disappear in a moment. She tried not to think about the white man's food; they had not eaten much since yesterday.

She and her mother and her grandmother squatted near the trees so that they could not be seen above the swamp grass, and her father melted against a tree so that she could hardly make out his form. Where were her two brothers? She felt irritable that they hadn't given the safe sign. Ah, there now. Her father waved to her mother. They arose and went on, walking northeast to the beautiful springs where she and her family had bathed when they first moved to this southern place. Now Ouithlacoochee was home and she could no longer remember the places in the north.

"Do you know, Grandmother, that I can no longer even remember the places in north Florida where we used to live?" she said.

Her grandmother shook her head and frowned. "You must search your mind and say aloud what you remember and teach all of it to your children." The old woman gasped for breath as she always did after a long hard walk. "For a long time I couldn't think of the villages I knew in Georgia. The shock of leaving them drove them away. I even forgot their names. But as I began to remember them, I sang the names, and then I remembered the villages too. This minute I see a beautiful field in Cow-e-tugh where the corn is ready to pick, and I hear friends laughing there, all because the name came back."

"Did you live there?" See-ho-kee said.

"No, but I knew the town. All of us visited and traded back and forth." She became quiet, and See-ho-kee, accustomed to these silent times, waited. "All those villages are empty now, burned and rotted. No more cornfields, no laughing friends. That's why I taught you to say the names, so they won't be forgotten."

See-ho-kee felt some guilt, for she had listened to her grandmother's recital of names all those times for the music in them. She wasn't sure she could still say them.

"You want me to sing them?" her grandmother asked.

"Dear old woman," See-ho-kee's mother interposed, "rest your breath for a moment, and say the names tonight when there are many to hear."

The grandmother nodded in agreement. See-ho-kee resolved to pay careful attention tonight, to set the names in her mind forever.

Now she saw Eemathle lift his arm and motion them to come, and in moments Hitchiti-hajo was back to help protect the party.

She stepped into the sun, lifted her face gratefully, her eyes closed; she felt the sun's good touch. Her mother saw to it that they had their burdens, and the men moved ahead with their guns ready, Hitchiti-hajo with his bow and arrows. Soon, he had told her, he would take a gun from a white man and have his own. But more than likely, she had thought, he would have to buy one that would come by ship from far away.

Hitchiti-hajo's lack of a gun reminded her of the embarrassment suffered by Yaha Chatee, her Wahoo Swamp lover since they were children, for he also had no gun. And not much else either. For this reason her relatives had cautioned her against him as a husband. Take Fixonechee, they had said. He will keep food on the table. He is older and more settled.

What else could she do? Yaha Chatee had never spoken to her of marriage. She recognized the difficulty he had, lost from his own family and raised by Nuff-kee's family, too poor to have a hunting gun or a horse. Still, she wished he would speak.

Yaha was so different from Fixonechee. Yaha was pleasant and fun-loving; he dearly loved dancing; he ran like a deer, and his legs were heavily muscled. He was smooth, silken, lovely to touch. His body had only a little hair, and she loved him as a playmate and lover.

But Fixonechee, older, firm in his opinions, courted her with vigor, tried many times to persuade her to lie with him. She tried to think how it would be to let him love her. Yaha Chatee's hands upon her could make her open with desire, and even now, thinking of him, she felt lustful, and she planned to keep him for her lover till her marriage to Fixonechee, for afterward there would never be another chance.

To her amazement, Yaha Chatee would have no more to do with her. His cheerful optimism disappeared, and he became somber and hurt. Why hadn't he spoken if he felt that serious about her?

She was very curious about Fixonechee's love-making and sometimes thought about it with some excitement. But he had an eye for other young women, she noticed, and she would wait till they were bound. He was a thin, taut man, almost angry. When he talked about the white man, he laughed harshly, his teeth gleaming brightly, and she discussed this with her mother. "He is weeping, not laughing," her mother had said. It was true. She observed the same kind of grating, coarse laughter from her brothers and father sometimes, and she always remembered that they were actually weeping.

Fixonechee wore glasses which he had taken from a home at a sugar mill on the east coast, and he loved them though they sometimes made him miss a shot at game. Indeed, he was vainer than most other men about his clothes; he loved costumes. She half-believed he didn't really care what she thought; it gave her a feeling of frivolity and stupidity, for it took away her responsibility.

But he was considered a good catch, and she had agreed to marry him.

She must put Yaha Chatee out of her mind. She couldn't think of him as a husband and father, though she wondered why he hadn't given her a baby, for they had lain together twice after her periods began. He seemed too young to be married, too lighthearted, too smooth, too amorous. He did well for a person his age — her own age, but he still seemed to be a boy, while she thought of herself as a *woman*. You didn't choose a husband on his ability as a lover.

Yet, these days sadness had come to live with her — sadness for the babies, sadness for the loss of Yaha Chatee, who could make her shout with pleasure, who would lie close to her and hold her afterward, who would grin at the teasing of her family. She didn't worry. It was her right to meet Yaha Chatee. Only her mother frowned, for she feared See-ho-kee was getting too serious about the lovemaking.

The cookpots and blankets had been lifted again.

See-ho-kee didn't mind the load, was glad to carry all she could, wanted to do her part to hurry the visit with Apayaka, who had sent for them and who must be eager to see her too. She also wanted to see Silver Springs again and to stare down into their clear beauty. They were getting close now, a shivery thought, a stomach-wrenching thought, for she would not only see her uncle and the wonderful spring lake; she would see the great log fort the white soldiers had built; she would see her first white person. Women were too protected, she sometimes thought, never to get to see a white person, even at a distance. She was bursting with curiosity about them, and no matter how afraid she was, she intended to look till she was satisfied.

She studied the hundreds of tracks on the trail, felt the sweep of humanity moving to the cantonment, *Fort King*, those strange harsh words. Sometimes the children of her clan said the ugly words in mockery and laughed in imitation of the angry laughter of their warrior-fathers. *Fort King! Fort Brooke!* But under See-ho-kee's quiet smile traveled a feeling of sickness when she heard the childish jeers.

The trail crossed another path from the south, and they began to meet other Indians, some of whom spoke Creek so that she couldn't understand them. Her father greeted the men in a slow, hesitating voice. Her own language was Mikasuki. All continued on the trip. The council would begin tomorrow, and they must hurry. There was one woman tending two small children; See-ho-kee smiled and her mother nodded. The woman smiled and spoke in Creek.

The sun was approaching the treetops in the west when they at last saw the stockade, a marvel indeed. Twenty feet high. Split logs, the flat side in, a platform against the inside wall where the soldiers could stand with their guns and shoot through little holes at the enemy.

The enemy: her father, her brothers, herself. She stood a

distance away and stared through the great open gates, amazed to think that the white man, so stupid in battle, so helpless in cypress canoe-carving, could build this strong barricade.

Her family stood at a safe distance looking at the fort. It stood on a high knoll overlooking forest, where the white soldiers could look down upon the oaks, sweet gums, and hickories. No Indians could approach the fort without being seen.

In the middle of the stockade was a tall building with an open space at the top where a white soldier moved constantly around, looking out. She wished she could see him closely. Two Indian men, dressed in knee-length robes and loose turbans, approached the gate. Neither carried a gun, she saw, though both wore powder bags like her father's. As they reached the gate, a great tuneless clamor sounded, and See-ho-kee jumped. Her mother laughed and it was a welcome sound. "It's a cowbell," she said. The two Indians saluted and went in.

She still had not actually seen what a white person looked like. Now she saw a column of them marching across the gate; only a quick glimpse, and they had gone, leaving her with a confused impression of their strange sick color, of their dirty blue and white uniforms and their tall dark caps. Even their walk was peculiar; choppy, heavy, unnatural. Some had heavy beards, and she wondered whether they were ashamed of it. They were different and foreign — awkward, heavy men.

Her mother called her away with a swift motion before she had looked half enough. They would go to find Apayaka now.

They went past the fort toward her uncle's cheke. Inside the fort she saw several men, both white and Indian, building a high platform, standing ten feet into the air, where the notables would sit tomorrow in council. The wood had been hacked from the forest, and the platform was still decorated with fresh twigs of leaves. She sniffed the sweet smell from the wounds on a camphor bough.

They arrived at Apayaka's town, saw here the look of permanence which Ouithlacoochee Cove villages now lacked. There they must be ready to run at any moment, grabbing up what goods they could carry and leaving everything if it were necessary. But here children played and worked with quiet happiness; women gathered at neighbors' chekes to sew or exchange foods; a man brought in a string of fish and a great land turtle. Ah. There was Nuff-kee from Wahoo Swamp. Her mother's sister's daughter, her own sister-cousin. Nuff-kee turned and saw her in the same instant, and they ran to each other, smiling. See-ho-kee felt immediate happiness, for here was the sister she could talk to when they had a chance to get away from the old ones who kept reminding them they were women now and to work more.

She looked about for Yaha Chatee, Nuff-kee's adopted brother, adopted from another clan when he was a baby. *Yaha Chatee.* Oh, Yaha, Yaha. She dismissed the times she and Nuff-kee had whispered that maybe someday they would be still closer kin. It hadn't worked out. No arrangement had been made. Yaha hadn't spoken for her. There had been no time for normal living, for talking about the future; there had been too much change, too many miles of fleeing from the whites. He should have spoken. She sighed. He wasn't here. Anyway, Fixonechee would be a better husband. A man with two horses.

"Will they let us hear the council?" she asked Nuff-kee.

Nuff-kee shrugged. "Who can stop us from listening, so long as we keep hidden in the trees?" Her voice was so sad and low See-ho-kee had to strain to hear. She studied Nuff-kee, saw how thin she was, how she drooped.

"You seem different this time, Nuff-kee. Are you growing up faster than I am? Are you thinking only of marriage and serious things now?" See-ho-kee laughed softly in triumph that she had made a joke on Nuff-kee. She saw then that Nuff-kee's face was drawn up in a weeping grimace though she made no sound and allowed no tears to come to her eyes. Something frightening plucked at See-ho-kee's heart.

"What is wrong, Nuff-kee?"

She waited while Nuff-kee struggled for words.

"Your little sister died last month?" Nuff-kee said, her voice rough and tight.

"Yes." Tears were in See-ho-kee's eyes now.

"My baby sister, who was born the same day as your sister, died this morning. Yesterday we got food from the white soldiers, but it was too late for her." See-ho-kee stared with anguish at her sister-cousin's twisted dry face.

The two girls sat and stared at each other, See-ho-kee thinking that she must never again allow herself to be happy, for each time she did, it seemed another baby died. Again she felt the painful plucking at her heart. She hid her face in a sudden storm of weeping, and in a moment she heard Nuff-kee weeping with her. When they had cried awhile, she felt more comfortable, felt as close to her cousin as if they had exchanged many words.

Now her heart-plucking spoke a sentence to her: *Maybe all the Miccosukee babies will die.* But she would not say this to her cousin who had probably thought of it herself. She wished that they could be young and playful and independent again, that they hadn't reached the age where they must be responsible for caring for the younger children of the tribe. She wished they could be silly and free, giddy as young deer. She wished she could stay in her mother's house and keep Yaha Chatee.

Still she felt better for having cried. She looked about the village. The women were at the cookpots now, her own mother sharing labor with Nuff-kee's mother. They had meat now, brought in by Apayaka men. This food would last a few days, though See-ho-kee hoped the council would go on for a long time, till they could fill their bellies and hide food in the woods where the white soldiers would stumble over it and yet not find it.

Her mother waved to her, a dismissing gesture like tossing a bird into the air and saying to it, "You're free now. Go where you wish."

See-ho-kee was delighted. There had been very few times since she was seven years old that she had been given a few minutes freedom from child-tending. It was her duty to tend any babies in the clan, not just her mother's children. Her mother smiled as she gave her this gift.

Nuff-kee waited, hopeful for a sign from her own mother, and See-ho-kee squatted by her, unwilling to leave her. Her mother's solemn face turned toward them, and she spoke to Nuff-kee's mother, who turned and lifted her hand in the same gesture. Go, little bird.

They were up and running back toward the fort. "Stay away from the white soldiers," her mother called. They wheeled as if they were on a long string and circled back. "I want to see a white person close," See-ho-kee said regretfully.

Nuff-kee's nose wrinkled with distaste. "You won't like it when you do," she said. "They are ugly, they wear strange clothes, and they have a bad smell."

They went around the village, stopped to play and talk with other children. Even while she played, she thought, maybe her father and Apayaka could make peace with the white men. Maybe they could agree not to fight, not to steal each other's cattle, not to take each other's slaves. Maybe the white men would understand that this land was home to the Miccosukees and Creeks and blacks who had moved here years ago. Maybe the white men would learn that Miccosukees would die before agreeing to follow the sun to a far-away, unknown square-ground, where there were night terrors, for the spirits of their ancestors would stay in Florida and the Miccosukees in the West would lose their gentle protection.

It was peaceful that night. Before she slept, she remembered that she still had not seen Apayaka. It didn't worry her, for she knew he was still her close friend and that he would come as soon as the talks with other Indians had ended. Now he must prepare for council. She stayed at her cousin's cheke and rested her chin on her fist as she listened to the night talk. At last she caught a glimpse of Apayaka, a tiny man with snow-white hair, his brown arms threshing the air as he talked to the other men. He shook his head, shook a small fist in the air. She caught a few words. No, they would not move. The Miccosukees would stay here.

But, Great-Uncle, the babies are dying while we run. Maybe it's wiser to go to a different place where the white man will let the babies live.

She could only *think* this; she hardly dared say it to Apayaka, for he was old and wise, an Owaale, a medicine man long before he became a chief. Not a warrior by nature. Later they would talk, and maybe she would have courage to speak about the babies.

Her belly was contented; her heart was happy at being with Nuff-kee and her other relatives; she rested with peace after crying and laughing. A chuck-will's-widow called to tell her it was time to hear her grandmother's stories, and she listened for a while and suddenly slept.

There was noisy excitement in the morning. The fort gates were closed, but See-ho-kee listened to the white soldiers crying commands, heard the strange foreign sound of their drum and their feet stamping in time. She wished she could watch them march, for it was impressive, she had heard, a thing they did to frighten Indians. Indian children now played the game of marching, their feet slapping the earth noisily. Occasionally the cowbell gave out its clunk of alarm.

She and Nuff-kee and the other children and women of Apayaka's village sat at the edge of the woods and peered through the leaves at the activities. She still had not had a chance to talk to Apayaka, though she watched him with love as he talked up the spirit and rage in his warriors. Oh, Great-Uncle. Old and thin. Some men would look pitiful at his age and in his frail body. Not Apayaka. His eyes blazed with passion. Not a warrior, a great leader. He was much like his sister, her grandmother.

Now See-ho-kee, her mother, and her grandmother waited in the trees near the fort. Their cookfire burned well, and the pot was full of stew from deer meat and fry-bread, very delicious.

Coosa came down the path, calling a greeting. The three women stood, eager for news, glad to feed him their own food, pleased to have him eat with them instead of with the other elders. Her father often did this and joked with them when he was away from the formal structure of the village square where he was obliged to spend most of his day with other warriors in the square. He ate quickly. "The food up there is no good," he said by way of thanks. See-ho-kee's mother and grandmother smiled slightly but remained modestly silent.

"Apayaka will not take part in the council," he then said. This was the news!

It was terrifying. Just when peace seemed to be bound to come, her old uncle stepped aside and refused to speak with the white man.

Her father continued, "Apayaka says it is dishonorable to think of anything besides what we agreed to. The Moultrie Treaty has not run out, and the white man is already at our heels to move away now. He is right."

Her mother sat on the ground, rocking back and forth,

her eyes closed. She asked, "Will you take part in the talk?" Her eyes were still closed so as not to influence her husband in his thinking.

"Yes, I think we must continue to talk. But he is right."

Coosa-amathle returned to the group of men near the fort, and the women waited patiently despite the lack of something interesting to watch. Many Indian men were now near the fort, lounging on the ground and gossiping. A few Negroes joined them. These were not the leaders; their clothes were not the most elegant; they added nothing of interest to the watching women and children.

Now suddenly something funny happened. The great gates swung open and a soldier came out with a dog on a leash, taking it to a little distance away from the fort, waiting as it stopped. It was a strange and comical dog. Even from this distance See-ho-kee could see that it had a huge jaw, a broad sad grin, and bow legs. Conversation began at once among the laughing Indians and the white man, with a black man interpreting.

What was he? What sort of strange dog was he? Had he had an accident to make him look like that?

The black man yelled loudly to overcome the language barrier. "It is a female dog," he howled.

The knowledge that it was a female made the Indians laugh more, and one or two of the black men began rolling on the ground and whooping.

But what kind of dog? How did she get into such a state?

"She is a bool dag, a very fine bool dag."

Bool dag? What did it mean in real words? The interpreter spoke rapidly to the white soldier who was getting irritated by all the fun at the dog's expense. His fierce mustache seemed to puff up.

See-ho-kee could hear the interpreter very distinctly, could see his broad gestures; she wished she could see his face and see whether or not he was smiling.

"Ah-h-h," shouted the Negro. *"Bulldog."*

What does it mean? What is wrong with the dog?

"It is a *bulldog*," he explained in a roar. "A female male-cow dog."

More puzzlement. More questions. The laughter had now reached the hidden women and children. The soldier had given up on the walk and now tugged the dog toward the fort, but the dog had great strength and yearned toward the woods.

Now See-ho-kee became aware of Eefe's strong interest in the bool dag. He left the group in the forest and strolled toward the bool dag, and to the amusement of all except the white soldier, the bool dag broke away and ran to meet Eefe. Eefe walked stiff-legged around the dog once, sniffed her thoroughly, took his time, slowly mounted her just as the soldier got to her. The soldier shouted and clapped his hands at Eefe, shouted unintelligibly to the black interpreter who yelled back and finally shouted to the Indians, "He says call your dog off!"

But why? Nobody could understand this. Wasn't it a natural thing to do? Were white men's dogs not allowed to do it? The Indians watched the two dogs and smiled.

The soldier, for whom See-ho-kee was beginning to feel pity, shouted at Eefe, tried to kick him, but Eefe adroitly danced the bool dag around so that they faced the soldier, and both of them made growling noises.

Now the Agent himself came out. He saw at once what had caused the loud laughter and he roared at the soldier, who tried again to beat Eefe away. It was too late, for a very strong connection had been made, and he must wait till Eefe broke the connection.

The Indians had the black interpreter to ask the soldier why it had maddened the general so. None of this made sense. Would the soldier please make it clear?

"It is a very fine *bulldog*," the interpreter at last explained. "Her lineage is superb, going back many years to good parents. Now she will have bad pups."

The Indians studied this astounding reply, and at last one man stood up to defend Eefe's dignity. "This also is true of our dog," he said. "He is a very fine Indian dog; he had Indian dog parents all the way back to the first Indian dog."

Eefe was finished with his work. The soldier sulkily took the bulldog back into the fort, and all the Indian men patted Eefe before allowing him to return to the woods.

The laughter finally became silent; all attention returned to the council, except for occasional outbursts of laughter as one man or another remembered the bool dag.

See-ho-kee understood well enough what was to be discussed; the Moultrie Treaty and Payne's Landing Treaty. She had heard these cruel words all her life, had watched the mention of them — *Moultrie Creek Treaty . . . Payne's Landing Treaty* — stir the Indian men into arguments and anger with each other, finally into helpless rage at the white men. *Moultrie Treaty:* the Yakitisee, whom the white men call Seminoles, including her family who continued to think of themselves as Miccosukees, would move to the West to good lands but not for twenty years. Even by the white man's way of keeping time, twenty years had not passed. The white men would honor Indian rights, the treaty said, would pay them for the homes they must lose when they moved into a smaller place called a reservation. There they would wait in peace for the twenty years to pass. The reservation would have a tract of land north of Pease River. The white men would pay them, would give them food, would keep bad white men off Indian land, would hire an Indian agent and interpreter to help them understand, would pay a thousand dollars a year for twenty years, would pay every year for a school on the Indian land. The land cut deep into Florida but did not at any point touch the ocean. This angered her father and Apayaka and the other adults in the tribe. How would they get their weapons and other goods that came by sea? And what if they wished to *live* by the sea for a while, as they sometimes did? How could they do that now? The reservation, she began to see, was a confinement place like the most horrible of the white men's inventions — a jail, a great jail.

Moultrie Creek Treaty. It had been agreed to three years before she was born. By the time she could walk, she understood the three ugly words to be evil. There were still years to go on the treaty, but it was no good, for the white man dishonored it.

Payne's Landing Treaty. It was signed by many Yakitisee miccos, including Apayaka himself, and had replaced the first treaty. Many times she had heard her uncle talk of the signing with rage. This treaty was even worse. It said they must move to the West in only *three* years after the government in Washington agreed to it. They would be paid in white man's money, which they desperately needed. The treaty wiped out the twenty years they had agreed upon.

At first, Apayaka and her father had thought that the Payne's Landing Treaty would not be so bad, for it stated that honored Indian chiefs, seven in all, would be taken to see the new country in the West. Arkansas. If it were good land, the chiefs would tell their people; if it were bad, the treaty would be thrown away.

The land was bad. It was dry and scrubby, unfriendly to animals and man. Even worse, near their designated home place lived their old enemies, a group of Creeks who had once been their neighbors, who had attacked them and stolen their slaves.

Apayaka was too old to go to look at the new land, though he had been chosen by the Indians, and his place was taken by Tuckose Emathla. He was called John Hicks by the white man. In this way of stealing the Indian names from strong men, the white men tried to steal their spirit too. The Indians laughed about it. Their medicine protected them and made the name as strong as the man. Sam Jones was now a very strong name. While they were in the West, afraid they would never get home, Tuckose Emathla and the other six chiefs were tricked into putting their marks on another paper which agreed to the Payne's Landing Treaty. What was worse, they would live with the Creeks whom they had fought in 1814, indeed would *become* Creeks. Not Seminoles. Not Miccosukees. Creeks! Here in Florida, Creeks were joining the Miccosukees. The white major said, "Sign this paper, or go home alone, without food or help from us." They could not live in that strange, dry land. They were used to lakes and springs where deer came to drink. And so they signed. The tricky white men had deceived them. The treaty said that if the Indians were satisfied that the land was good, they would move. But after the treaty was signed, the white men changed it to say that if the seven chiefs were satisfied, then the Indians would move.

Many times Pi-co-yee had told See-ho-kee about the furious gathering when the chiefs finally reached home. First to speak out against going to the new land was her great-uncle. "You have let the white men trick you. They have teased you the way they would play with a puppy," he told the seven men. Others had agreed with him, and the chiefs themselves denounced the signing and said they had been deceived about what it said. When at last the Indians believed that the seven chiefs had been deceived and coerced, their anger turned away, back to the white men.

To this day the Miccosukees were angry, and so were the other Florida red men who were their friends.

Worst of all had been the white men's determination to force them into becoming part of their old enemies among the Creeks. There would have been another Indian war.

"Those people would steal our slaves and work them too

hard or sell them to white people," Apayaka often said. "Will we allow our friends to be sent away from us like dogs?"

And the answer in everybody's mind had always been: *No. Our slaves are our people too, with the right to live to themselves, in their own villages.* Many of the Negroes had escaped from white masters and come to the Indians. Their little village in the Ouithlacoochee Cove consisted of slaves who belonged to the Miccosukees and also were friends of the Miccosukees. They gave part of their crops to the Miccosukees to work out their slavery and in return were protected by the Miccosukees against white Georgian slavers who came searching. Sometimes See-ho-kee wondered how they felt about being slaves; it was a condition she would have considered intolerable, though there were some Indian women in her clan whose parents had long ago been captured and enslaved. A few times she had tried to talk to the black children about it, but their language difference made it too difficult. Once, her black friend Marcy had almost understood what she had said, and her face had filled with pleased understanding.

Slavery in Georgia, she had told See-ho-kee, meant long hours of hard work. Here, it meant that she could live free except that some of the food she raised went to her Indian friends. Greedy white men will come; the Miccosukees will protect their slaves. All this she told See-ho-kee with much gesticulation and many one-word questions between them. It took a long time, but afterward See-ho-kee felt some satisfaction that they understood each other a little.

See-ho-kee also taught Marcy things she must know. When Marcy whistled a song into a strange whistle-stick, cut with holes, See-ho-kee quickly silenced her. *Don't blow into a wind instrument. It is bad to imitate the wind.*

Marcy seemed not to understand the reasons, but she put the whistle-stick away.

The Miccosukees would never surrender their slaves. It was one more thing to make them angry.

But See-ho-kee thought to herself, *I am not as angry as I am afraid. Some day the white men will drive us away from here to the western square-ground.* Many times Apayaka had assured her that they would never go. Yet she often thought of it and tried to visualize the square-ground. She could not. After they had bathed and eaten, they went back to the fort where the council was congregating.

At the council, the Indians would listen to the reading of a paper addressed to them by the white president, Andrew Jackson.

The council slowly began to form. Still she had not been able to speak to her uncle. "Nuff-kee, where is Apayaka? I want to greet him."

"Not a good thought," said Nuff-Kee. "He is angry. He is talking to the other chief."

See-ho-kee had waited long enough. "Where is he?" she persisted.

Nuff-kee shook her head in disgust. "If you must make a fool of yourself, look down that path. He will come in a few minutes."

See-ho-kee got to her feet and ran down the path, had gone only a short way when she met Apayaka, dressed in his finest clothes, and with him were other Indians, all very beautiful, for it was understood by all that the chiefs must always dress so as not to shame the tribe. She hesitated. Apayaka's eyes had a strange sharp look, like the one his sister, her grandmother, often wore.

"Uncle?"

"Eh?" He turned and looked. "Oh, little daughter. How are you? What questions do you have for me?" It was always his joke that See-ho-kee had more questions than a mockingbird who filled the woods with his wondering.

"What does a square-ground in Arkansas look like?"

Some chiefs would have been angry at her for interrupting them at such an important time. Her uncle was not. He deliberated. "Fort King is like a western square-ground. There are few plants and much dust." He touched her head, and he and the other men went on.

She followed at a respectful distance. Fort King? Suddenly the square-ground came into her mind with clarity. A square-ground would be a huge grassless meadow with a twenty foot wall around it. She didn't like the picture, and she agreed with her uncle. She would never live there. She would hide in the swamps forever rather than live in such a dusty place. First to speak out against going had been Apayaka, and if children were allowed to speak too, she would be the first to say no. Apayaka would never move; her people would never move; she would never move.

She returned to the seat by Nuff-kee, who touched her in quick greeting, now that she had got back without trouble. She looked quickly to see whether her mother had noticed her absence, but no, Pi-co-yee and the other women still talked in low, troubled voices. See-ho-kee thought about the long time it had been since the women of her family had talked and laughed together all day as they worked, as they did in old times. She could not accustom herself to her mother's solemnity.

The council was about to begin. All the Indian warriors now went into the fort. Suddenly See-ho-kee's mother arose. "Come," she said. "It is now safe for us to stay near the fort. No one will notice us now."

All the women and children went in a tight group to the great gates and seated themselves outside, where they could see inside. See-ho-kee stared with fascination at the houses inside. There was a long building to one side. Her mother pointed. "Barracks!" she said. "The soldiers sleep there."

See-ho-kee looked and laughed. There was her uncle, lounging against the barracks, contempt on his face. "He is close enough to see what goes on," she whispered to Nuff-kee who smiled and nodded.

Now the chiefs — all except Apayaka — and the white men mounted to the top of the platform to sit in council. The green wood cried under their weight, and See-ho-kee bowed her head thinking of its pain. The men settled themselves, arranging their clothing to show its richness properly.

She watched with tremendous curiosity, hoping to catch the glance of a white person, perhaps to see the strange look in his eyes which she had heard her parents describe.

There were no weapons on the platform though white soldiers stood in rows at the front of the platform and leaned on their guns, while Indian warriors lounged in groups on the far side of the platform, their weapons lying against their bodies.

A big muscular white man stood in the center of the platform and began to speak. "Agent Thompson," whispered Nuff-kee. An important white man. He could see that Indians received food or went hungry. See-ho-kee smiled, thinking of Agent Thompson's ugly dog.

Agent Thompson read the letter, and Abraham, a huge squint-eyed slave, roared a translation of the President's words. The Seminoles must go, the message went. They must leave this country and go to their new land. Florida was no longer their home, according to their agreement signed by their leaders. There was much land waiting for them in the West.

The Indians listened in silence to the long statement.

See-ho-kee felt sick with excitement, could barely endure the words pouring out upon them. Suddenly, there was a great ripping and cracking sound, a coming-apart sound, and she smelled pungent camphor again. The platform hesitated drunkenly and collapsed slowly, slowly into separate pieces, the green wood bending in pain, and as the men, white and Indian, hit the ground, they began shrieking with fear and distrust.

"It's a trick, a trick, white man's trick!" an Indian screamed.

There they were now in a great tumble on the ground, all the beautiful clothes tangled and dirty, a squirming mass of people, all trying to disengage themselves from each other. A few got loose and began to run away from the rest. "Run!" yelled a chief.

See-ho-kee's hands kept her mouth from screaming. She could not run, for her father was still there somewhere in the pile of people and tree limbs. Now, white soldiers were racing about the fort. Where was Apayaka? He was not at the barracks now.

There now. There was Apayaka, standing in the center of the broken platform, his turban over one ear, his eyes swiftly darting. He took his time looking around. He grinned suddenly. "It was an accident," he said in a mild voice. He fell forward and hit the ground with both fists and laughed aloud.

All the others grinned a little and then began to laugh. The soldiers came back, grinning with embarrassment. See-ho-kee was glad she now had an excuse to laugh aloud, for who would notice in all the laughter filling the clearing?

The meeting was over. Apayaka said to Agent Thompson, "We will think for one month on this matter."

Abraham roared the words. Thompson shook his head. "Three weeks," he said. "April 20th."

There was agreement. "Let everybody be here, and let the agreement be known by all," Agent Thompson said.

See-ho-kee was glad. She liked council, and it would be even better if her whole clan came next time. She thought about the walk home. Nuff-kee and her family would walk with her on their way to Wahoo Swamp, and Yaha Chatee would walk with them. Oh, Yaha Chatee, she thought. He was so handsome and amiable, perhaps not quite as amiable as he used to be before her marriage plans were known. Her breast suddenly hurt from strong feeling for him. It would be pleasant walking back with him, and she had much to tell those families at home who had not ventured out to the great meeting.

As she thought of this at the gates of the fort, she suddenly realized she stood alone. She looked in fright at the forest, saw her mother give a commanding gesture for her to come. She ran to safety, thinking with shock that she had not had the sense to run when danger presented itself. She must guard herself against such carelessness.

She was anxious to be at home, needed to know that all was well. She prayed that the Breathmaker would allow no more babies to die.

three

Yaha Chatee had gone home, taking his sister Nuff-kee, after ruining See-ho-kee's long walk with his sulkiness. Nor was Fixonechee here courting her and begging her to lie with him. This gave See-ho-kee a chance to be herself again, to forget the strain of being wanted by a man and the strain of trying to please another. She was almost like a child, back here with her family and neighbors, enjoying the slow pace of the village and the constant chatter and joking.

Not until the second night back in Ouithlachoochee Cove was See-ho-kee's grandmother given a chance to sing the village names, and even then she was asked out of courtesy after other tale-tellers had had a chance. This was a special thing she did, unlike any of the tale-telling at night or happy chitchat during the day, and she did it out of need, for as she sang the names, the villages lived again for her. As she sang, she emphasized an occasional syllable and stomped her foot. It had the effect of making the listeners remember, and sometimes they sang along with her.

Tonight See-ho-kee decided she would sing too, to see whether she could remember the stomps, and she wore her rattles on each knee. Her mother shook her head, and See-ho-kee removed them. They were for Busk only.

"Cow-e-TUH (stomp), Cow-e-tuh Tal-lau-HAS-see, Cus-se-TUH, U-chee, Oo-se-OO-chee, Che-AU-hau, Hitch-e-tee, Pa-la-CHOOC-la, O-CO-nee, Sau-woog-e-lo, Eu-FAU-lau."

The grandmother paused. "Those were the old towns on the Chat-to-ho-che. Next are the old towns in Florida.

"Sim-e-NO-le-tal-lau-HAS-see, Au-LOT-che-wau, Oc-le-WAU-hau thluc-co, Mic-co-SOOC-e, We-cho-TOOK-me, Tal-lau-gue chapco POP-cau, Cull-OO-sau-HAT-che.

"And next are old towns on the Coo-sau and the Tal-a-poo-sa.

"Tal-e-see, Foosce-HAT-che, E-cun-HUT-kee, Sau-va-no-gee, Mook-LAU-sau, O-che-au-po-fau, Ki-a-LI-jee, Coo-sau, Tus-KE-gee, Took-au-BAT-chee, Coo-Sau-dee, Nau-chee, Eu-FAU-lau-HAT-che, Hill-au-bee, Aut-TOS-see, Hoith-le-WAU-le, Coo-loome, We-WO-cau, Woc-co-coie, Puc-cun-TAL-lau-HAS-see, Hook-choie, Eu-FAU-lau, Hook-choie-OO-che, AU-be-COO-chee."

They sang them through twice, and smiled as the others sang with them. Nobody objected if an enemy town name were sung.

Then for a while her grandmother talked about the old towns and the villages that belonged to them. Some tales were not new, for she must recite them over and over, so that all would learn them, and they grew dearer in the telling.

One small story enchanted See-ho-kee.

"The old town of Ok-mul-gee was dead before I moved down here, but my grandmother said it was once a big important town. We used to camp there on the way to trading days or Busk, and we found ghosts there." She looked around to see that she had their attention. See-ho-kee sighed, heard the children sigh with her.

"We heard the old townspeople singing at dawn. They sang happy sacred songs, and they danced their way to the river to make themselves pure, and then they came back to the townhouse."

Now the grandmother was pensive. "Ok-mul-gee. I never knew those people, except for my grandmother, but they are our people too. Every dawn they sing and dance in that place."

See-ho-kee suddenly saw Indian towns stretching out into the distant past, suddenly saw herself and her family dancing at dawn in the far future, saw her children's grandchildren listening. She had a strange, lonesome feeling.

They sang the names again, adding Ok-MUL-gee this time.

There were other names See-ho-kee wished to sing: Palat-ka, We-TUMP-ka where Charley Emathla was chief, Peli-kla-ka-ha where many Negroes lived, O-ki-HUM-ky, Pico-la-ta, Ok-hol-wa-kee, Ou-ithla-COO-chee, and Micco-SOO-kee, over and over.

But she was afraid to sing the names of these villages, for they were still alive, and maybe the singing of them would bring evil spirits of white men to kill them.

It was on this night she began to see the tremendous value of her grandmother who carried the history of their people in her heart.

four

In April of 1835 fifteen hundred Yakitisee gathered at Fort King near Apayaka's village at Silver Springs. The women and children went to the spring while the men met the white soldiers at the fort. See-ho-kee wanted to go to council but listened obediently when her mother said, "No women must go there this time. This may be a bad council. We don't know what will happen.

It was true, See-ho-kee thought; they might begin a fight. She and Nuff-kee and the other young women walked to the river to wash their clothes and to bathe and finally to swim. Barely had they got into the water when Nuff-kee caught a shining fish with her hands, scooping it up as easily as if she had used a net. She flung it on the river bank with a subdued whoop. "There," she said. "I will cook this for our dinner."

Nuff-kee looked better since their last meeting. Her medicine man had good medicine, and she was healing from her grief. See-ho-kee observed that their laughter was still open and real, not angry and sharp as their fathers' laughter had become, not like Apayaka's derisive cackle which hit her like punishment.

See-ho-kee held the fish while Nuff-kee strung it on a piece of willow and dangled it in the cool water till they were ready to go home.

"The white men call Apayaka 'the fisherman'," Nuff-kee said with a smirk. "Sam Jones, the fisherman."

See-ho-kee laughed. Her uncle had sold many fish caught by the villagers to the soldiers of Fort King and also Fort Brooke in Tampa, and he often walked out of his way to their village Ouithlacoochee and showed them the treasure he got for fish that were free for the taking, and they laughed together over the white men who *paid* for them.

"I never once saw him fish," said See-ho-kee. "Did you?"

"No. He thinks it is work for girls and for boys who have not proved themselves yet. He thinks it is funny that they call him a fisherman, but he lets them think what they want to." Nuff-kee's eyebrows went up in puzzlement. "Who can account for the way white people think?"

"Nobody," See-ho-kee said at once. "They make a mistake though to call him fisherman and Sam Jones. One day they will learn that he is a great leader of warriors." She spoke these words in anger and at once had a shiver to go over her. She didn't want her great-uncle ever to have to fight the white men. And still her words poured out. "They're making a mistake to think he is a foolish old man."

They swam and bathed in the water with the children they were tending. They felt free to talk normally, for the white soldiers would not bother them now when they were engaged in council. While part of See-ho-kee's mind enjoyed the cool water, another part worried about the council. Her family would not have come at all except that it was annuity time when the white men paid them for the land they were taking away. This year, the white men had hinted that they would give no money, but See-ho-kee understood that their talk was frivolous, that they wished to frighten the Indians into giving in and moving west.

See-ho-kee saw her grandmother sitting on a high dry rise, huddling on the brown grass, as brown as herself: her face and hands, her dress, her shoes, all brown which gave her white hair prominence. She stared at her grandmother, wondered what she was thinking. Her grandmother was here to watch over the young ones, she knew, but the old woman lived much of the time in her dreams and seemed unaware of what the children did. Was she worrying over the council? See-ho-kee wished she would change her position, wished she would not face west where the dead spirits had retreated, almost as if she were readying herself for the journey.

At last, See-ho-kee got up and went to the old woman.

"What are you thinking about, Beloved Woman?"

"I am thinking of the old town of Cow-e-tuh Tal-lau-has-see and the white agent who lived there. He was such a worrisome man; he kept at the townspeople to plant, plant, plant and to build fences, fences, fences. It nearly drove them mad, and yet they wanted to be courteous to him."

She bent forward in a sudden convulsive laugh. "He told the men they were lazy to sit in the square and talk. They were angry at this and told him he didn't understand our ways. It was true. He didn't see that they were tending to our medicine. They were making decisions." She laughed again. "And yet I knew another place where it was the law that everybody had to plant before hunting or sitting in the square. It worked well."

"Were the Cow-e-tuh Tal-lau-has-sees hungry?"

"Oh, no. We didn't know hunger then as we do now." The grandmother suddenly slept, and See-ho-kee went back to the river edge.

She sat in the water like a frog and thought of the council. Yesterday her father Coosa-amathle walked with her mother and talked over his worries with her, for he regarded his wife as a wise woman, and he liked her opinions. This had nothing to do with her wealth; her two good houses and her cook house, and their clothes and jewelry and their other goods; all these belonged to her. He valued her thoughts, and whoever laughed at him for this had better keep his laughter silent and hidden behind his face if he wanted to laugh another time. Coosa-amathle would go to Micanopy's village to talk with the other Indian leaders so that they could speak with one voice to Agent Thompson.

Yaha Chatee would be there. Oh yes, and Fixonechee too. But Yaha was the one she would like to see.

"I think we should simply tell them that we won't go to Fort Brooke, that we refuse to take the ship to New Orleans, and that's all of it," Coosa-amathle said. "Do you think that is the right way, Pi-co-yee? We'll face them down on it. Don't you agree?"

See-ho-kee listened for her mother's answer, held her breath. For her father's way would certainly mean war, and yet what else could they do if they were to keep their home in Florida?

Her mother took time to think, as she always did when she and Coosa-amathle debated big problems. "You are right that we will not go to the West and that we should tell them so," she said, but her voice trailed as if something sticky were bothering her thoughts. Coosa-amathle waited respectfully for her thought to clear itself.

"We have no food now," she said. "Our crops won't be in for a while; our cattle died in the freeze. If we anger the soldiers, they will war upon us so that our warriors can't even hunt, and the women and children will be running so much they can't take time to dig coonte. How will we live? First our medicine man must protect us with good medicine. And then I think you must be courteous to the white men, explain in a soft voice what we think, keep your anger down. It will give us time to get more food, to collect our pumpkins and corn, to get meat, maybe get more food from the white soldiers. And then we will not be quite so weak."

See-ho-kee shivered. She knew what her mother was thinking. Fight, if we have to, but fight when we are strong and ready.

"You are right," Coosa-amathle said. "If the Indians will keep their temper, and if the white agent will be calm, maybe we can put off a quarrel. Later, we can decide the time and place."

There was no question about it, See-ho-kee had realized. Both her parents believed there would be another war. Since the last trip to Silver Springs and Fort King she had put away her fears that all the Miccosukee babies would die. But if there were another war, how could they save them?

She now watched a two-year-old strutting man-like past Nuff-kee's fish which flipped its tail in the shallow water. He stared at the moving fish, stamped his foot at it, lost his balance and fell. He sat up and thought of crying, remembered the scratches on his arm, and wept silently. See-ho-kee smiled with amusement and sympathy. She went over and swept him up, took him into the water and bobbed him around like a pig bladder till he laughed his hurt away.

Don't let this little boy die. She sent her thoughts to her protective ancestors, sent them again to the four winds, sent them to the sun. It was foolish, for there was no threat here; he was a healthy boy. Still she wished for good medicine to overcome all danger.

After her parents' talk, Coosa-amathle had taken a different path to Fort King. First he had gone to Micanopy's village where he and other warriors had met to deliberate. Last night her father and the other warriors had come to Silver Springs and camped with their families.

"We made an agreement," Coosa-amathle said over the campfire. "We will be peaceful; we will speak with pleasant words; we will agree with the agent whenever we can. But we will not agree to move to the West." See-ho-kee looked quickly at her mother, saw the quick gleam in her eyes, felt proud that her mother's words were worth listening to, not only by her father but by the rest of the warriors.

Now at the river that gushed from Silver Springs, See-ho-kee regretted that she was not there to watch the drama at the fort. The drama and Yaha Chatee too.

"Nuff-kee!"

Nuff-kee turned in wonder at the sharpness of See-ho-kee's voice. "What?"

"Will you go to the council with me?"

Nuff-kee's long face became leaner and filled with surprise.

"Why, no, sister. You know we must stay here. Our mothers said that the men are angry and excited, that they may get into a fight. Our mothers said we could play here a while in the Silver River and then bring the children home. How can you even consider going? You want more scratches?

See-ho-kee tried to think of the scratches she might get if her parents caught her. Surely they wouldn't, at her age. Nothing was as exciting as the fort. She would go.

"You won't tell?" She gave a begging look to Nuff-kee.

Nuff-kee signed. "No, I won't tell. It won't be necessary, for you'll get caught all by yourself. But I will tend the children till you're back."

They glanced at the same moment at the grandmother, but she was now facing away from them to shade her eyes, and she seemed to be dozing. See-ho-kee shook herself free of water. "I'm going," she said.

Now Eefe, tired of playing in the water, crowded his wet rough body against her, aware from the tone of her voice that she was going for a run. He was ready to accompany her, and she felt safer when he went. She made a clicking noise with her mouth to signal her permission, and they ran from the river toward the Fort. Eefe stayed behind her and ran great distances back and forth, checking with her frequently.

See-ho-kee ran through the forest, ignoring the trails, for the path of the sun was so strong in her mind she would never get lost. She remembered laughing about the white soldier who got lost in the forest and was nearly starved when he was found by Indians who took him back to his fort. How could he get lost?

It took a while to get there, for the trails were easier and she had to watch for snakes and alligators. She spoke respectfully to those she saw. Ah, there was the clearing. The blaze of sunlight made her cautious; she darted from tree to tree until she reached the forest edge. At once she heard a roar of voices. She settled herself under a myrtle bush and became as motionless as a stone. Sat, listened, thought, but never moved except for her slow breathing. The run through the woods had hardly quickened her heartbeat. Eefe crowded against her, and she put a quieting hand on him.

Why were the men howling? Was this the peaceful approach Coosa-amathle hoped for?

This time there was no platform, she saw. The meeting was on the ground this time — no more dangerous platforms. A large group of people sitting in proper places around the speakers. Agent Thompson was talking and she could see him above the rest. A huge black man translated Thompson's words. She knew the black man. He was Abraham, a big squint-eyed man, very smart, very rich. A free Negro, who lived at Peli-kla-ka-ha. Agent Thompson was angry. "You are unfaithful to your white brothers," he yelled. "You are dishonorable and full of falseness. You have said you would move to Arkansas if your chiefs went to see the land and called it good. We took them to see the land. They signed a paper there that they would abide by the agreement to move. Now, you hesitate."

Another man stood up above the group, stepping up on a rock. This must be General Clinch, an older man with much dignity. She wished she could be close enough to examine his face, for her curiosity about the white people's look still kept her mind at work. General Clinch raised his hand and waved it over both groups, white and red, like a peace wish. She felt sudden hope. General Clinch smiled gently.

"We wouldn't want to fight our brothers, but our troops are ready here. More white soldiers with guns will come in great numbers if you do not obey the commandments of the treaties." His voice came in sharp stuttering bursts, and at once the smooth translation of the black man filled in the sense of what he said. As Abraham's voice lifted and fell with the drama of what the general had said, the Indians became absolutely silent, and now even the white men stopped muttering. See-ho-kee felt a sickening shiver again and inexplicably she thought of the little boy whom she had bounced in the water a while ago. She had the tingling feeling along her wrists which usually came with the sound of a rattlesnake when he spoke to her and warned her away. General Clinch talked in a calm and kindly manner; yet it was *war* he spoke of.

Agent Thompson talked again, louder and louder. Now she saw the young warrior Asi Yahola, angry and bold, rudely ignoring the agent and speaking to Apayaka and then to other Indians. She shook as he went to speak to her father. Now there was an occasional yell from the Indians who were being deprived of their turn to talk. Never before had See-ho-kee heard grown Indians interrupt a speaker like this. Abraham went on translating without taking note of what the Indians shouted except to give them a quick look out of his good eye. They kept yelling. Her own father got up and howled, "This is how you talk peace? You threaten us with your soldiers?"

Apayaka was so outraged he now began a long talk without pausing to think, a high-pitched speech of the injustices the white men had imposed upon the Indians. At last Thompson couldn't be heard.

General Clinch was up again. "My brothers, my brothers . . . " Abraham translated. "Be calm and peaceful. My troops will keep it peaceful."

They were going to fight. See-ho-kee had a sudden pain in her left temple, and she knew she would have a headache in a few moments. But the Indians calmed down, for after all, what fool would wish for war? This was not the way they usually talked. It was common courtesy to allow a person to consider and then to speak. White people interrupted; red people listened and considered and then spoke.

Agent Thompson went on with his speech. Even from here See-ho-kee could see that his face had reddened and bulged with his rage. She wished she could see Apayaka, for she knew he would be in a fit of fury, whether or not he spoke aloud.

"I speak now to honorable Indians," said Agent Thompson. "I speak to the Indians who honor their word, who honor the treaty they signed. I ask those men of their word to come forward and agree to the treaty they signed. I ask you, honor what you have already said."

There was a long pause, and a tall Indian started across the crowd. A low, angry sound rolled across the opening to See-ho-kee. Another chief stood and went toward Thompson. Slowly, reluctantly, another chief arose.

No Miccosukees had moved. Suddenly Apayaka was on his feet. *No,* See-ho-kee thought. *He will not do it.*

"Don't speak to me of honor," Apayaka shrieked. "We signed a treaty to look at the land, and the man you call John Hicks went for me to see the land. He told me it was bad land. Yet you made him and the other Indians sign a paper saying they wanted the land. If they did not sign, you would let them stay there and die, alone and away from their people. That is what you said. Now I say YOU are not honorable. You fight for our home and our lands with trickery and deceit. I will never go to Arkansas. I will never go. My people will never go."

Swiftly, smoothly, Abraham translated.

Apayaka sat down, and again General Clinch stepped forward. "Let men who mean what they say come to us. My troops will protect you. You will have till January first to come to Fort Brooke."

There was a long moment, and suddenly two Indians arose and walked toward the agent. Finally eight chiefs stood there and consented to the treaty. One man spoke to the other Indians, "If the land is bad, still we might live," he said in sad tones. "Our women and children will die if we stay here and try to fight the white people who are thick as leaves around our villages."

He spoke in a Hitchiti tongue, but See-ho-kee had never seen him before, and she believed he was not Miccosukee. Abraham looked at him with doleful courtesy and did not translate.

Who was left? See-ho-kee forgot her need to hide; she stood up and stretched. Who had not moved over? Five chiefs sat over to the side, looking obstinately at the ground. See-ho-kee felt jubilant to see Apayaka on his feet, arms crossed, eyes red with fury and the desire to fight. He was small, and the white agent perhaps did not understand that he was as dangerous as a hurricane wind. She wanted to scream at him, "Hey, Uncle! You tell them the truth."

"Well, you won't come up, you obstinate ones. Then we'll strike your names from the list of chiefs."

Strike their names? What could that mean? White agents don't choose red leaders. Red people choose their own leaders from the proper lines of inheritance or for bravery.

But Agent Thompson held up the paper and a pencil. "I will *strike out the names,*" he said. "If you come when I call your name, I will not strike it."

He waited. No one came.

"Micanopy!"

"He is sick today. He could not come," someone said.

Abraham translated swiftly.

"He is playing sick," Agent Thompson said. "He is lazy and shuffles like an old man. I strike his name." His pencil rose and slashed across the paper like a knife. See-ho-kee heard the warriors suck in their breath when they saw Agent Thompson meant what he said. "Micanopy can no longer be councilor for the Indians."

"Coa Hadjo!"

Coa Hadjo arose and glared. He turned his back.

"I strike your name!" Again the slashing pencil.

"Jumper!"

"I am Ote Emathla," a man said. "I talked for two hours against signing the paper to move, and I don't change now."

Agent Thompson struck his name.

"Holata Mico!"

Holata Mico, a Pease Creek Tallahassee, yawned and made a rude and vulgar remark about Agent Thompson's likeness to a pregnant hog. Abraham refrained from translating though his good eye slitted in mirth.

Thompson struck at the paper.

"Sam Jones!"

See-ho-kee felt her heart leap like a mullet. She leaned

against the tree in full view of the council if anyone should think to look.

"My name is Apayaka," her uncle said, greatly dignified and reserved. He stood with firmness, as tough as scrub oak. "I will not sign."

"I strike your name!" For the last time the pencil came down. See-ho-kee flushed with fury at the insult.

"I will speak," her uncle said.

"The time for speaking is past, Sam Jones. You cannot speak for the Seminoles any more. You are not a leader." Agent Thompson looked well satisfied, and General Clinch nodded and smoked his pipe faster.

Suddenly See-ho-kee saw both her men: Fixonechee sitting straight and bold, his spectacles shining, his teeth glinting in an amused smile; Yaha Chatee leaning with his elbows on his knees, his face full of anger and hatred. It comforted her to see her own feelings reflected on his face. What could Fixonechee be grinning about? His idiot glasses?

Apayaka screamed, "We do not choose your leaders, and you do not choose *ours.* Now you will see how Yakitisee fight." He stamped his feet and gnashed his teeth in a great angry grin. "You do not choose a chief. The chief comes through the bloodlines, and *we* choose." He held up a fist and screamed, "Yo-ho-eeee-heeee!" The war cry set all the warriors astir, as nervous as the leaves on a sweet bay tree just before a storm.

Agent Thompson turned his back. "Sam Jones is no longer a councilor."

Oh, Agent Thompson, you have turned loose a great wind. This little man is our spirit. You will see.

See-ho-kee was right. Already the red men were on their feet and talking war, right in the faces of the white soldiers with their ready guns. Suddenly a hand gripped See-ho-kee's mouth and an arm dragged her into the forest. It was her mother, looking a storm of anger. "Come."

See-ho-kee looked with shame at Yaha. Had he seen her embarrassment? No. She didn't think to look at Fixonechee until she was deep in the woods.

"Find a rock," her mother said. "A good sharp one. Maybe a shark's tooth. Or a stick."

See-ho-kee felt afraid and lonely. Never had her mother been angry enough to do something so impolite as to punish her. She hesitated.

"Hurry. Find one." Her mother's voice was low and guttural. Where had the voice like a singing bird gone?

She found a rough pebble, tested it, sighed, handed it to her mother. Pi-co-yee pushed her dress away from her arm, scratched deeply, watched the blood flow. The anger eased in her face.

And then, as if she had to explain, she said, "I took only a little blood. The white man might have taken more."

There was no need for explanation. See-ho-kee felt a strange weakness in the sudden knowledge that this unheard of punishment had been done for love.

They hurried through the forest to the swamp, on toward the trees above the springs. "Did you hear them, Mother?"

Her mother turned and gave her a bitter look. "Yes. I heard."

So her mother knew the plan had failed, a good plan that hadn't worked. Still, five chiefs had held out, and they would withdraw with their people into the wilderness, wherever they could hide. When they were ready to fight, they would come out.

five

She was to be married at Busk, a celebration for the four winds which had given them their old tales. The clan built a new fire in the square, using four logs which formed a cross that pointed to the four winds: east, south, west, north. They cleaned the whole village, burning old clothes and donning new ones, sweeping the square and the paths and every house, even putting new white sand on the paths as the old ones used to do, so that all was beautiful and clean. They danced and called upon the spirits, each dance done four times, each message sung four times, every move done four times or four times four in increasing complexity; yet no one forgot or lost step. There was forgiveness for all mistakes except murder, and when a sweating man who had killed his wife came to face this dreaded day, he knew, as all of them did, that he was a dead man.

Except for that, there was peace everywhere in the village, and everyone spoke in low and gentle voices.

Just before Busk, Fixonechee came with his sisters and mother and his mother's brother, a silly giggling man who had never married. Fixonechee tried to hide his embarrassment at having no brother to help him build See-ho-kee's first house. Her own brothers pitched in to help the silly uncle set the palm logs upright for corner posts, but Fixonechee, stern as an eagle behind the glasses he had stolen (taken in battle, he claimed, though there had been no battle at the sugar mill when he visited it), did the rest himself, except for gathering of the fronds for the roof. He stormed at his mother and sisters to hurry them in this job, and when the house was finished, the women swept it clean to the sand and left it to take refreshment with See-ho-kee's mother and grandmother, separate from the men so that they could relax and talk to each other freely.

Fixonechee went away to hunt, returning in two days with a good deer which he dumped outside the new house, which was already stocked with gifts for See-ho-kee from the women in his family. In front of the house were his two horses, one of which would be her own, and she gazed at them often. He laid four logs for their fire, lit it with fire received from a neighbor, and watched it catch up; then he left the house to join the men, and she moved in to become his wife. He ignored her all that day, staying with the men on the square. Meanwhile, she skinned the deer and cut meat for stew, and when it was dark, he came and ate hugely, though without comment.

See-ho-kee was in a terrible state of excitement, because she was at last doing her own work and also because of her burning curiosity about the way Fixonechee would give her pleasure when they slept together. Yaha Chatee had faded from her mind now, and all she could think of was Fixonechee, having his hands upon her, having his body on her, at last entering her. Tonight she would have to muffle her shouts of pleasure, she knew.

So she sat through the tale-telling, wishing for the first time in her life the long stories could be shortened. They seemed to last forever, almost as if her family were teasing her. She felt an emptiness Fixonechee must fill, and she nearly groaned with the thought, the whole time trying not to look at him, for, when she did, her breath caught and frayed out into a gusty sigh, and everybody near her laughed. He, on the other hand, seemed cool and detached, not at all concerned about what was coming. He looked away from her family, as was appropriate early in the marriage, and not once did he glance at her. She tried to look away from him, and for the most part she succeeded, but sometimes her eyes were as wayward as her desire, and before she realized what she was doing, she would be looking at his face, at his strong throat, at the hands that lay relaxed on his knees. He was beginning to look much better to her. He was a great hunter, a tremendous runner, unspoiled by owning horses. His legs bulged with strength. There was nothing soft about him. Oh, she wished this tale-telling would be finished.

And when at last it was, she went to her new cheke and waited until the stars blazed from the sky, until the fires were low, until she heard snores from all the other chekes, until the night birds whispered, all the time troubled with need and uncomfortable that he had not chosen to come. At last, she slept lightly, awoke, slept again.

So he caught her asleep. He didn't bother to awake her by touch or by putting his cheek to hers or touching her body. He simply ripped her clothes away, and she awoke, still needful and yearning.

He was drunk!

Not a word was exchanged between them. He simply

pushed her into the position he desired, plunged in and went to work, finished, withdrew, and fell asleep.

See-ho-kee felt a fury she had never known before. It was not supposed to happen like this! Yaha Chatee had taught her better than this. Oh, Yaha Chatee. What had she done to herself?

She went to sleep at last, and again she felt him coming wordlessly to her. Again he left her furious. This happened four times during the night and once just before dawn. She slept heavily then, still frustrated and smarting from his vigorous attack. He had to call her to get up and cook. She began to cook new food; left-over food was bad to eat, so she sliced more venison and made new bread.

She tried to think good thoughts about her husband, for Busk season was still upon them, and all must be peaceful and loving. She could not muster one good thought. She considered withdrawing from the marriage, for after all she had until the next Busk to decide this. She could not do it. She had accepted him, and somehow she must make it work. He was a good hunter and provider. Wasn't that what a husband was for?

But it was almost too much to endure when, two days later, he and another man from Long Swamp rode the two horses back to his home. There, he explained to her father and brothers, not to her, the hunting was better.

six

Green Corn Dance was past, a hurried event. It was early in summer when the days were long. See-ho-kee and her family joined others in the village in tale-telling about the sacred fire. It was comforting to see her two brothers push the fire-logs closer to the center, still in perfect line with the four lines of heaven, (east, west, north, south, where the four winds lived) tidily built to fit nature and not in the disrespectful and unnatural manner with which the white men built their fires. The white men didn't know to protect their fires. Often she had heard her brothers say to a fire, "I will protect you, grandfather."

Tonight, as had become the custom, the talk went to the white men and what they would do to the Seminoles with whom the Miccosukees had allied themselves.

See-ho-kee thought it was shameful, using the precious time to talk of war, though she wanted to know all there was to know about that too. But old tales were needed. You had to hear them to know where you came from, what you believed, who you were. They made you know there was a beginning, and if there were an end, it would be proper and natural and therefore not frightening.

War talk was frightening. She didn't want to think of the end that came after war.

"The difference between them and us is growing like a creeping sore," her neighbor said. "It is getting angrier and more dangerous till finally it will eat us all up. The only thing to do is to leap in and cut the sore out." Her neighbor was a good hunter and a kind man to his wife and children, so that it was hard to accustom herself to this new side of him, for he was sullen most of the time now, and anger poured often from him.

He suddenly stabbed his hunting knife into the ground before him, scooped out a great section of grass and turned it over, stabbed it with brutal force. "Cut it out. That's what I say."

Nobody had doubts about who was getting stabbed.

The night was going to waste. See-ho-kee thought wistfully of the old stories they usually told.

"Yet we must also think about whether we can cut the sore out or whether we will merely make it worse," her father said in a gentle voice, not to give more offense to his angry neighbor than the white man had already given.

"That's right," muttered See-ho-kee in a voice low enough that it could be ignored by the men if they wished. She thought better of her timidity, cleared her throat, spoke aloud, "That's right. Is war better? Will making us run like hunted deer be better? Maybe the white man is not as bad as they say."

"Sister, have you lost your mind?" asked Eemathle, who

at sixteen itched to get the war going. He turned his back on her and faced his father. "The runner didn't tell you enough yesterday when he told you about how they treated Asi Yahola, Black-drink Singer?"

Coosa then smiled at his oldest son. "Yes, I know about Asi Yahola and his rage. He can puke black drink farther than you can throw a rock." It was only a mild rebuke, but it settled Eemathle down to fire-tending again.

"He is a brave angry man," Coosa-amathle said, "but he has insulted the white men until they think of him as a mad man." He glanced around the circle, let his eyes glide past his wife as if he were not looking to her for approval, though that was exactly what he was doing. "We are still talking to the white men. So long as we can talk, we won't fight. It is a shame. People who used to be friends, white and red, are enemies now. They used to talk at Fort King to each other, pass the time of day. Now they barely speak. Asi Yahola insulted Agent Thompson so much that the agent put him into irons. A stupid thing to do, to put leg irons on a man, to insult him in such a way, for now Asi Yahola cannot rest until he has his revenge. Yes, I know all this. Asi Yahola raged aloud like a wolf for a day till at last his sense came back to him and he knew he must bargain."

"How did he bargain?" See-ho-kee asked.

"He told Thompson he would sign the document agreeing to the rightness of the Payne treaty."

The villagers gasped and shook their heads in astonishment.

"And," Coosa-amathle added angrily, "Agent Thompson would not accept that. It was not enough, he said. It had to be more than that. And so Asi Yahola agreed to bring in a band of followers who were willing to emigrate."

"So that's what last night's runner had to say?" said his wife reproachfully. "And what did you tell him?"

"Why, I said for him to leave while his hair was still attached. I said that we had nobody here who was willing to go to the West."

"So, Father?" laughed Eemathle. "You were so sure of us you knew we wouldn't go to the West; yet you also think we won't have to fight."

"Wait," said Coosa-amathle, lifting his hand. "I am saying that I *hope* we don't have to fight, that we should postpone it till we are stronger and have weapons and full bellies."

"The corn is ripe, Father. Green Corn Dance is past, and we are ready now."

"And the weapons?" Coosa-amathle asked his son. "And the full bellies?"

Eemathle subsided. It was true that food was very scarce, for the Miccosukees could not plant this year, thinking every minute they would be attacked and thinking too that they would be forced to emigrate. There was not much corn.

Suddenly the man whom the children called Bear because he lumbered and loved bear meat stood up and said, "I will take my family and go to stand for Asi Yahola."

Coosa-amathle arose in amazement and turned toward him. His mouth opened as he stared in silence. "Why, Bear," he said, taking up the insult of the children, "I can tell merely by looking at you that *your* belly is full. So why do you want to go?"

It was a worse insult to call attention to the fact that he was fat, when his family was so bitterly frail. The rumor had often gone around that he got half the food and his wife and their seven children got the other half.

"It is not because I am afraid or hungry," Bear said. "I will stand for Asi Yahola."

If it had been true, they would have admired him, but everybody knew Bear too well.

"I will not leave my home," his wife called out. See-ho-kee stared in amazement. She had never known a wife to live apart from her husband.

Bear looked at her sourly. "Then my children will go."

"*Your* children? They are *my* children. They will stay with me."

There was no answer to this, for the house and the children belonged to the woman. Everybody knew this.

Bear looked around at the solemn faces, shuffled in the dirt, lumbered off to his wife's cheke for his goods. "Tell Asi Yahola that we won't give ourselves up to go to the West for him, but that if we have to fight, we will fight for him," Coosa-amathle called. Bear stopped to listen, turned, went on. See-ho-kee could imagine his anger and embarrassment. To think that Bear could get the courage up to leave the village at dark.

"Will he go in the dark?" she asked her mother.

Her mother smiled, and it was good to see her eyes close with merriment. "No, I don't think so. I think he will go out about the distance you can hear the owl and there he will lie down, facing our fire so that he won't be afraid, and he will pray that the owl will not hoot." See-ho-kee shivered at her mother's mention of the dreaded owl cry, sign of death.

"Father, I will go and beat him for you, if you want me to," said Hitchiti-hajo hopefully.

"No, Son. Let him go. What you must do is to help feed his family when you catch fish or shoot game."

Poor Thlicklin, See-ho-kee thought. *Never to find a deed worthy of his new name.* She did not worry about Bear's family. They were all brothers and sisters here, and food would be divided as well as the work to get the food. When one ate, all ate.

They heard a sound on the trail from the east, got ready to run and hide. *It's Bear,* thought See-ho-kee in terror. *That's all. It's Bear.*

There was a soft friendly call. It was a runner, a young

man about as old as Eemathle. "Hello! I've got news!" he called in a voice that carried only to them and not to the woods beyond.

It was hard to wait for the young man to eat and drink before he talked, but See-ho-kee waited in silence with the others. He looked around at them in apology, his eyes gleaming white in the firelight. He chewed, gulped, washed down food with water, and before he was through, began to talk.

"There has been a bad fight. Six of our friends were going to Deadman's Pond, and they stopped to slaughter a cow."

"That's Alachua. Right?" said Coosa-amathle.

"Yes."

"White man's place. They went out of our land."

The runner considered this and shrugged. "When they stay out of our land, we'll stay out of theirs. They cooked their beef. Who knows? It was probably Indian beef. And white men came and fought them, got them before they knew what was happening, took their guns, beat them with rawhide. One man got a gash here . . . " He ran a finger across his right eye. "That eye is bad, swollen. Blind, I think. Then while they were beating our brothers, two more Indians, Lechotichee and his friend, came up and started shooting, and they shot back, killing one, wounding another."

Lechotichee. It was not a name she had heard.

"Were any white men killed?" asked Coosa-amathle.

"No."

"Damn," said Coosa-amathle with quiet passion. See-ho-kee felt proud that her father knew a foreign word.

"But they wounded three," the runner said.

"Good. Then what?"

"The headmen turned them over to white chiefs for punishment, and now the white judge in Alachua will judge them.''

The young messenger, haughty and swaggering with importance, received food and drink again and ate with passion.

See-ho-kee's father was angry. ''That was an evil thing to do. I would not have done it. I would not turn our people over to their people to judge.''

See-ho-kee herself felt angry; she watched as her brothers stirred with rage. ''Will we fight them, Father?'' she asked.

''I will consider it. What do you think?'' he asked the man beside him.

''I think the Indians were wrong to cross our agreed boundary, but the white men are worse for punishing our people. We can punish our own in our own way. But I don't see going to war over it. They have more weapons, more soldiers, more food. We need to protest, not to fight.''

''I will rest now,'' the messenger said, like a command. He was led away to a sleeping cheke.

The argument went around, the older men cautious, the younger ready to go at once for revenge. See-ho-kee tried to keep her fear and excitement from making her mind slow. She wanted to think what was right. At last, when she was realizing that most of her village was ready for war, her father gave the final thought, which was proper.

''We must wait till the crops are harvested, whatever we do. If we fight, we will need to hide food in safe places, so we must wait.''

The adults of the village nodded in agreement. It was settled, for the time being.

''When will we have tale-telling?'' a small voice pleaded, and children who had been quiet and obedient now crowded against the old people and pressed softly for a story.

''You are right,'' said See-ho-kee's mother, looking a polite challenge at Coosa-amathle. ''We can't use the rest of our lives talking war and neglecting the stories about the old people. Grandmother, are you ready to tell a tale?''

The old woman was always ready for this; she had sighed with impatience that all the time was being wasted on passing things like wars, neglecting the lasting legends. She began the story of the way the Miccosukees got corn, and the children settled thankfully, knowing it would be a wonderful story — they had heard it many times, knowing it was always a little different and even better than the time before, knowing that the grandmother in the story was the bringer of corn and that would help *this* grandmother to make the story sing.

See-ho-kee studied the beautiful, wrinkled face with love and respect, not only for the old woman's genius at recalling their sacred history and the funny stories other grandmothers had passed down, but also because of her high position. At Green Corn Dance she had always led the other old women into the square to dance. She was the wealthiest and most important person in the clan, the oldest woman in the village; every child here, every woman here was part of her body. Until the white men came, her grandchildren were busy all the time in caring for her cattle and horses, in keeping her houses repaired.

See-ho-kee's grandmother had outlived her first husband, about whom she still spoke as if he stood near her. After his death she had traveled on horseback with her oldest son to the north where there was a man she remembered from her young days. She had proposed marriage to him, and soon they came riding home, he astride the horse she had given him and wearing the shirt she had made. Her second husband lived a long time and treated her kindly, but finally he died of old age.

Once in a while someone teased the old woman about marrying again, and See-ho-kee believed she considered it; though, when she spoke of it, she laughed and put her hands over her face.

Her grandmother's lively tales were interrupted by the messenger who suddenly stepped back into the firelight; he was urgent to tell something he had forgotten to say, and the grandmother quieted instantly, while all the people shifted positions on their cheke boards and faced him, courteous and still.

"Maybe you know the man who was wounded," the messenger said. "He was a Long Swamp man."

See-ho-kee felt a stricture in her breast. Her thoughts scurried. Fixonechee, her husband, was a Long Swamp man, and he was there now, hunting with his friends, as he often did, coming home only when he had game. Last week he had brought her a deer, and she had felt proud to give meat to the tribe. Yaha Chatee and Nuff-kee had come to visit that day, and she remembered the taut, unnatural look on Yaha's face when he refused some of the meat. This tense look had never left him since she married at the Green Corn Dance, and it saddened her.

"What did you say his name was?" asked Coosa-amathle.

"Lechotichee."

See-ho-kee's breath came forth with a full sigh.

"And the dead man's name?"

"Fixonechee. He is also from Long Swamp."

There was a doleful silence, and See-ho-kee felt something strange and strong run into her head and make it swell and ache.

He couldn't be dead. They had been married less than a month.

"He was killed," the messenger half-chanted. "A great hero who fought to save his brothers, a marvelous warrior."

Her head whirled with the horror of it. Any day now, she had thought, he would be home with food, and he would take her in silence to their cheke for love-making, and there they would stay for the hours it took him to exhaust his need. She had lost her husband before they had learned to speak easily to one another. And excited as she became over intercourse, she had not yet received satisfaction from it, as she had with Yaha whose gentle ways never failed to give her pleasure.

Fixonechee was dead. *Fixonechee was dead!*

And she was bound to him, even more now than before, for she faced four years of mourning, four years of looking away from Yaha Chatee, even in casual friendship, lest he be accused of sleeping with her. Four years of guarding against bathing downstream from Yaha, four years of never allowing him to approach her for so much as a drink of water. She must guard against all these things so that he wouldn't be accused of adultery and beaten for it or even have an ear cropped, though *she* would more likely lose *her* ear or even her nose.

And what else must she do?

Suddenly she looked up at the members of her family, saw their eyes upon her, her mother sad and sympathetic, her father and brothers stern and watchful, waiting to see that she followed the path of duty.

Oh, she wished that Fixonechee had had an older brother who could come to sleep with her tonight and free her from this terrible duty.

They waited for her to move. Her family waited. Tale-telling was over. Their neighbors went quietly back to their own chekes and to bed, their backs turned to her while she began her preparations.

She unpinned her hair, let fall the most glorious hair arrangement in the village, and she stretched it forward till it hung, loose and ugly, over her face. She realized she hadn't cried out a word of sorrow, and she still could not do it. Instead, she stooped and grappled with the earth for some black loam, and she rubbed it over her face and dress, and then she turned toward her cheke to begin her four years of prison. She must put her dress aside for a sheet, which would now be her only garment, summer or winter, except for her shoes and her sash for carrying things.

She kept her face down; yet she caught the nod of approval her grandmother sent her; she saw Yaha Chatee, whose face turned steadfastly away.

seven

Charley Amathla from We-tump-ka, a high chief of all the Florida Indians, the Yakitisee, persisted in saying that the Indians should give in to white demands that they be removed to the West. The Indians were suddenly divided. The old and the weak thought that the only safety was, as Charley Amathla had told them, to go to Fort Brooke on the west coast of Florida and wait for the white people to take them aboard a ship.

But there were angry people who thought the other way. Apayaka, See-ho-kee's great-uncle, was old but not weak, and he was bound to stay and die in Florida, he told everyone. And there was Asi Yahola who still fumed from the insults he had suffered at the hands of the white men.

The anger built up among the restless people in See-ho-kee's village, for there was no food. Hunting was bad because of the animal still-births after the freeze last spring, and the crops had not come to much; only small patches had been planted. Everybody had thought they would have to move again, either farther south to escape the white men or to the West. No use to plant, they thought.

Charley Amathla's village still owned cattle. In her own village there was only her grandmother's one cow, which they hoped to have bred in the spring to build up the herd again. In the meantime, See-ho-kee's belly ached for something besides fish and coonte. She thought much of food these days, and she remembered with longing that there had been more food at Okihumky where Apayaka lived, or so it seemed now.

Suddenly her father showed his thoughts were like hers, and he announced to the family his thought that they should return to Big Swamp, near Apayaka's village, where they could be with other family members. It was her grandmother's old home to which they had moved when they had fled from Georgia, and it was the village where her mother had grown up. She remembered clearly the day they had left it, had felt the same sadness she saw on her mother's face, but fear had driven them to the good hiding places in the Ouithlacoochee Cove, where there was water, then land, then water, an easy place for the white soldiers to get lost.

"I think we should go," said Coosa-amathle. "It is dangerous to live there so close to Fort King, but we will starve here. The soldiers are closer to our hidden places every day. Who knows where we can live safely? And it is proper to live in your wife's village."

The family discussed the idea at great length; each person was heard with courtesy and thought, down to the youngest children. They decided to go. See-ho-kee watched the lines in her mother's face curve upward in happiness, and the grandmother's smile spread through the group. But See-ho-kee had a quick thought of her mother's dead baby, and she wondered whether a small spirit would hover near their empty cheke, looking for them. She tried to put the thought away. No doubt the small spirit had gone westward. She thought too of Fixonechee, whose death she still mourned. Oddly, she could no longer conjure up his face, though she easily pictured his heavy brows and the glinting spectacles. She was already sick of her ugly hair and the dirty sheet she wore now.

Yet the sadness at leaving the spirit of the dead baby sister mingled with her hidden delight of moving away from the cheke her husband had built for her. In the new place she would live in her mother's cheke again.

"If it doesn't work out," her father said, "we can come back in time for the planting in the spring."

The move was undertaken at once, and four nights after Coosa-amathle's suggestion, they had slept in one of their old houses. It had been wonderful, and since her grandmother went with them, as well as her sister- and brother-cousins, including Nuff-kee and Yaha Chatee, it had not been hurtful. Except for the soft touches by the small spirit before she left, and the worry that it wandered alone and afraid in Ouithlacoochee Cove.

They were accustomed to moving. When she was a little girl, they used to leave Big Swamp frequently to find better hunting or ocean fishing or anything for a change, but they never stayed away more than a month or two at a time. Nuff-kee's family sent word from Wahoo Swamp that they were coming too, and she and See-ho-kee had a joyful reunion at the cove, the evening before their trip.

Now that they were back home in Big Swamp, See-ho-kee discovered right away that there too the men met daily on the square to discuss what they must do, whether to move to the West or to stay and fight if attacked. It must be decided, for in two months all Yakitisee must leave Florida, according to the way the white men interpreted the treaties. Her father wavered from day to day in what was right to do, and his inconsistency fed See-ho-kee's nightmares.

The subject of going or staying became so dreadful that it was now forbidden at the nightly tale-telling sessions, but the men discussed it with each other and then told their wives in bed, and the wives whispered it to each other later, and the children listened and worried. Fort King had become a fearful place, now that the Indians had stopped visiting there, and See-ho-kee realized that the same terror that affected her at Ouithlacoochee had followed her to Big Swamp.

On a cool, pleasant day, See-ho-kee and Nuff-kee and other Big Swamp young women went out to dig in the coonte ground. Coonte was now a staple in their diet, for it did not have to be planted, and it took the place of sofkee which was made from grated corn. The women worked hard and fast; they must feed the village, now that the men were more involved in war than hunting, now that food was so scarce that the only way Indians could get enough to eat was to raid white villages. So the women dug and probed industriously, getting warm in the sun after the long cold night.

Nuff-kee couldn't bear uncertainty; she could die without fear, she said, if she just knew when it would be and how and where she would die. Especially where. "If I knew that I was going to the West and would be killed by a Creek lover and die a scandalous death, why, I would go without complaint," she said.

See-ho-kee grinned. "If you take a Creek lover out in the West," she said, "your own family will probably kill you and pitch your lover to animals."

This remark didn't bother Nuff-kee nor slow her down in her speculations. "They should simply tell us what will happen," she went on. "We wouldn't worry then."

"What worries me is not when I die, but whether I'll die without ever seeing a white person in the face," See-ho-kee said. "I haven't seen one yet."

"Think of that as a blessing and not a curse," Nuff-kee said sourly, "for they are not very beautiful." Her words jarred See-ho-kee. Nuff-kee seldom spoke maliciously, and she had caught the disease of perpetual anger from her parents. See-ho-kee resolved to resist anger in herself.

The coonte bed was northwest of the village, just off the trail to We-tump-ka. See-ho-kee stood up at last, ready to go home. She had all the roots she could carry in the bag her mother had made for this purpose. She stretched, felt her sore back creak into place. Nuff-kee's bag was full too, she saw, which was lucky for their families. The coonte ground was nearly used up. What would the Big Swamp people do when that was gone too?

"You ready to go?"

"Yes. Hey. Wait. Look over there."

Nuff-kee pointed to the trail. There went Charlie Amathla with a few of his men going north from Fort King.

"Oh. Let's run ask the news."

They shouldered their coonte and started out, leaving the other girls who had not worked so fast.

"Wait," said Nuff-kee. She pointed.

From the forest trail several other Indians suddenly burst into the sunlight. See-ho-kee felt her heart begin to beat very fast. Something terrible was about to happen. Now many men came out of the forest. There was her great-uncle, Apayaka, talking in his high-pitched voice, and there was Asi Yahola, parading and stamping his feet like a nervous horse. They marched ahead very swiftly, caught Charley Amathla by the arm, whirled him around and confronted him. Ah, there was her own father and her two warrior brothers. And Yaha Chatee. Her heart moved, to see him so thin, so solemn.

All the men were quiet and unmoving now except for Charley Amathla, who said in a loud voice, "I will not act as a child. I will act as a man. I signed that we would remove, and I will do what I said. I will be honest and go, as my father has said he will do too."

See-ho-kee suddenly understood what the whole thing meant. The Indians must stay together or be swallowed by the white men. They must agree to do the *same thing,* even if some had to die to convince the others. Terror arose in her when she finally understood. Charley Amathla was surely about to die.

"Charley Amathla, you're not a weak and crying old man," Asi Yahola said. "Act like a warrior. *Be* a warrior on your brother's side."

"No. I have said what I will do, and I will do it. And the people of We-tump-ka will go to Fort Brooke with me."

"Your time is over," screamed Asi Yahola. "I will kill you myself." He ran at Charley Amathla, while See-ho-kee waited trembling.

Abraham, big and black, pushed between the two men. "Wait, brother," he rumbled at Asi Yahola. "Should we use our little strength killing each other? Let's decide by council. I call for council, now in this place."

It was his right. Asi Yahola must allow the men to deliberate before they took action.

Argument ceased, and the council began. The Indians seated themselves as if they were on their own square-ground in the village, leaving a rectangle of space in the center. Now that it was quieter, the girls could no longer understand the grumbling voices. The two glanced at each other, and moved, as if they had spoken and agreed, through the saw-grass closer to the council, moving carefully so as not to leave a wake in the grass that would attract attention.

Asi Yahola spoke. His speech went on and on; his fists hammered the air; his body turned and turned as he faced each set of men. Each thing he said four times.

Nuff-kee punched See-ho-kee. "Look."

Charley Amathla moved away from the group and went back to the trail that led around the swamp, between the water and the thick hammock. In a moment he would be in the woods and hard to find.

"What is going to happen?" Nuff-kee whispered.

"I don't know. Nothing, I hope. But I am afraid."

Asi Yahola's angry voice went higher. "If we cannot depend upon our *brothers* to be loyal to us, how can we expect anything but treachery from the white men? I say we should kill him now and be done with it. He is carrying money the white soldiers at Fort King paid him for his cattle. Those cattle would have fed all the Miccosukees who must steal to live."

Another warrior stood and spoke. "But it is true that Charley Amathla has said since the beginning that the chiefs who went to Arkansas were forced to sign and thus the treaty was wrong. He argued against the white agent many times."

"Then he should help us fight instead of working against us," her uncle suddenly shrilled. "Asi Yahola is only a young man, not a great chief. Yet he has courage to speak the truth, and we should listen to him."

The speaking went on, one after another of the chiefs rising and going to the center. At the edge of the group Asi Yahola and three men moved quietly away.

See-ho-kee felt her heart begin to race again. She looked north, saw that Charley Amathla was still visible, a distant figure now starting into the hammock.

The four men followed him, running swiftly up the trail, never seeing the watchful women who huddled in terror in the shelter of the grass. The men carried heavy flintlocks, longer than See-ho-kee herself. She strained to hear. At last she stood up.

An ugly sound came from the hammock. *Kuh-blung.* A distance away, another *kuh-blung.* Shots. Heavy gunshots. Charley Amathla was no longer visible. Asi Yahola bent over, hitting down with his gun, swinging it up into the air and hitting again. The other men bent and struck. She heard them. Grunts and yells. Asi Yahola's whoop.

There was never a word nor sound from Charley Amathla.

The council warriors were on their feet and running up the trail. See-ho-kee moved that way too, moved silently across the edge of the swamp, not so much afraid of being seen now, for she believed she could have run with the group now and not be noticed, so great was their excitement. The killing was done; her fear was subsiding. They would not kill her. No Indian warrior would kill a woman. Asi Yahola said this himself. Warriors killed only warriors.

On the edge of the woods Asi Yahola stood up holding his hands high. "Look," he said. "Look at this money. This money comes from the blood of Indians. No one will have this money."

He cast the money into the air, turning the while. He cast it in four directions. "There and there and there and there," he said. "Let no one touch this evil money."

See-ho-kee now saw Charley Amathla, dead near the trail. She felt no fear now, but the warriors, including her father and brothers, suddenly looked so frightened, cowed by Asi Yahola's grand rage, that they began immediately kicking a new trail, hacking at the underbrush, clearing a new way around the body rather than touch it and honor it with burial.

See-ho-kee felt sorrow for Charley Amathla although he was wrong. His body would lie there, for nobody would dare move it. His spirit would roam in anguish.

"Let the wolves eat him," Asi Yahola said.

In the next two days there was a swift movement of Charley Amathla's villagers, led by his father, to Fort Brooke. They were mostly women and children, but there were also some men, seeking protection from the other Yakitisee warriors.

There was still a cruel division among the Indians, but now all of them were afraid to speak for removal.

The tension in the constant meetings on the square at Big Swamp spread to the children. See-ho-kee understood what it meant; they were going to move again. It was no longer safe to live so close to Fort King; the women and children could not be protected here in the swamp, and indeed, they now saw that it was no safer here than it had been in Ouithlacoochee.

The day after Charley Amathla died, the Big Swamp and Long Swamp Seminoles moved away, some to Wahoo Swamp, See-ho-kee and her family back to the cove. A few of the most terrified went all the way to the Everglades. A bad choice, Coosa thought. Nobody could live there long.

The women grieved deeply to leave Big Swamp. See-ho-kee walked with her mother and their joyful Eefe beside her grandmother's horse. She looked often up into her grandmother's ancient, mysterious face and wondered at the old woman's thoughts. She believed her grandmother was gathering her strength to overcome her grief at losing forever a beloved place.

Or perhaps she was thinking of Charley Amathla's village of We-tump-ka, now also a place with only spirits in attendance. Maybe her grandmother was saying to herself, *We-tump-ka! Say that name!*

eight

There was a great meeting and celebration at Wahoo Swamp three days after the white peoples' winter festival for their god. Runners had crossed Florida, to the east, north, and south, and had told them the news. Asi Yahola had killed Agent Thompson and would come to tell how it happened.

See-ho-kee sat alone, dirty and untidy, and watched.

Jumper and Alligator had trapped some white soldiers led by Major Dade and had killed them. Jumper was at home in Wahoo Swamp, ready to boast of their deed.

A runner had come from the east coast to tell of the destruction of most of the sugar mills. Soon they would burn the rest of the mills.

Suddenly the red people were taking the offensive in the

little battles that had been going on for many years, ever since General Jackson burned the three hundred houses of the Miccosukee villages years ago. Now, the Yakitisee were saying, *All right, white soldiers, we will fight rather than go to Fort Brooke on January 10th. We will fight, and we will decide* where *to fight.*

"The white man is finished in Florida. He will not show his face again." The boast came from her brother Eemathle. "He knows we can kill him, we have the right way. We have medicine to keep us strong. The white man is a savage, and he will die." Her brother chanted the words, and the Indians began to group around the square-ground, ready for the recital and celebration to begin. Asi Yahola was nearby, and they waited, eager to see the hero. As more and more chiefs and warriors seated themselves in the square for the celebration, Eemathle ceased his singing and the little dance he had begun. He moved to the tier of chekes where the young warriors with more strong spirit than distinction must sit. See-ho-kee saw that her great-uncle Apayaka sat with the important men. People walked across the square and back, anxious for Asi Yahola to come. *Everybody* would be at the celebration, even the women and children. Someone passed a bottle of liquor, and See-ho-kee watched her father drink. Her mother would drink later, so that one of them kept a clear head, but See-ho-kee would not drink at all. Her mother did not like the liquor, and she drank it only to feel the good fire that ran through her veins and to make her husband laugh.

But liquor was bad, See-ho-kee knew. Some Yakitisee squandered a whole season of trapping by giving the pelts to the white traders on the edge of the reservation for liquor. Agent Thompson had told them time and again not to do that, that he would take the liquor away from them. He did that to Asi Yahola, and saw what this had brought him to. She often wondered why Agent Thompson allowed the whiskey sellers to get the Indians' animal skins without punishment, and then he punished the Indians by taking their liquor away, so that they were left with nothing, not even a celebration with drink to make themselves feel better.

There was Yaha Chatee, beloved friend. He would not look up.

She heard loud voices and a burst of laughter. Asi Yahola! His laughter was as distinctive as the shrill yelp he used to call his warriors to battle. There they came now, Asi Yahola in front of his party. All of them were swaggering and dancing and holding their booty high in the air. "Hey," said Asi Yahola. "Here we have the agent." He held up a tiny bit of scalp, and See-ho-kee shuddered. It was a strange feeling; she was curious to get close enough to examine the scalp, but also felt she would have sick-belly if she did. Of course, she had seen the scalps on the pole before, but they were so old the hair had fallen out, leaving white papery skin.

"And *here* is Agent Thompson," shouted another warrior, holding up another bit of scalp.

The crowd laughed. Agent Thompson had got himself separated. Suddenly Nuff-kee was there, nudging her over to make room. See-ho-kee felt tears of appreciation for someone so real, so normal.

"And *here* is Agent Thompson." Another bit. The laugh again.

They gathered to give all the pieces of scalp to Illis-higher-Hadjo, the great medicine-chief, and he accepted them and fastened them on the central pole. He was solemn. He did not give in to the jubilance of the warriors; he did his work with quiet words whose meaning was known only to himself and the spirits. Then he waited for the next trophies.

Asi Yahola was a brave man who could look and know. He didn't need to talk in council for three days like Micanopy; he saw and acted. See-ho-kee had always liked him for his beauty, for the sad half-frown, for his gentleness with children and with women. Now, seeing him as a triumphant killer, bedecked with scalps that dripped blood from his girdle onto his legs, seeing him wear another man's hair on his head that let blood trickle to his face and neck, seeing him hold up the red silk sash that had distinguished Agent General Thompson from ordinary soldiers, listening as he gave his talk and his war cry in demonstration, seeing and hearing all this, she felt inexpressibly afraid and sad. If it were true, as some people said, that Asi Yahola was the spirit of the Indian, was she also like this? She moved closer to Nuff-kee, leaned against her. She thought: *She is thin. I feel Nuff-kee's bones.* She remembered: *The white men did this. They kept us from our lands, pursued us till we couldn't plant. They are killing Nuff-kee.* She felt better, now that she had remembered the reason for Asi Yahola's angry celebration. He stopped to drink liquor, and she felt almost glad, knowing he would soon relax and the wild face would soften.

"The white men taunted him when he was a boy," she whispered to Nuff-kee.

Nuff-kee nodded. "I have heard this too. And did you hear that his wife, who was part-Negro, was taken from him and sold as a slave and that General Thompson did not help him?"

"No. I hadn't hear that. Is it true?"

"I don't know." Nuff-kee was honest. She would tell a good tale and then admit it might not be real. She didn't know how to lie, but See-ho-kee did. If it were to prevent getting a scratching, she would think about lying. So far she had only thought and never lied, for it was truly a disgrace to do that, but she knew how and kept in mind that she might do it someday.

As See-ho-kee stared at the men who were now getting

noisy with liquor, she saw that there was a difference in them; some had a certainty, others a hesitation. Asi Yahola was as certain as sunrise. There was no pause or question in him; he believed the white men would never leave them alone, wherever they fled to; he would hate and fight till he died. He would not forgive.

But in others among the warriors there was uncertainty about what to do, what was right to do. Micanopy had that hesitation; yet he was not a coward. *Are we to risk all our lives?* he seemed to ask. *Is it right to let our wives and children die while we fight?*

Her own father had the hesitation, though he spoke out and fought bravely.

She herself was on the side of the hesitators. Yet, she believed she could kill a white man to save a baby from being murdered. If she *had* to.

Halpatter-Tustenuggee, whom the white men called Alligator, now spoke. "Asi Yahola is a strong man. When we planned to fight the white agent, he told me, 'No, you will not do it. He used to be my friend, and he put me in irons. The insult is on me, and I will take care of that matter.' And this is how he took care of it. He went to Fort King and got ready to attack it. But then the general and another man came out; Asi Yahola had such strong medicine that Agent Thompson came out to meet his death."

Suddenly Asi Yahola gave his shrill scream, sending a cold feeling over See-ho-kee. "That's the last sound he heard," Asi Yahola yelled. "The agent knew, oh, he *knew* who was there." He shrilled again. "He knew this call. And we shot him and shot him." He strutted up to the pole, held up his liquor bottle. "My brothers," he said to the bits of black hair, "will you listen to our good words? We have been patient with you. Our father in Washington is patient with you. But now you must consider removal." He had become Agent Thompson. See-ho-kee laughed with the other listeners, a bad thing for a widow to do.

He strutted and talked, catching Agent Thompson's personality and gestures so perfectly that the laughter broke out again. He danced alone around the pole, crying out the story. When he was through with the tale-telling, others joined him, warriors only, in the wild noisy dance around the pole, and before long, the whole group fell to the ground in a drunken laughter.

See-ho-kee looked at her parents, saw they were stern and embarrassed at the lack of dignity. She immediately stopped laughing. Her father leaned toward Jumper and suggested something. Jumper looked uncertain, and Coosa-amathle hit his right fist into the open palm of his left hand. It sounded with a sudden smack. He repeated his words to Jumper, and Jumper arose.

Over the laughter his voice lifted. "It is time now to hear of our battle with Major Dade and Captain Gardiner."

All attention was on him at once, for it had been a great victory, but one of Asi Yahola's warriors stood up at the pole and cried out, "No! Not yet. We have not yet told you about the sutler."

Jumper contained his anger if he felt any. He stayed near the pole and looked with his small bright eyes at the men who now struggled to their feet, giggling occasionally. Jumper had an ugly face, See-ho-kee thought, but it was easy to see his sharp intelligence. He was known to have two faces and to laugh at fat Micanopy behind his back, yet praise and coax him into doing what Jumper thought was proper. Now was a time to be gracious. He spread his hands in an open, generous gesture.

"Yes," he said. "Tell us about Erastus Rogers."

The strange-sounding name set the giggles off again.

Asi Yahola sprang to his feet, eager to tell it, though he was becoming thick-tongued and uncertain of movement. "Erastus Rogers and his two clerks ate their noon meal at his house, not knowing we were near, not knowing it was their last meal. And we sprang upon them and shot and hit and hit." Asi Yahola began hitting down with an imaginary weapon, then swung down with an imaginary long knife. Then he signified a separation of limb from limb and head from torso by a harsh look and a swift swinging of his hands apart. He turned and kicked the imaginary body parts away from each other, finally lifted the scalp on his head and made a scalping movement.

When the appreciative whoops died down, someone asked, "What goods did you get?"

Asi Yahola looked sour. "We got what you see here. We have some food and the clothes we wanted. But the sutler had cleared out his store of goods." Again he chopped the air at the sutler and his clerks, and he recommenced his dance, the others of his party of Miccosukees joining him.

Jumper waited. He had time. What he had to tell was so much grander that he could afford to be generous. They had all night.

At last Asi Yahola's enthusiasm slowed, and he announced that his brother Ote Emathla, whom the white man called Jumper, would speak of his victory. *The red man too,* See-ho-kee thought. *Everybody said Jumper, for the word had a lovely drum sound.*

Jumper proved his graciousness. "I will let Halpatter-Tustenuggee speak."

Halpatter-Tustenuggee came at once, seeing no reason for modesty. He stood near See-ho-kee, no taller than she was, his face amiable, his eyes alight with mischief. The audience brightened at once, for he was always funny and he made fun of the pomposities of the other chiefs.

"If you call him Jumper, then call me Alligator," he said. They laughed in agreement, for this word of the white men was comical and not at all like the real word *hal PA te* which sounded just like the animal itself.

"We took a year getting ready," Alligator said. "The white soldiers tried to make us move, and we waited and argued till we were ready. Then we heard from the Negroes at Fort Brooke that two companies were coming, and we readied ourselves. We wanted to wait for Asi Yahola, but he was delayed. . . ." Here Alligator motioned to the scalps decorating the pole, and the crowd grinned with appreciation.

Asi Yahola nodded with much dignity and gave two jugs of whiskey to be passed around.

They will be drunk, See-ho-kee thought.

"Micanopy wanted to wait for Asi Yahola, to give him the pleasure, but we saw the time had come, for the white soldiers were almost at the swamp. At dawn we slipped out of the swamp into the pines. We took our places near the road, each man behind a tree or clump of palmetto. We waited two hours. When they came, we waited till all the soldiers were between us and a pond, and Jumper gave a whoop."

The story must cease now, while Jumper demonstrated his whoop which was drawn out and could be heard a mile away. See-ho-kee believed. After Alligator took up his story, the whoop still went through her mind.

"Micanopy fired the first rifle, and then every Indian fired. It was a great fight. The white soldiers shouted too and fought bravely, especially one little man who roared, 'God-dam! No rifle ball can hit me!' But one did."

"What did he look like?" Asi Yahola asked.

"Short and broad. Very brave. Very angry."

"That was Captain Gardiner," a warrior said. "I knew him."

"It was easy to hit them. Their clothes are the color of the sky. See this one? It is dirty now, but it was easy to see." Alligator held the tunic up, poked two fingers through bullet holes. The people grunted a little, knowing what a bullet hole like that did to a human being.

"We thought we killed them all and we took a few clothes and some food and ammunition. We left. But an Indian told us they were building breastworks, and we went back and killed the rest."

"I think one was still alive," said Jumper. "It's all right though. Somebody needs to tell the others what they can expect if they keep nagging us to go; they need to know what we will do to them if they keep trying to take our slaves away."

"Where are the scalps?"

"We didn't take any," said Alligator.

There was no embarrassment in his voice and no hint of criticism toward Asi Yahola. It was simply a decision they had made on the spot.

"The blacks went in and found three whites alive. They talked to them and killed them, I think. Many Negroes were there looking down at the white men when we left."

The celebration took on a more exciting aspect now; it was not only that the Yakitisee had taken revenge but that they had now had a powerful victory that would stop the white men from their outrages. The dancing now involved half the warriors. Yaha Chatee danced; his face shone with fervor.

At last Jumper held up his hand for silence. "Let's hear the rest," he said. "Let the runner from Miccosukee Philip say what they did over in the eastern part of Florida."

Everybody knew this of course, but it was good to hear it again from somebody who had been there and seen it himself. Philip's warriors had destroyed five sugar mills on the day the white men usually celebrated their god's birthday.

Alligator jumped up and shouted, "Not the sort of celebration they're used to having."

All the great deeds had been told.

"Let's hear from Beloved Man Apayaka," a voice called.

Yes. Ehee. Yes.

Apayaka stood and looked at the faces of his people. "My father used to tell me of the old town of Cus-se-tuh," he said. See-ho-kee immediately envisioned her grandmother doing her stomp-dance.

"It was a very large town," Apayaka said, "and they were friendly to the white people. But the chiefs were old men like myself, and they liked order; they began to notice that their young men became rude or disorderly when they were with the white people very much, and the chiefs complained about this. They worried about the morals of the young. And now I say that it will no longer be a problem. If a white man tries to associate with us, we will not need to be polite. We will *kill* him."

The warriors roared agreement.

"The morals and manners of our young men will not be threatened again," Apayaka said. "That is all I have to say." The singing and dancing and drinking would go on all night. The women were drinking now, and the children were falling asleep wherever they could find a bit of room in a cheke. The men would stay away from their wives tonight, See-ho-kee knew, for it was not proper to sleep with a wife after going to battle. It worried her a little that only liquor had been drunk tonight and not purifying black drink. This was a white man's custom, and it was wrong, as her uncle had said.

See-ho-kee stayed awake all night. When only two men were still staggering around the pole, she stared at the swamp around their hammock and waited.

She had a sudden terrible vision. What if Asi Yahola were wrong? What if these attacks did *not* defeat the white men? What if they swarmed into Florida like the northern birds, wave upon wave of them, in numbers beyond counting?

nine

By the time her father had stirred himself out of heavy sleep the next morning, it was too late for See-ho-kee to tell him of her vision, for scouts came into the village and announced that white troops were coming for revenge. As soon as See-ho-kee heard it, she knew that her vision was a true one.

The troops were coming down from Fort Drane which was northwest of We-tump-ka Hammock. The scouts talked very fast, heard questions, tried to answer. How many troops were there? They didn't know exactly. Two hundred regulars at least. Four or five hundred volunteers. Were they moving fast? They smiled. No. They carried all their belongings; they moved like old men.

At once, the village became awake and active. Alligator

and Asi Yahola gathered the warriors about them, two hundred and fifty, a strong group. Thirty of them were Negroes as eager to fight as the Indians, for they had much to be angry about.

Several others were Uchees who had only lately given up trying to live in north Florida and moved to the cove. They lived near See-ho-kee's family, and many times she had tried to overcome her ignorance of their language so that they could talk to each other.

They were good people but angry. As soon as weapons were gathered and readied and the women had brought them all the ammunition the village owned, the warriors ran north to the ford in the Ouithlacoochee River where they could ambush the whites. It was the only place the soldiers could cross without boats.

They waited all night and all next day.

See-ho-kee told her mother about the vision; her mother was attentive and treated her words seriously. "It could be a hunger dream, or it could be real. If it is real, my husband needs to know it so he may tell the others. They need to be warned." Her mother's solemnity and fearfulness made See-ho-kee afraid too.

Her mother would never allow her to take the warning to her father. She knew that. It was too dangerous. The battle might be going on by the time she got there, and it was inappropriate for a widow to go out among warriors, but *someone* must go.

Months of never having enough to eat, a sleepless night, a frightening vision — all these things set a tremor going in her legs. She was too weak, too afraid to go see her father. But the decision surged up from somewhere in her mind, as relentless as the vision had been, and she knew she was going. She tucked her sheet tightly into her sash.

It was a long run back to the cove. She ran swiftly, listening for the birds to change their songs to friendly warnings, for the Florida jays always did this when something was wrong. She hoped she would not hear an owl. She slowed down, became cautious as she approached the ford across the Ouithlacoochee River where the Indians would be hiding, waiting.

Ahead of her a sabal palm bowed in invitation toward the northwest, humbled by years of wind. She ran up the palm to the point where it curved up and grew toward the sky. She saw to her horror that the white men had already crossed the river, some of them, the regulars. On the north side there was a large group of ragtag volunteers, their guns stacked.

But this is not the ford! she thought. *What are they doing here?* She clung motionless to the tree, watched, saw more men crossing, only six of them in somebody's discarded old cypress canoe. *All those men crossed in that boat?* She waited. *They did! It's the only boat they've got.*

The regulars had learned. Their shirts had been dirtied so that only a hint of the sky color remained. Their white belts had been blackened, and no longer could they be considered easy targets. They blurred into the earth, into the shadowy water, and only their white faces were easy to see.

In the distance she saw her people, dark, also part of the earth, blending into the protective foliage. They were waiting at the ford, too far away to hear all the noise the whites made in their moving about. It was a dangerous situation. Two hundred soldiers already on the south side of the river with nobody stopping them. She came down the tree much faster than she had gone up, cut across to a trail which she knew would lead her to her father. She ran as fast as she could down the trail, a long run, slowed when she came to two outside scouts, said, "Hsst, hsst!" Got their attention. Saw them turn and look. She waved and ran to them. "I must talk to my father," she said.

"Leave this place, young widow. Your father is too busy

now. Go home.'' The men were impatient, and one seemed ready to give her a cuff, proper or not.

''No. I must talk to him. You're guarding the wrong place. The white soldiers are over there, *this* side of the river.'' She pointed with authority.

The two men stared at her, mouths open. One suddenly turned and ran, and by the time she got within sight of the main group, Asi Yahola was standing near her, giving close attention. ''What? What do you say?'' he asked. He was gentle and very soft-spoken, but his eyes glittered with intensity.

''They're on *this* side of the river. They have an old canoe.''

''How many?''

She looked around at the warriors. ''As many as we have here. And twice as many on the other side.''

The men moved quickly into a strong place, each with his own tree or clump of palmetto. They were silent as death.

Now in the distance there were sounds from the white men, trying to be quiet but crashing like a herd of panicked cattle.

''I have to see my father,'' See-ho-kee softly told Asi Yahola as he turned away toward the coming fight.

Asi Yahola stared at her a moment, nodded, for he owed her something. He motioned her father to come. ''Talk to your daughter,'' he said, ''and then send her home.''

She told her father about the vision. He listened, shook his head.

''It might be a false dream.''

''How can it be a false dream when already all these men are coming, like the first wave of birds from the north?''

''Still it could be. But it is good that you have told me, and I will tell it to Asi Yahola so he can take warning. And I will tell Illis-higher-Hadjo so that he will protect us with medicine.

"But now, go home. Tell your mother to be ready to hide. And you, *you,* be ready to help take care of your little brothers and sisters. Mothers will need help with the babies, to keep them from crying out and letting the white men know the hiding places."

All the children in the clan were considered her brothers and sisters; all were to be protected.

She felt a quick wave of gooseflesh to hear her father voice the worst fear she had, and she loved him very much because his thoughts were the same as hers. She wanted to ask him, *How many more babies will die, Father?* But she knew he was worried now about the fighting and she must not distract him.

Surely white soldiers wouldn't kill babies.

When she got back to her leaning palm, she ran up the trunk again, watched the battle begin. The sun was at the high point. Noon. General Clinch and his soldiers came into sight. She heard Asi Yahola's whoop, saw Asi Yahola and Alligator begin the firing, listened to the booming guns, heard Asi Yahola's shrill encouragement to his men, heard the general's roar.

General Clinch. She had heard much about him. There he was riding a horse, looking superior to white soldiers and red warriors. There were three quick gunshots, and the general's hat suddenly tipped back. He looked around, this way, that way, to see who had shot, quickly leaped from his horse and stood among the ranks. See-ho-kee smiled. General Clinch was corpulent; his face was young and handsome despite his silvery hair, and when she first saw him, See-ho-kee noticed his muscular build and did not think of him as fat. But he was ponderous enough to slow his movements, and it had been so long since See-ho-kee had seen a fat Indian (except for Micanopy) that General Clinch seemed strange to her.

The general roared again, a second man repeated his

strange words immediately, and suddenly the white soldiers got into a line and ran toward the Indians. Now she couldn't see the Indians who faded into the woods. She watched and trembled. There was a long cry of hurt and sorrow, a wail in Mikasuki language. She could not see the man. Her people disappeared into the woods, and she could breathe. She heard shots, knew they were still fighting, wondered who had been hit. *Not my father, Breathmaker. Not my brothers. Not Yaha Chatee.*

It happened again, the soldiers ran in a line toward the woods, held their guns that had spears on the tips so that any Indian who didn't run would die. And then again they ran.

This time she saw an Indian die. He was the U-chee who spoke only a few words of Mikasuki, who searched frantically for words when he met her father, a good man who cuddled his children and worked without embarrassment in the fields with his wife. The U-chee stepped from behind a tree, took aim, and as his gun sounded, a white man caught him on a gun spear, lifted him a little; the U-chee called one strange word, then kicking and waving in silence fell to the ground out of sight. The white man stabbed the gun downward twice, looked quickly around, fell back into the brush where he couldn't be seen.

See-ho-kee felt a sickness come over her. She would look no more. Through closed eyes she saw the U-chee holding his little boy and laughing with him, as he had done last night.

She thought constantly of her father and prayed again that the Breathmaker would not let his breath be taken from him. Not my father. Not my brothers. Not beloved Yaha.

Now she saw from the sun that over an hour had passed, though the excitement and drama before her had made the time shrink into moments. She came down from the tree very fast and started her long run back to the cove where she must warn her mother and the other women. She believed there were more white people hurt or killed in the fight than red people, and she was glad to have this to report.

Her feeling had changed since watching the line of white soldiers charging against her people. She felt hatred and fury. She felt savage to think that strangers could come upon their lands and try to kill them. She wished she had a gun that would send a bullet from that palm tree all the way to General Clinch. For the first time she understood the way Asi Yahola felt. The white men had more goods, more guns, more powder and bullets, more food, more wagons than her whole village owned. Yet they would come and kill for more.

ten

Two months later there was another battle at Ouithlacoochee with many more white men and many more Indians. This time the Miccosukees were ready, as were inhabitants of other Seminole towns nearby. See-ho-kee was more afraid than the others, because she alone among the women and children had seen death from the white men.

She now knew all she hadn't seen that day. Asi Yahola had been wounded in the arm and had retired from battle, leaving Alligator to lead. It took the heart out of the fighters, seeing Asi Yahola downed, and they retreated with three dead and five wounded. Two of Micanopy's Negroes had been killed and he still complained about it when anyone would listen. "From now on," Micanopy said (till they were tired of hearing it), "none of my Negroes are going to fight."

This outraged her father who couldn't see why Micanopy's black men were more valuable than the dying red men. "He's afraid of losing Abraham," Coosa-amathle said, "and then who will do his thinking for him?"

So it went with Micanopy who had inherited the right to rule but not the natural ability that Asi Yahola and her great-uncle had.

But the battle she had watched had not been so bad after all. They had survived as a village. They were no hungrier than before.

Actually, she had barely known the three dead men, who had lived in Wahoo Swamp, so she felt no grief except when she saw the faces of the widows who now would withdraw for their mourning time. The village would mourn for four days. To See-ho-kee's amazement, her grandmother — that unflinching little woman — broke into tears over the death of one man. "His father came from my mother's village," she said. "He is Che-au-hau, like me. His wife came from Oose-oo-chee. One more person who remembered the stories of my mother is gone." She turned fiercely to See-ho-kee. "Say it. Say Che-au-hau." And See-ho-kee obeyed. She said it twice.

Yaha Chatee, Nuff-kee's brother, was one of the wounded, and See-ho-kee had gone to Wahoo Swamp twice since the battle to take gifts to him from her family. Nuff-kee presented them, and he accepted the gifts without comment. One of the gifts was a rabbit she herself had caught in a trap, an embarrassment to her mother who said that meat-gathering was still a man's chore, hard times or not. Yaha Chatee liked the rabbit though and refused to let his mother kill it for food until finally there was no meat left, and then they ate it. He was a man; yet there was still much of the boy in him. See-ho-kee took pains that their eyes never met; nor did they exchange a word.

For this battle, the Miccosukees had a plan. Again Alligator, Asi Yahola, and Jumper were leaders. Again the white men searched for the ford; again the Indian guides couldn't seem to find the ford. This time their leader, General Gaines, came with inadequate supplies, for he was on the way to Fort Brooke and wanted only a quick slap at the Ouithlacoochee Indians, hoping to waste the villages and make the Indians give in to being removed.

The Indians knew exactly where the soldiers were from the moment they entered the Ouithlacoochee area. As the white men waded into the water in search of the ford, the Indians began firing, and the battle was on. It went on for several days, with much noise, many shouts and shots. The soldiers began building rafts; the Indians howled and shot; the soldiers shouted (from behind shelter) that the Indians were too cowardly to come out into the open for a good fight.

The soldiers built a protective breastworks of logs and settled in for a long stay, for the Indians slipped in very close and screamed warwhoops, each time from a different side to make the soldiers think they were surrounded.

Soon the white soldiers would learn to their horror that more Indians were on the way, for Asi Yahola had in his possession many bundles of sticks, each stick a promise that a certain warrior would come and do battle. There were seven hundred sticks in one bundle and another one hundred in the bundle from Apayaka. Everybody knew this, and See-ho-kee knew she would soon see relatives from Apayaka's village, the men with their weapons, the women with supplies. It was very exciting, almost as enjoyable as a festival, except that somebody (maybe she herself) would die. And, of course, there was no feast to eat.

All the women and children, all of the old sick men, away from the village now, hid in a hammock three miles from the battleground, where they formed a supply line for their men. They ran bullets, prepared food, measured out powder from sacks, which were open for anyone's use. They were ready to pick up the wounded and bring them in for treatment. By now, bullets had heavily marked the trees around the battleground. See-ho-kee managed to become a runner rather than a worker, much more interesting to do, since she was able to gather battle news and on her return be the instant center of interest. It was gratifying. She was getting tired, the good cowhide shoes loaned to her by a neighbor now had a hole, her sheet sagged with water from the creek she ran through. Yet she felt lucky to have this job.

On Saturday at dusk, See-ho-kee and two young boys took some cooked fish to her father and brothers and the boy's father. It wasn't enough. She had eaten a fish herself before this run, had done so at the insistence of her mother who looked at her and frowned. "You're thin as a cornstalk. Eat something. You're using more food than Coosa-amathle is, for he isn't running, just standing or sitting."

So she ate, and while she cleaned the last bones, she studied her mother, wondered at the swollen face, the different look. It suddenly struck her. Her mother was pregnant. She felt her heart dip with gladness that another baby would take the place of the one who had died. Her joy was instantly replaced by terror. How could her mother survive with so little food? How could a baby survive the kind of wandering life they now lived? She wanted to talk to Pi-co-yee and couldn't. Maybe the truth her mother told her would be worse than what she knew now.

"It will be dark before you can come back," her mother had said. "Stay there with your father till dawn." Now her father drew her into a safe thicket and had her sit with her back against a big oak which would catch any stray bullets. Her brother drew close and began eating. She noticed that the yelling and shouting seemed to be coming all from the

Indian side now and that the whites were quiet. "What has happened?" she asked him.

"We believe they are hungry. They are killing their horses now, but this may not be enough. Maybe they're like us, tired of the whole thing and ready for a good meal and sleep at home." Coosa-amathle ate with enjoyment. "Good catch. Who got these?"

"Mother. Some old women. Even Grandmother."

"Good. You want to give your friend a fish?" He tilted his head toward Yaha Chatee who crouched behind a tree, carefully tending to his fighting work and not looking at See-ho-kee.

"Certainly not. It would not be proper." She thought about it. "*You* can give him one if you want to."

Coosa-amathle almost smiled. "Yaha Chatee! The women sent you a fish."

Out of the corner of her eye See-ho-kee saw Yaha Chatee lean his gun against the tree and bound over, his face alight with pleasure.

"How great!" he smiled at her father. "I've been hungry for a fish." He kept his head toward Coosa-amathle, and See-ho-kee felt invisible.

What a good face you have, Yaha Chatee.

Cold misty rain began falling, and they crowded under the big oaks.

They ate and talked easily, nobody in a hurry to do anything, for the work had been done back in the hammock by women and children. Here in the battle camp were all the Miccosukee men from the cove village, every boy over eight, every old man who could walk fairly well, and all were armed with guns. For months now, small boys had strengthened their arms until they could hold a gun steady. Now was the reward time, when they could lounge with their fathers and occasionally go to the edge of the woods and fire at the white men behind their protecting logs. See-ho-kee began to feel sure of victory. After all, this time the Miccosukees had had time to purify themselves with black drink, and although they had been in the field so long that they must have food, they were still in an exalted state of assurance.

Tomorrow over eight hundred Indians would come for a final battle. Then the white soldiers would at last leave her people alone.

The rain slowed and stopped, leaving traces of mist.

"The moon has pulled a bearskin over her face," someone said quietly.

There were nods of agreement.

She relaxed and went to sleep, sitting against an oak, then slipping down and curling in a tight knot against the cold.

A loud clear voice awoke her. She recognized the voice. John Caesar. She sat up in great excitement.

"What is he saying?"

Her father was furious. "He says we are tired of fighting. He says we wish to treat with them. He says he will shake hands. That fool. Why does he do this just before our forces come? He will ruin the whole plan."

Coosa got to his feet and hurried to Asi Yahola who stood nearby, giving his attention to the black man. Firelight made Asi Yahola's face fade and reappear.

"He will cause us to lose our chance," her father said loudly. "Let me kill him for you."

"No. Wait," said Asi Yahola. "Listen."

The sentinel at the opposite camp called back at last. Asi Yahola translated, "It is too late to shake hands tonight. Come tomorrow morning under a white flag, and we will talk."

"All right. We agree to that," John Caesar yelled.

"Will you have me shoot him?" her father asked in rage.

"No. We will hear what the white men want to say," Asi Yahola replied. "Nobody must touch him."

Several other men now shouldered in, angry and ready to fight Caesar. There was a quick scuffle as they reached for him, and See-ho-kee stood to see what was happening. There was Asi Yahola still, both hands uplifted, fingers curved in warning. "Nobody touch him! I will see what the white man has to say. Maybe we can live here in peace."

Coosa now loomed over See-ho-kee, his body tense, his brow lowered with anger. "Go to sleep, daughter. We'll see what comes tomorrow."

She stayed at the camp, sent word back by the small boys she would stay and help her father and brothers until afternoon. By then the thing was finished.

At noon Asi Yahola and Jumper, having dressed themselves elegantly enough to shame the white soldiers, led a band of warriors under a white flag to the council. Coosa, Yaha, and many other Indians were still in a fury and they refused to go. Instead See-ho-kee's father sent Eemathle to the council, not to take part but to listen and run back with the news.

Eemathle was soon back with the first news. Asi Yahola had said they wished the white soldiers to withdraw from the Ouithlacoochee, that they wished to have council, that they wished to treat. But, he had cautioned, their chief, Micanopy, had gone to his home, so that no agreement could be binding. When Coosa first heard this, the stern look on his face lightened a little, for everyone knew that Micanopy was chief in name only. He was too fat and lazy to hold respect. He was a good excuse to get out of a bad bargain, if the council turned out wrong.

What was more, Asi Yahola had told the white captain that many more warriors were on their way and would be here any moment, over eight hundred men with good guns. The general had looked only a little surprised and he had said that *he too* expected more soldiers, indeed that General Clinch was bound to be very close by now and that when he came, they could fire at the Indians from all sides.

Furthermore, the white captain had told them, the general could not treat with them, but, if they would go to their side of the river and stay there and not bother any white people thereabouts, why, they would not for the present be disturbed.

Eemathle finished his news and waited. "Go back and listen," Coosa-amathle said. "There's more to it than this. I don't trust them."

Eemathle ran without a word. He barely had time to get back when they heard shots. Screams arose from the group of Indians. In a few moments Eemathle came running back, wild-eyed and dirty from a quick fall to the ground to escape the bullets.

"It's worse than I thought," said their father. "They got our people there and attacked. Right?"

"No. Even worse than that," said Eemathle. He vigorously brushed himself clean, for he was something of a dandy and hated not to look his best. "It was all a plan. General Clinch and his troops came out of nowhere and started shooting the council Indians." He stopped brushing, looked up in the direction of the white camp. "They'll be here in a minute. Everybody's scattered."

It was just as he said. The battle was over. Two Indians died, one shot in the head with a cannon ball, and one Negro died.

The greatest group of Yakitisee ever to gather for a battle separated and went to their own villages. But before See-ho-kee's family left, they watched from the woods when the white soldiers left their breastwork and marched away. They were extremely thin and pale, ready to be defeated. A great opportunity had passed. Coosa-amathle would not forgive John Caesar for this day.

eleven

See-ho-kee's family was no longer safe in Ouithlacoochee Cove which was such a great challenge to the white men, so when they heard that Fort Drane had been abandoned by the white soldiers, they moved there, all except the very old and very young, the crippled, and a few women to care for them. Apayaka and Asi Yahola also moved them with their warriors to gather crops. The fort had been built on land claimed by General Pierce as his plantation, but of course the Indians still thought of it as their own land. There was a wealth of food around the fort, planted by the soldiers and General Pierce's slaves. Thousands of acres of sugar cane and corn waited the harvester's knife. In a few weeks at the time for gathering beans and peanuts, it would be appropriate to have a skunk dance. The white men had planted neither beans nor peanuts, but See-ho-kee remained hopeful that the dance would be held; she loved the drums and dances as well as the opportunity for the women to sing. It turned out there was no dance, not that she could have participated, dressed in widow's sheet.

And there was no peace. The Miccosukees had hoped that each little fight was the end of it, that the white soldiers would see that they would not give up. And still the soldiers, hoping to find the Indian villages, came in great numbers. They planned to attack women and children in order to draw out the warriors. The Indians watched for every chance to attack small groups, to make life so miserable for settlers they would give up. They were careful with their forces, fighting only where there was an excellent chance of winning, and if they lost, there was always a familiar swamp or hammock as a haven.

The hammock at Fort Drane was over half a mile away.

Apayaka directed all the people who were able to pick in gathering the crops. Among the pickers were Miccosukees, Creeks, Chee-au-haus, and Hitchitees whose grandparents came from Hit-che-too-chee — Little Hitchitee — a village that belonged to the old town of Hit-che-tee. These people were kin to See-ho-kee. Back in the old days, her grandmother had often said, their Hit-che-tee relatives were very rich, and they got all their great herds of cattle and hogs and horses from their own hard work.

Their descendants worked equally hard today, alongside the Miccosukees, all of them Seminoles now (according to the white people), but there were no riches. Now they moved the food to the hammock where women worked to get rid of the husks and trash and to hide the good food. Each woman had a map of the caches in her mind, so that they could come back and get them.

Pi-co-yee, almost at the time for her baby to come, stayed in the hammock, and See-ho-kee pulled grain on a stretcher of hide from the field back to her mother.

It would have been a pleasure to pass a few words with one of the guards posted on the outer edges of the fields. Yaha Chatee. His back was turned to her. Why, she sometimes thought angrily, *why* hadn't he asked his adopted aunt to approach her family for her? When this thought crossed her mind, she at once belittled it and tried to put it away, for it was not proper for her to think of what might have happened. She couldn't stop the insistent question.

Yaha Chatee's duty was to call a warning and then fight any soldiers who came, not that Asi Yahola or her great-uncle expected any. They had left Fort Drane because of a fever that had killed many of them. This was not a source of worry to the Indians who had the protection of Apayaka's medicine against the fever. He believed the spirits of dead Miccosukees had sent the fever to make the white men leave, but See-ho-kee was still afraid, and she never entered the fort.

If the whites did return, the women and children were to drop whatever they had and run to the hammock, while the men picked up their weapons and covered their retreat.

On a cool August morning they went to work at dawn. When the sun came up, the instant warmth comforted See-ho-kee, and she relaxed a moment. Suddenly Yaha Chatee's alarm whoop shrilled over the fields, and at the same moment she heard horses' hooves beating the ground, heard barbaric howls from the white men, heard a gunshot. She dropped all her corn and ran, glanced back at the other women and their children also running.

The soldiers were already in the field, her father and brothers shooting at them! Yaha Chatee backed toward them.

Hitchiti-hajo suddenly threw his gun away, stood tall with his hands high in the air, leaned slowly down, leaned, leaned, fell to the ground like a palm that had rotted at the root. Thlicklin! She stood for a dangerous moment and yearned back to her brother, watched her father shoot a soldier off his fast-running horse, saw her father give her brother one look and recommence shooting. She ran on, as she had been ordered to do, looking back when she reached a flat, safe place where she was not likely to fall.

The soldiers were coming in three sections, she saw; there was a large group on the right, a large one on the left, and between them big guns were drawn toward the Indians, guns that boomed and boomed. She saw Miccosukees go down before the guns, and now the warriors were in retreat, following her and the women. She could no longer see Hitchiti-hajo. *He is dead,* an inner voice told her.

Thlicklin, brother, if your spirit is here, lead us out of this danger.

At once she felt more energy, as if he had given her his strength, and her feet barely touched the earth till she came to the shadowy trees.

Shots were hitting into the hammock. Her mother met her there, her face tight, her eyes large and wild. She grabbed See-ho-kee's hand. "Let's go," she said. They ran down the path as fast as Pi-co-yee could go, burdened as she was with a baby who was ready to come. A bullet sang a quick trill and thumped into a tree. Another splatted past her, and she couldn't decide where it had hit.

Her mother stumbled, turned around and gave a surprised look, and sat down. She cried out in pain, lay down, rolled on her side, folded up, got up and moved off the trail where she would not be seen.

"You'll have to help me, daughter." She had her skirt back now, and See-ho-kee could see blood making a long slow curl down her back. Pi-co-yee sat up again, tried to get into a position of comfort, had to lie back down.

"A bullet hit me," her mother said in a soft voice. "I have been in labor for a while; now I must push the baby out before my strength leaves me.''

Her mother couldn't stand or squat to have the baby; she must stay in this unnatural position.

Why would they shoot my mother? What harm could she do them?

Pi-co-yee wasted no time with useless wondering as See-ho-kee did, but put her whole self into getting the baby safely out. She called out to some unknown spirit, ''Help me. Quickly!'' She heaved and groaned.

See-ho-kee was ready to catch the baby; she wished she knew what else to do to help her mother. The terrible thinness of her mother's legs and body gave See-ho-kee more hurt than the blood from her wound had. This thinness had been hidden all these months. Her face was gaunt, her arms like willow whips.

Thlicklin has died. Now, my mother, you will die. She had a sudden knowledge of her mother's coming death, as she had known the white soldiers would come like flocks of birds.

Thlicklin. See-ho-kee hoped he had not been scalped, for he would have to wander in the wilderness forever unless her father could avenge his death. Then he could go to the blissful regions. Thlicklin's ghost *must* be placated.

There was her father running the trail now, Eemathle with him. No Thlicklin.

''Father!''

He came directly to her, and she pointed to the struggling woman. Her mother breathed lightly and infrequently. Her eyes were closed. Suddenly the baby's head was out, and See-ho-kee got her hands around the tiny slippery shoulders and eased the baby out. A gush of blood followed.

Her mother was dying.

Coosa then lifted the silent baby to catch her dying breath, which was right and proper to do. The baby gasped as the faint breath touched it and cried at its loss, continued to cry at the burden of daylight against the tiny eyelids.

See-ho-kee's mother went out of her body and left a terrible stillness in her place. Coosa put his head on her breast and listened. In a moment he wept. He handed the baby to See-ho-kee.

"Here, little mother."

She knew what a charge he laid upon her, this small, thin crying infant. Her father cut the cord and tied it, as handily as a woman would have done. See-ho-kee herself shook so that she could not have done it, though she was able to hold the baby tightly against her body.

See-ho-kee was now responsible for the breath of two people as well as her own, for the Breathmaker had given her mother's breath to the baby. Nothing was more precious than breath.

Her father slipped off his shirt and gave it to her to wrap the baby in. He paused one instant to touch his wife's face, to close her eyes, to arrange her hands. See-ho-kee touched the hands, and suddenly couldn't bear what was happening to them. She ran down the trail, back where the white men would not dare to pursue. Coosa-amathle followed. Once he stopped, and she heard his gun fire. She ran until there were no human sounds except her gasping, her father's pounding feet, the baby's crying.

She began to plan. She would save this baby. This baby would not die. She would find a mother who was nursing and would give most of her own food in return for milk. This baby would live.

"Wait, Father. I forgot to notice something."

"Keep running. I noticed. It's a girl."

She felt a strange quick happiness. Her mother had given her a sister.

twelve

They stopped in what seemed a safe place, hidden in the trees, separated from their friends and family. Coosa-amathle paced in agony, decided at last that See-ho-kee and the baby were safe in this place, and left to see to the bodies of his son and wife. He didn't insult See-ho-kee with instructions, and she was grateful, for she didn't want to be burdened with demands that couldn't be met in the face of unimaginable dangers. She would stay here until she had her breath, but soon the baby would need food, and she must return to the village.

She grieved for her brother. If only she had been near him, she could have given him a cup of ginseng tea, and he would have drunk it, and she herself would have sung the Yahola cry to prolong his life. She dozed suddenly, sat up with a start, felt the baby's foot twitch, looked at the small frowning face. Good. The baby still slept.

The air was sultry now. She believed a storm was coming.

She got up and started homeward, leaving bent twigs for her father's notice, hoping the white men would not see them, if they dared come into these woods.

Winds came, and the rain began. She moved over the baby to protect it.

Who would be at home now? Her grandmother and the other old people, if nothing had happened to them. The three youngest babies and their mothers. But who had survived this battle and run home? She worried over the question, but she didn't hesitate in her careful run through the trees. She paused often to rest, lest her running become ragged and frightening to the baby. Once, as she rested, she heard a sound, and at the same time a jay called a friendly warning to her. Instantly she melted into the shrub, holding her hand over the baby's mouth.

"See-ho-kee?" A soft voice.

Her father. She peered around a tree. Her father, and beside him, Thlicklin! A strange and stern Thlicklin, now so manlike she must think of him as Hitchiti-hajo. He had a great brown bandage around his knee, a rough crutch braced under his arm. She stilled herself. It would not do to disclose the fierce sweep of joy she felt at seeing him, but her smile was irrepressible. They reached, touched hands.

"You must rest before we go on, Hitchiti-hajo," she said.

"No, Sister, it's not needed," he responded with equal dignity. Then his normal buoyant spirit reasserted itself, and he smiled and mocked her, "You must show me the baby before we go."

She unfolded the wrapping and showed him, and he looked at the tiny girl with love. See-ho-kee admitted aloud, "I'm glad to see my brother." She studied him, felt sorry for a second that he had indeed become a man, a warrior. She would miss her childhood playmate. She realized he was giving her a strange, hungry look, and she had sudden knowledge that he was thinking similar thoughts about her.

Now she turned to her father and waited. "I found a good tree with a fork," he said, "and I put her there, her head to the west, and I left her turtle-rattles there so that she may continue to dance, and I took out her sofkee ladle and broke it and left it, and I tore up her blanket and left it for her. When we get home, I will burn her house, so that it may come to her through the smoke."

See-ho-kee nodded in silence. It was not too much to do for her mother, although they would miss the house. She wished more could be given to her mother's spirit.

Now they hurried toward home with an urgent need — milk for the baby. Perhaps they might even meet someone on the trail. All the way See-ho-kee thought of names.

"What will we name her?" See-ho-kee asked.

"We will not name her at all," her father said. "The medicine man or Apayaka must do this. We will wait till we see them."

They started and very quickly arrived at a clearing. "Look," said Hitchiti-hajo, nodding toward the west.

"Where," asked their father.

See-ho-kee saw it, a great dark cloud, a funnel like a moving finger reaching down from it. She knew not to point, lest the funnel see her and come toward them.

"There, to the west," she said.

"Oh," said her father. They waited a few moments till the finger bunched and flattened into the cloud.

She was proud she had remembered. Never point at a tornado.

Ah, in the north a rainbow came; again she would not point. The rainbow was a great snake named Cutter-off-of-the-rain. No need to attract its attention.

The rain had stopped.

thirteen

The feeling of quiet happiness See-ho-kee used to have at Ouithlacoochee Cove was no longer there. White soldiers ceaselessly probed the swamps for them, and there were several terrifying times when the soldiers were within hearing distance, but they didn't find the people. At first, Coosa-amathle was uneasy about burning his wife's house, fearing the smoke would bring the enemy, but at last they managed this. Then there was no reason for them to stay longer, and they moved to Wahoo Swamp. See-ho-kee hoped this would be the last move; even as she hoped, her mind said it couldn't be so. The white man would drive them forever.

Under unrelenting pressure from the grandmother, Coosa-amathle and his sons built two houses, one for cooking, one for sleeping, both open to the winds, unlike the solid log houses they had owned in Ouithlacoochee.

See-ho-kee felt at home in Wahoo Swamp the first day, felt happy to be with her grandmother who had waited at home for them, who grieved now over her daughter and whose every other sentence began with "Pi-co-yee used to say. . . . " See-ho-kee was glad to be in the same village with Nuff-kee and Yaha Chatee. She resisted all offers from older married women to take the baby for their own, though she smiled in appreciation when they helped her. Many people brought little gifts, for her and the baby, for the use of the family. It was a way of saying, *We are glad to have you here. We wish you good luck in raising the baby.*

Otulkethlocko, the medicine man, who was called Prophet by the white man, came to name the baby. He looked with tender concern at her, comforted her when she began to cry. "Ooshtayka. Daughter," he said softly. At once her face relaxed and the crying ceased.

See-ho-kee, her father, brothers, and grandmother leaned anxiously toward him. He hesitated; no name came to him.

"She wants to be called Daughter," he said. "I wonder why that is true. What did she see first?"

Coosa-amathle leaned over the baby, his tears flowing steadily. "Her mother. She took her mother's dying breath. Her mother kept a hold on life until she was safely born."

"And what was the girl-name of her mother's favorite aunt?"

"Anatho-yee," said the grandmother.

"Anatho-yee?" Otulkethlocko said, a question in his voice. It was a strange name, if that's what he intended. A beautiful name. "Anatho-yee," he said with conviction. He nodded to See-ho-kee who lifted her sister into her arms.

"Anatho-yee?" See-ho-kee asked her father, as if he had a right to name the baby.

"Yes. Ehee. Yes." Her father and brothers gave their

agreement in pleased voices.

"Anatho-yee?" she questioned gently. The baby squinted up at her and blinked. The name had been accepted.

See-ho-kee looked at the small hands with tiny bags on each finger, each pulled firm with a drawstring. The baby's nails could not be cut for four months. She was getting the best care See-ho-kee could give.

Raising a baby had always been difficult; now it was almost impossible. There were tales now of babies whose mothers had to smother them rather than have their cries disclose the tribe's location to the white soldiers who came deeper and deeper into the swamps and hammocks.

This was See-ho-kee's old nightmare, that the babies would have to die or be abandoned to save the rest.

It was early fall, and a cooling rain had swept across the swamps before daylight. See-ho-kee awoke as light came from the east. She listened to the water softly dripping from the trees onto the woven palm frond roof. The trickle made whispering sounds. But she listened with only part of her, for her mind was, as always, focused on Anatho-yee, who slept beside her on a blanket. She was a solemn baby, she frowned over all the attention she received, frowned over the milk she got at the breast of a good neighbor, frowned when See-ho-kee talked to her and tickled her. "Don't be so nervous," her grandmother said. "Babies who smile at that age are only trying to get rid of stomach gas. They don't really smile. It's too early."

But her brothers teased her. Only Yaha Chatee paid no notice to her. "The poor thing," they would say. "Anatho-yee is so gloomy she will never get a husband."

When they went too far in their teasing, she talked back in rage and said more than she really thought. "It's all right if she doesn't have a husband. This will be her home, and she can still live." Her brothers laughed aloud at her rage, but Yaha Chatee frowned at them, and she was suddenly shy around him, realizing he was sensitive to her feelings.

She was fifteen, a mature handsome woman; she did a woman's work; she cared for the family; she cooked and mended; she tended the baby when no girl was available; she tended her grandmother whose leg and back pains sometimes made it hard for her to work or even sit up to eat. Usually the medicine man could relieve the pain in a day or two, but in the meantime her grandmother became silent with melancholy.

See-ho-kee thought of these things as she looked with affection at her grandmother whose bright eyes had been open for some time now, though she had not made a sound that would disturb the sleep of others. See-ho-kee reached over to touch her and received a smile.

Hitchiti-hajo was missing. Out hunting, she felt sure. He was responsible. When everybody else gave up on the hunt, even Coosa-amathle, he still stalked the fields.

Her thoughts called him in. She heard a quick footstep, a rustle, and Hitchiti-hajo laid two rabbits beside her. She was up at once, took the rabbits to clean, motioned to the place where she had slept so that he could catch a quick nap. She was glad to have new food, for last night's food could not be eaten, lest the spirits had touched it.

She cleaned the rabbits outside of the cooking house, her attention partly on Anatho-yee who slept in a small wooden box that had been tossed from Fort King. The Indians had gathered many good things the white men discarded, such as this box.

Part of her attention went to the day, the weather. The rain still dripped from the roof fronds, but already the sun was heating the earth. She glanced around, saw that the roof was still watertight, felt proud of their cheke, felt glad to be in this place. Here, with her family, with the baby, it was still a happy place, and it was possible sometimes almost to forget the white savages.

When the rabbits were in the stew-pot, the others stirred and began the day's work: the men prepared for the hunt, the grandmother brought a few vegetables for the stew and then sat near Anatho-yee to guard her. The small sad baby had not yet forgiven the world for her bad beginning, and she awoke with her usual frown.

See-ho-kee stirred the stew, glanced toward Yaha Chatee's cheke, tended the baby, looked for Yaha Chatee, chatted and laughed with her grandmother, wondered about Yaha Chatee. Where was the man? He always came to hunt with her brothers and father.

Ah. He came now. He held out a gift to the grandmother, looked at the smiling faces of her family, said quickly, "It is a gift for Anatho-yee."

See-ho-kee regarded it with pleasure, for the gifts he brought were always interesting and beautiful, taken from white men's belongings, either from wagon trains or from white houses or even from forts. Some Indians called this stealing; her own family used to frown upon it, but now the argument was that the white savages had driven them from their homes, had rounded up their cattle and taken them, had burned their mothers' homes, had stolen their slaves and their black friends who were not slaves, had taken their game food away. And so most of the clan had come now to think that it was appropriate to take back from the white men what they could, however small.

Once Yaha Chatee brought Anatho-yee a bundle of colorful cloth scraps, too small to make much of anything. A gift from his mother to the baby, he had said. He had apologized for the paucity of the gift, but the baby was so small, he said, that maybe someone could find a way to make something.

Since it was from him, she had an inspiration. She studied the scraps; a design came into her mind, one that would protect like good medicine. She began at once to sew the scraps together to fit her vision. She sewed the flame from the sacred fire into the garment, and lines for the four winds, and medicine from a certain tree to protect the wearer. She had to get dyes from the forests to complete the work, and it took a long time. Finally it was all together, a piece of cloth big enough to make a little robe.

Anatho-yee wore the dress and Yaha Chatee exclaimed with pleasure over it, said it was the most beautiful robe he had ever seen. He wished he had one too. A design for his robe began to form in her mind. From then on she put away whatever cloth she had, and she watched for every chance to get a new piece, even from feed-bags which she herself had worn for some time now, for they were tossed aside on the roads to the forts after the soldiers fed their horses.

She couldn't think what today's gift was, finally realizing with pleasure that it was a cake of soap, used only a little, pink as a swamp mallow, fragrant as a water lily. It was a wonderful gift. Did Yaha remember it was a month ago she had been allowed to bathe? Now it was her widow's right for another bath. There were no words for thank you, but there was the determination that the rear quarter of one of the rabbits would be carried to his cheke later on, as a gift from Thlicklin. He would understand the gift was from her, just as she understood the soap was for her, once she had given Anatho-yee a bath with it.

"I will go bathe her right away," she said. "Then I will wash the clothes, but not with this gift."

She noticed then that Yaha Chatee's neighbor was there, smiling and pleased that her friend had brought such a gift. "I will help you bathe her," she offered. "I know much about the care of children."

Now the grandmother groaned and got herself down from the platform. "It is good of you but not truly necessary," she said. "I also am experienced with small ones, and I can teach my granddaughter what to do." She caught herself sounding rude and added, "Of course, we wish you to come to watch."

"And help too," the other woman said pleasantly. "And learn from you, Old Mother."

See-ho-kee recognized that she had a problem, was beginning to get angry at the silly grin on Yaha Chatee, who didn't know the way of women and didn't understand that his stupid gift had caused a problem. She considered postponing the bath, and while she was thinking and seeing the two older women looking at her anxiously, she sniffed the soap. Ah, it was lovely. She scooped Anatho-yee up, gathered some clothes, and headed for the water. She felt hot and half-angry at all the interference she was getting over the bath. All the way down to the water the gentle argument heated up. First from Yaha Chatee's neighbor, "We must be careful, you realize, or we will burn the child's eyes with the soap."

From the grandmother: "And you think we don't know that? We have had soap. Many times before, we had soap. In the old days up in Georgia we *made* soap, just like this, except it was not colored like this nor did it have this smell, but very good soap. We made it. We didn't depend then altogether on sands and herbs to wash with."

From Yaha Chatee's friend, "Oh, we had soap too! I hope you didn't think I was talking without experience! And we made it too. Why, even my grandfather was accustomed to soap, and when the white people drove them south out of O-co-nee, he wept because he could never again have a soap bath in the river there. But he had his wife carry a pot of soap all the way south. But, in knowledge, I defer to you, Old Mother."

From the grandmother: "Sniff! I hope so."

See-ho-kee maintained her silence, but she suddenly recognized the human need that set the two friendly women to bickering. Everybody loved to bathe a baby, and with the luxury of soap added to this pleasure, it was no wonder three women were determined to have a part in bathing one small baby. See-ho-kee grinned and began to enjoy the prospect. She looked down at Anatho-yee who frowned with her eyes closed.

By the time Anatho-yee's dress was off and she was eased into the warm water at the shallow edge, they had reached a compromise. After all, the grandmother must be honored as the child's oldest relative; See-ho-kee must be given deference because she stood in for her mother, and this left the third woman begging. It was all foolish, but See-ho-kee understood it, so she yielded her place.

"Let Grandmother do the soaping, and you may do the rinsing, and I'll dry her," See-ho-kee suggested, keeping just enough question in her voice not to sound authoritative.

"Good. Good," agreed Yaha Chatee's friend, but it was easy to see she wished to do the soaping, to feel the squirming little body covered with soap. That was the real pleasure of it.

The truce held until the actual bath began, and suddenly the three of them began bathing her; the grandmother, unable to stoop or squat, had to sit in the water, and when the others saw her advantage, they too sat down. All three passed the soap around politely enough, but their words told their true feelings:

"Don't you know enough to start with the head?"

"Use this bit of rag to clean the ears, not your big clumsy hands."

"Watch her eyes! Watch her eyes!"

"You see now? You've got soap on her tender parts down here! Move aside, and I'll rinse her."

Anatho-yee screamed her rage. They murmured and fought for the soap.

When she was soapy all over, Anatho-yee suddenly spurted out of Grandmother's hands like a slippery bullfrog. She quit crying. She was still in midair when Yaha-Chatee's friend caught her, held her only a second before she squirted loose again. See-ho-kee lunged for her, missed, watched in horror as she went under water.

See-ho-kee recovered her at once, fished her out, completely rinsed and no longer slippery. Her jet-black hair had flattened out on her face, and See-ho-kee pushed it back and wiped the water away from her eyes. "Ah, now, baby, you're all right. We wanted only to clean you, not drown you. Don't cry, little sister."

Anatho-yee was not crying. She opened one eye and studied See-ho-kee, got the other eye open. She smiled, a broad, ragged, beatific smile, undoubtedly a real smile and not a gas pain.

The three women looked at her and laughed in relief, tickled her a little, decided that no matter how much she enjoyed being squirted into the air or being bathed with real soap, she had had enough. They put her into her box.

And since they were all wet head to foot anyway, they decided to bathe themselves rather than wash clothes. They did. It was a wonderful bath, and when See-ho-kee took the thin blade of soap that was left and put it on a leaf to save for Anatho-yee's next bath, they all agreed that the soap had been well used.

fourteen

It was January, the first month of the white man's year. Anatho-yee was five months old, a wiry little girl with her mother's smile and her father's frown. See-ho-kee hated to see her become so stubborn and spoiled, but her old teacher, Apayaka, was never at home any more, nor were there any other uncles to do the punishing, so it was up to her, and she could not do it. There were days when she bitterly needed her mother's advice in raising the baby, for her grandmother was as weak and unable to scold as she was, so the three of them played and teased whenever there was time away from the worry their lives had become. These were her only happy times.

She often thought of Ouithlacoochee Cove which they had left forever. Their old home would be easy to find, once the white man became fully determined to track them down. Knowing that the cove would be the first to be attacked had convinced her father to bring them here to Wahoo Swamp.

See-ho-kee sat with the women in the center of the village; she needed their company and chitchat to keep her courage high. She gave Anatho-yee quick proud glances that wouldn't interrupt her pounding and pounding at the mortar where she was reducing coonte root to a powdery starch. Other women gathered the powder and washed it through coarse cloth. They let the sediment fall, poured off the water, and there was their gruel or bread, ready to be mixed.

See-ho-kee worried because Coosa-amathle had blackened his face and let his hair grow long; he had become slovenly. His mourning time was long past; a wife mourned for years, a husband for months. But he still grieved for his wife. See-ho-kee, on the other hand, grieved not at all in her heart for her dead husband, though her dress was still a sheet and her hair could be combed only infrequently.

Her father had tied his scalping knife to his sash, and he wore it everywhere except to his sleeping place. All these were signs of a man in grief, a man preparing for war. Once he caught See-ho-kee looking at his knife, and he said, "I will have satisfaction from *two* white men for the murder of my wife."

She agreed with him that a higher value should be set on her mother than on most people.

When Coosa-amathle saw that she could manage the household with the help and advice of her grandmother, he returned to the cove to fight.

Daily reports came to Wahoo Swamp, and tale-telling at night deteriorated again into war stories. These stories became part of the children's lives, a sick and sad thing to hear them talk casually of killing and to see them playing war games.

The Indians had come to think of the scattered fights as a war, and they called it the White Man's War. At this time, many wild white men, called Tennessee men, came into Florida. The Tennessee men fought with fervor equal to that of the Miccosukees who were, after all, fighting for their homes. There were small, savage battles all across Florida.

The Tennesseans were on their way to the Ouithlacoochee Cove and Wahoo Swamp, but the swamp was deeper, darker, harder to invade, easier to defend. First they would go to the cove, nearly deserted now except for warriors. See-ho-kee thought often of the cove and wondered what would happen to their cabins there, built like the houses they had owned in Georgia in the days of her grandparents' youth. Warm cabins that lasted a long time. The chekes here were open, protected from above but not from the sides, very cold this time of the year, though they were wonderfully cool in the summer.

Her father was with Asi Yahola and Jumper in the cove. They planned together and tried to make themselves ready for the white men. Philip and Micanopy were coming, they had heard, and Asi Yahola hoped they could combine forces before the attack. But the wild Tennesseans moved more swiftly than earlier white men had, for they had learned from the red men how to fight, how to move. They swept into the cove, captured fifty blacks, chased Asi Yahola away. Only three warriors were with him, and he was sick.

Coosa-Amathle helped Asi Yahola to safety, sending his whoops against the trees, so that they would echo and confuse the white men as to the number they pursued. Asi Yahola had become very weak and distraught, and Coosa-amathle had undoubtedly saved his life. Now Coosa-amathle was an important leader, listened to with respect.

Bad things happened everywhere. East of them, on the

Oklawaha River, the white men destroyed a Negro village and captured the inhabitants. Three of the young women were See-ho-kee's friends. On the east coast the plantations were still being destroyed by the Indians. John Caesar was killed just as Micanopy had feared. The blacks were now fighting strongly, terrifying the white people, who had never believed they would do that, to the amusement of the Indians who had understood it well enough. There was a battle near Lake Apopka, and Chief Osuchee had died with four other warriors. Sixteen Indians and Negroes had been captured. See-ho-kee heard that Osuchee's widow had watched stoically as her husband was buried but that her son, fifteen, a little younger than See-ho-kee, had not been able to hold back his tears. See-ho-kee understood and wept too, remembering her mother.

The white men would not let them live in peace, anywhere. They found an Indian camp, stole their ponies and the packs they carried, then followed the Indians into the swamp, and at Hatcheelustee Creek they captured many Indians and Negroes, mostly women and children. The captives were taken to Tampa to board ships and from there they went to New Orleans; they had to walk the rest of the way. It gave See-ho-kee a fever just to think of it, to ponder what the captivity and the long boat ride and the long walk were like. She knew that many had died.

The Indians at last asked for council, and Jumper, Micanopy, and Abraham met the white leader. Both sides agreed to stop fighting for three weeks. They had time to catch their breath.

There were other incidents:

Philip and Coacoochee led a big battle before dawn at a lake across Florida.

North of Wahoo at Crystal River, a town of Creeks was attacked, and their homes were destroyed; the people escaped.

In mid-February a council began between the whites and Micanopy, Jumper, and Philip. A truce was drawn up. There was disagreement among the Indians about the truce which said there would be no more fighting. It said the Indians would leave at once for the land set aside for them, west of the Mississippi. It said they would be allowed to take their allies to the West, and this meant their slaves and the free black people who were their friends. Philip sent word that all Indians must obey.

Coosa-amathle came to talk to his people about it, not trying to hide his grim hatred of the truce agreements. "We won't go," he said. "We will *not* go. To leave our land, to leave Florida which holds my wife's bones, would pull my heart out. I will never go of my own will."

Tears stood in See-ho-kee's eyes as she looked at her father. He was no blood-kin to Apayaka, but they seemed much alike now: fierce, nervous, willing to kill or maim, passionate for a collection of scalps. See-ho-kee knew Coosa-amathle would not let a white soldier die gently. Already he wore two scalps at his sash, his grim victories in his wife's memory.

Now they heard that Apayaka would not heed the order from Philip; he sent out angry words that they could not be so foolish as to trust the white man again. Hadn't they seen Indians go in with the white feather and even with a white flag as the white man insisted, and hadn't those same Indians been captured and sent away?

As for himself, Apayaka said, he would rather die in Florida than be killed a little at a time on strange trails, for they all knew this was happening. For Apayaka, for her father, for *herself,* it was not only a matter of staying in their own region, but also there was fear that the slave-hunters would hunt down their black friends as soon as they started west; the hunters would claim them, separate them from their Indian friends and from their families, sell them in Georgia, Alabama, Virginia. Who could protect the Negroes out on the trail? The Indians had no proof of ownership of their slaves although the Negroes were *willing* to be owned by the Indians, to escape a worse slavery. The Indians never won in court against the white men; they had no civil rights.

Yaholoochee and two hundred of his people went to Fort Brooke, defeated and abject, as a first step on their way to Arkansas. A few others went. None of Coosa-amathle's people left.

The women and children of their village were now alone in the Wahoo Swamp with women and children of other villages, except for three or four old men, crippled and near senility, who scouted the edges of the camp at all times, armed and ready to defend. At unexpected times they blazed away at palm trees when no enemy was there.

Hour upon hour, day after day, the women talked about these things, never tired of seeking out the last bit of rumor or truth about the fighting. It was a ceaseless picking at themselves, an endless worry and pursuit of knowledge of what was happening to their men. Were they alive or dead? Had their sons been hurt or (even worse) captured? Were the white soldiers near them, or were they safe for another day? Whatever work they did, they gossiped and questioned too.

It was a cold afternoon after a morning of speculation when the white soldiers finally came. See-ho-kee heard them, saw the shock on the faces of the women standing near her as the scout ran in with his warning. She swept Anatho-yee up and ran from the village clearing to the woods, saw that the nearest woman had also snatched her own baby up from its little hammock and was following her. She glanced back. The village was already empty, though she could see people disappearing into the woods all around its edges.

She and the other woman moved through the small grove of trees, came out into the swamp which was safer, gave more ground cover, was threatening to the white men who never knew whether the black water was deep or shallow and therefore hesitated to try it. See-ho-kee had personally tested the depth of the water all around there in case a time like this would come. Now she was thankful. She plunged ahead, heard the other woman splashing near her. Water left no tracks. "Be careful not to bend a path of grass down, sister," she told the woman. There was a grunt of agreement; the woman's baby fretted aloud.

See-ho-kee wished with all her heart that her father and brothers were here to help them, rather than in Ouithlacoochee waiting for soldiers. How had these men got by the waiting warriors?

Now they were close to a good hiding place, and they must keep very still. She motioned silence to the woman, for there was a sudden foreign voice crackling into the air like a series of little gunshots. Its noise offended her spirit as much as it frightened her. She put her hand over her mouth to caution the woman to control herself and her baby. It was a tiny baby, not a week old, as thin and puny as Ana-tho-yee had been at birth.

See-ho-kee had still never seen a white person in the face, and this would surely be the time it would happen.

A soldier laughed, very near them; there was a murmur; he chuckled in a more subdued way. She couldn't see him or the murmurer, but she wondered whether they knew she was there, whether they were laughing because she had brought another woman and two babies into their trap. She scolded herself to make her mind think better, held motionless. She and the woman were very close to each other, touching, each holding a hand over their children's mouths.

The soldiers came around the shore, nearly at them, one splashing childlike at the edge of the water. The other woman kept her head down, controlled the baby's squirming and crying, waited to be discovered. The soldiers moved on. When they were a distance away, See-ho-kee stared at the woman, saw that her terror had half-crazed her. A foot stamped nearby, and she froze, readied herself to run. The feet now splashed in water right at her, and she could hear each drop of water hit the water, in terrifying warning. The man moved on, a rear guard, she realized.

They were out of sight now. She smiled grimly at their efforts to be still. She nudged the woman to let her know they were safe. The woman sat up, smiled, released her hand from the baby's mouth. She stared at the baby, and See-ho-kee stared in horror and sympathy.

The baby was dead. The mother had smothered the baby in her agony of fear. She began a wail, stopped at once by See-ho-kee's hand. The mother now held the baby up, stared at it, began shaking the baby, shook it, shook it, kept shaking and then looking to see whether the violent action had awakened it. Splashed water on the small placid face, shook it again, till See-ho-kee couldn't stand seeing the arms flapping loosely. Finally she hugged the baby to her shoulder, commanded it to be alive.

Whatever she tried, it was too late, and See-ho-kee knew it. Another Miccosukee baby had died. She looked at her small sister and thought how marvelous it was to hold a living child.

fifteen

See-ho-kee's worst fear now was that there would be no Busk this year, no Green Corn Dance, and she could not imagine how life would continue without it, for it was the time for cleaning the whole village, for starting anew, for contracting marriages, for healing with the medicine bundles, for judging and punishing wrong-doers, for scratching and bleeding the males who were not naturally purified as women were. Besides, she loved to watch the feasting and dancing and laughing, though her mourning set her apart from Nuff-kee and Yaha. She wished she could see Yaha Chatee right now; he used to be a good friend. But now he was away with the warriors. Indians from scattered areas in Florida straggled to Fort Brooke in Tampa, gave themselves up for removal, according to the truce signed in

March. Other Indians, particularly the Miccosukees, were distrustful, even more so now that they had seen General Jesup waver in his promises. There would be no doubt that the Negroes would go with them to the West, he had sworn. Yet, *now* he said that Negroes who belonged to Georgia whites and were captured during the War, must be released. Now *any* Georgian could claim he owned a certain black, and the Indians could not prove otherwise. If Jesup lied about this, what else would he lie about? Maybe the Indians would be killed in Fort Brooke, or maybe the white soldiers would kill them when they were away from their brothers' protection; maybe they would sink the ship that carried them toward New Orleans. Maybe Jesup would let them starve in the West. Who could say what a man who did not keep his word would do?

Every day or so, runners came to them with terrible news.

The worst news came. Many chiefs were ready to surrender: Coa Hadjo was ready, Philip (a Miccosukee!), Tuscinia who was Philip's brother, and Philip's son Coacoochee who fought like a mad man — all these were ready.

Even *Asi Yahola* and *Apayaka* were ready! When See-ho-kee heard this, the earth trembled under her feet, and she thought for a little while that it was truly the end of civilization. If Asi Yahola and Apayaka were ready for surrender, then all was lost; her father would go with them, and she and her brothers must follow.

"What else do you hear?" her grandmother demanded of the runner.

"Why, all those great fighters are at Fort Mellon."

"Why? What are they doing?" her grandmother scowled with disbelief, stared so fiercely the young man was flustered.

"I don't know it all, but they say outside the fort that the chiefs are inside filling their bellies with food and liquor. They have sent out food to their people too."

There was a long silence after he said this and no one asked anything more, but as they moved away from him, See-ho-kee and her grandmother began to grin. What else the chiefs were doing they didn't know, but mainly they were making a fool of the white general and eating his food. It was naughty and funny, causing the old woman and young woman to chuckle, and finally Anatho-yee laughed to see their faces break. They went peacefully back to their cheke, no longer stirred by the news of surrender. See-ho-kee felt embarrassed that she had believed the runner for a few moments. Why, her father, uncle, and the great Asi Yahola would *never* surrender.

Another runner told them there was sickness at Fort Brooke, a white man's disease called measles, and many Indians were very sick; some had already died. Until this happened, a few people left each day to surrender. That flow ceased.

The next morning a messenger came with word that General Jesup was bringing bloodhounds from Cuba to pursue the Indians who refused to surrender. Those who were flushed out and caught would be hanged. More of their friends lost courage, and they slipped away at night and went to Fort Brooke. Close warrior friends left each other. Families broke apart.

One night there was a commotion, a loud exclamation, and a prolonged squawling near her family's shelter. When all was quiet, they went out and searched but could find nothing. At dawn they saw that their man slave Julius had gone. Julius! Black man as proud of his heritage as was See-ho-kee of her own, for his great-grandfather had come by ship from a land where only blacks lived, and his grandfather had been given to the Indians of Eu-fau-lau many years ago by Great Britain for their help in the war. His grandfather's family were called King's Gifts.

"I am King's Gift from Eu-fau-lau," Julius would describe himself. "My grandfather saw to it that those Indians had good farms, good crops; we were good to them and they to us. That's what my grandfather told me."

Now Julius was gone, captured by whites whose fathers had fought his grandfather's owners. And being King's Gift had not helped him at all.

Fort Brooke now bulged with people, and word came back that there was a sickness of spirit from being too crowded. People there failed in health without a cause. A medicine man gave up his freedom to help them.

A few warriors came home during this time of negotiations and pleas from the general, and life in the villages was a little more normal though still a mockery of the life they used to know. Coosa-amathle stayed away with Asi Yahola or Apayaka, and people kept asking See-ho-kee where her father was, what he and the others were planning to do, as if she had personal runners to keep her informed. There was even a feeling among some of the most frightened people that these men kept the war going out of love for excitement. It was not so, she knew, but since no one dared to say it openly to her, she had no defense against their accusatory looks and curious eyes.

"Do you think they plan to surrender?" a man asked her.

She was sure they did not, but she shrugged and said, "I don't know any more than you do. You heard the runners. But I have confidence in my father."

What *were* they doing at Fort Mellon? There had been no word of fighting for a long time; yet it was not a peaceful time; it was rather a waiting, tense interval. She would not have said what was happening, even if her father had somehow got word to her, for there were spies about the camps now, Indians who would take messages to the white men for food.

This was a warm June night. Three Indians suddenly appeared in the camp, not runners from a chief, but a woman, tall and scrawny and strong, and two men. She talked very fast in Creek so that See-ho-kee could get only a few words.

"Can you speak Hitchiti or Mikasuki?" See-ho-kee pleaded.

The woman paused, began again in slow broken Mikasuki. "Free from Fort Brooke. All free there now."

"Who? Who's free?" See-ho-kee shouted. Now most of the adults of the camp were gathered around them.

"Everybody free."

Nobody could believe this. "How did you get free?" a voice asked.

"Asi Yahola and Apayaka brought many men, two hundred men, and they got us out."

A shout went up; an impromptu dance started. The children were all awake now and piping questions like little night birds.

"How many were freed?"

"Many." She puzzled for a minute, turned to her two comrades, and chattered in Creek. They gestured, argued briefly, settled on a number.

"Seven hundred."

Now the whole camp involved itself in shouts of triumph and dancing. Miccosukees had released them; the fathers and husbands of this village had done it.

The woman held up her hand, grinned with delight. "Listen, you'll hear."

They heard people coming, heard many voices talking without fear, the sounds as shrill and persistent as swamp frogs singing after a rain. They came steadily as if they knew the way into Wahoo Swamp, led by Miccosukees.

Nuff-kee came to See-ho-kee. "The women want me to ask you how we will feed them. What can we give them?"

See-ho-kee had a brief childish resentment that the women would put this big problem on her, for she was younger than they were. Then she thought pleasantly that they did it in apology for their distrust of her father. They were saying, *Your father is a good chief. You are a worthy daughter of his.*

She accepted their delicate apology. "Have they eaten lately?" she asked the woman.

"There is no worry," the woman said. "Everybody has food. They carry much food with them. They will feed *you.* Every skirt, every sash has food, every blanket."

"Are all of them coming here?" It certainly sounded like it to See-ho-kee.

"No. They go in different directions." She swiftly pointed to the homes of the four winds. "All ways. Some come here but go on east or north."

The people came pouring into the camp, hundreds of them. Every cheke was full of sleeping people in a short time. Others on their way had stopped to rest and would come in the morning.

The war was over, they told the villagers jubilantly. The white men had at last learned their lesson.

At last, Coosa-amathle came. He led old Apayaka who had no patience with his help but whose eyes were not good at night. Other warriors came in, including Yaha Chatee. Ah, there would be Busk this year. If only her mourning period were over now, their marriage could be contracted. If only *he* had spoken before she married. This wayward thought, all unexpected, made hot embarrassment storm over her face, and she was thankful for the dark. She must mourn nearly two more years.

Yaha Chatee stopped to speak to Nuff-kee. "Asi Yahola has gone to his own village. He is still sick. A very great brave. I am practicing to be like him."

See-ho-kee could not speak. Her mourning left her mute before him. She would like to have told him that he was fine just the way he was.

Now that the warriors were here, the celebration began,

the eating, the boasting, the dancing and laughing. The exhausted travelers regained their strength and joined in.

Apayaka danced with Anatho-yee who was now ten months old, a toddler who had survived much longer than most Miccosukee babies nowadays. It was the first time he had seen this grand-niece, and he was delighted with her, and she laughed very much at him.

Everybody went to sleep with full stomachs that night, and See-ho-kee slept peacefully. In the middle of the night a good dream of the Corn Dance awoke her, and she thought with delight that they would be able to celebrate Busk after all.

sixteen

See-ho-kee's family decided to stay together, no matter where the fighting took her father. Hard as this life would be, her mind was relieved, for too often she had to make decisions alone about where to run and how to care for Anatho-yee.

"We can't leave you here alone any longer," Coosa-amathle told her. "Our brothers hope the white men are through with us, that they won't be back, but I believe you had a true vision. They will come again, and the first place they attack will be this swamp, for they know now that the cove has been emptied. Families will fight together from now on. If we no longer have a home, we must stay together rather than lose our families. Later, when we get settled again, we'll worry about building another house.

The family began a life of wandering. The women hopefully carried seeds of corn and pumpkin.

Her father and brothers caught horses a distance away from Wahoo Swamp — they never cared to say exactly where. They were wild horses, Hitchiti-hajo said, lost from their masters. See-ho-kee recognized the false look on his face, but she realized that her grandmother and Anatho-yee could not possibly cover the tremendous distances on foot, although the men, burdened with heavy guns but unencumbered by household goods, did it easily. Her grandmother gave a strange whistle to the horses, and one came to her instantly. She winked at See-ho-kee and whispered, "That's a white man's whistle. You learn that, and they'll come to you."

See-ho-kee was delighted to see her grandmother sit on the horse with perfect comfort. She leaned forward, let the horse follow the trail, drowsed most of the time. Once, when she awoke, See-ho-kee asked her how she could sleep and ride at the same time, and her grandmother laughed and replied, "When I was a child, I never walked, until my mother forced me to, so that I would be strong. We had great wealth then: good houses, good planted fields, cattle, horses. We had boats for the water, horses for the land. We always rode."

"I am having trouble staying on," See-ho-kee confessed. "Anatho-yee is hard to hold." Anatho-yee whimpered with discomfort.

Her grandmother was wide awake now. She pulled her horse over and reached for the little girl. "Here. Let me have her till you learn." She looked critically at See-ho-kee. "Watch me. Do it this way."

See-ho-kee followed, checking occasionally to see whether she rode in the correct manner. It was embarrassing to see how quickly Anatho-yee had settled into a peaceful attitude, how she seemed even to enjoy the ride. She curved into her sleeping grandmother so that now they made a small inseparable hump, while See-ho-kee clattered and bounced miserably. Even Eefe seemed comfortable to trot alongside her horse, not at all threatened by the large strange creature.

In this way they followed the men all the way to the east coast of Florida in the sugar mill country. The women and children tried to settle; the men prepared for war and tried to encourage each other not to give up.

There was not much fighting that summer. The Indians knew that General Jesup was very depressed over his humiliation of losing seven hundred prisoners, and they realized that he was like a wounded rattlesnake, very angry and dangerous. They waited for his revenge.

A few things happened before fall. In August John Philip, who was King Philip's slave, deserted the Yakitisee, took his wife (who complained of the bitter life in the Florida scrub) to the whites, guided nearly two hundred men to Dunlawton plantation thirty miles south of St. Augustine. They went in at night, safe in the knowledge that Indians did not post guards at night, and waited till daylight. They took the Indians by surprise, captured King Philip and all the other Indians but one, including pitiful, ragged, hungry women and children. Philip was the first big chief to be captured, a heavy blow to the Indians. The news came to the camp where See-ho-kee's people had joined Asi Yahola near St. Augustine.

Tomoka John was also captured. He led the whites to the camp of Yuchi Billy whose entire village was taken, after which the captured Indians watched with deadly loathing while Tomoka John looted their homes. Tomoka John became a name of evil in all of Florida, and See-ho-kee sometimes thought of it, and wondered how words you could not see or touch could arouse such anger and hatred within her. *Tomoka John.* She made a face over the words; she spat a bad taste out of her mouth. Finally she had to talk to the medicine man who then cured her of her painful anger.

King Philip needed someone to bargain for him, someone who could persuade a few Indians to give themselves up, a sacrifice so that a strong chief could stay and help his people. He sent for his son Coacoochee to come, to enlist help from others, and this led to a terrible happening. Coacoochee was called Wildcat, a ferocious warrior who was loved and admired by the Indians, feared and hated by the white men. He was young, bold, swift.

See-ho-kee had seen her grandmother grin at Coacoochee many times. "He is ruled by the spirit of his ancestors from the town of Tal-e-see on the Tal-la-poosa River. That man was a great chief who helped the people of the United States and was loved by them. But after the war he showed his true nature, just as Coacoochee is doing."

"What true nature?" See-ho-kee had asked.

"When peace came back, he opposed the new government as hard as he had the old. The whites warned him and warned him, but he was the voice for all Indians. And gradually we have come to see his courage and sense."

Coacoochee's fury was fed by the white men. When he heard his father had been captured and was being held at Fort Peyton on Moultrie Creek, he immediately called Blue Snake to accompany him, and they approached the white leader Hernandez under the perfect safety of a white flag, torn from cloth General Jesup had given them to use when they asked for council.

Hernandez ordered soldiers to seize them. Indians watching from nearby told others that from then on Coacoochee was amazed, then furious, and that he had a moment to trample the white flag before he was dragged away. But in a few days they released him, with the warning that he must bring in *many hostages* to take his father's place, if he wanted to keep his father from being killed.

See-ho-kee heard Coacoochee tell all this to her father and brothers and to Asi Yahola whose sick eyes glittered dangerously. They had a hidden camp not far from St. Augustine, but in October Asi Yahola decided he would go to bargain for Coacoochee, and the Indians promptly broke camp and went to the fort, reestablishing a camp in the woods.

They fastened some of Jesup's white cloth high in a tree over the camp, where it could be seen easily, and they waited for Hernandez.

See-ho-kee's father was full of distrust, and he sent her and Anatho-yee and her grandmother away from the main body. "Stay here till all is settled. They dishonored the white flag once. Who knows what they will do this time?"

The soldiers came. See-ho-kee saw them clearly from her hidden place where she and her grandmother clung to the horses. Eefe sat near her, alert and quiet. She saw the argument, saw Asi Yahola choke with sick rage and motion to Coa Hadjo to speak for him, saw Blue Snake led in, saw him shake his head and deny what the white men tried to make him say, saw the white soldiers surround the Indians in a swift serpentine movement, so that there was no time to shoot, no time to run. The soldiers rounded them up like cattle, captured all of them, even the blacks, even the women, and marched them toward St. Augustine. She saw her father go, her brothers, her friend Yaha Chatee. She saw Asi Yahola wearing his bright blue shirt and elegant red leggings. He stumbled from the sickness which still sapped his strength.

She watched them go and when they were gone, she leaned her head on her grandmother's shoulder. Her grandmother cried quietly, reached to touch her and Anatho-yee.

It was treachery beyond belief. See-ho-kee sat and shook, thinking of it. Exaggerations, she could understand; distortions were a normal part of bragging, a daily thing; lies and treachery were beyond her understanding. The way the white man thought was a mystery.

Before she could decide what she was to do, she thought of what would happen to the Miccosukees. Who was left to lead? Not many. But there was Apayaka, somewhere in the south near the great lake. She wondered what he was doing. And she thought that he needed to know about what had happened. Who could let him know? There must be someone she could tell so that the word could be sent to him.

She led her grandmother and little sister back to their last night's camp where the white flag still waved overhead, and they searched for anything they could use. She found her father's bag of food which he must have tossed down for her, and she hid her tears from her grandmother. There were other treasures! There was Hitchiti-hajo's scarf which he loved so much, and here was a mortar with which she could grind the dry ashpe — corn — to make gruel soft enough for her grandmother and for Anatho-yee. She considered the mortar a moment, rejected it as too heavy.

"Help me load the horses, Grandmother," she requested, packing everything so that it could be strapped in bundles. They took all they could carry; she swung Anatho-yee upon the horse with their grandmother and the three went back to an earlier hiding place, where they would wait for a day or so in case any of her family escaped.

Nobody came. And still they waited in the solemn quiet of the woods.

On the evening of the second day they heard someone running on the trail. See-ho-kee cautioned the old woman and the little girl to silence and went to the edge of the trail to look. In a moment a runner neared her. Hitchiti-hajo!

"Thlicklin! Brother!" she called.

He stopped, turned, looked. His mouth dropped open and he looked like a great gawking fool. "You're here, little sister? I can't believe you're here. We thought you had probably gone back to the cove."

"No, we waited to see what would happen. Did you escape? Where are our father and Eemathle? And Yaha Chatee?"

The name slipped out before she knew it was in her mind.

His face was sour. "They're under guard at the fort. I am sent out to call Asi Yahola's wives and children and his other relatives, his warriors, his slaves to come to him. They will send him to prison in Charleston, and he believes he will die there. He wants them to come. Maybe, he thinks, *maybe* the white soldiers will let him go with them to the West. I do not think so. They will never let him go."

"And what about you, Hitchiti-hajo? Are you going back? Can't you stay with us so that we can go live with Apayaka?"

Now he no longer had the look of angry warrior, but rather merely his own look of young brother, a sad young brother.

"If I don't go back, they will kill our father."

"Oh." She pondered again about the two faces of the white men, the way they smiled and bargained, then lied and betrayed.

"But what we plan to do is to go with them without protest toward Tampa till we come to trails we know well, and then we will escape, one way or another. Don't worry about that. And if you have gone to Apayaka, we will come and find you. Don't worry, See-ho-kee. We will be together again. Now, you have work to do.

"Our father needs you to do him and the other prisoners a great favor. They want herbs gathered for black drink and brought to them at the fort. Will you do it?"

"Certainly." As soon as she answered him, she thought, *What if they capture me? Who will take care of Anatho-yee and our grandmother?*

He examined her face closely. "Outside the fort, there

are Indians of other tribes. They fight with the white men and want us to be captured, but if you tell them you are bringing herbs for the health of the captives, they will honor this."

"But what if they take me into the fort?"

"They won't. They get rewards for what they do in battle, not for stealing women."

He cupped his hand around the back of her head, gave her head a little shake, patted Anatho-yee, smiled at his grandmother, turned suddenly and ran down the trail.

Despite the limp from his old knee wound, Hitchiti-hajo's running was so swift and silent that not even a bird complained. It gave her a feeling she had dreamed he was there. She wished she had thanked him for his comforting words, though she understood that he had given her the only thing he had, words that pretended all would be well.

See-ho-kee told her grandmother that Coosa-amathle had requested black drink and old woman looked up at once with a bright grin. "What, Grandmother?"

"They plan to escape. They will have loose bowels and sick stomachs. Ah, they will be very pure." She laughed aloud. "They will also be very *thin.* They plan to escape, that's what."

See-ho-kee took on immediate hope. It made perfect sense. "Well, let's go find the herbs. Help me to get the right stuff."

"Oh, I will, I will. We'll get plenty of cassine yupon to make a-cee. Anybody knows that. But there are other things, plants good for certain reasons." Her grin was constant now, and she winked. "Your father will know what to use."

For hours they gathered herbs while her grandmother talked constantly about the old days, the good days before the white savages drove them away from the Flint and Chattahoochee rivers.

"We knew exactly what to pick, and we could find all necessary herbs there for bad health and other trouble. We knew the sacred proportions to use. In the good days before the white savages came, we had time to do things right. We *took* time to do things right, looked for just the right plant. Now you listen, dear girl, and I will teach you what you will need to know."

See-ho-kee was tense and afraid about going to the fort and about the long, long journey to the big lake in the south. But she listened.

Finally her grandmother was satisfied with what they had, and she took over the care of Anatho-yee when See-ho-kee gathered up the herbs.

It went as Thlicklin had told her. The white men were inside the fort, the Indians and one or two black men were outside, lounging about the ground. One was drinking from a whiskey bottle. "Hello, woman," he said.

"Will you take these herbs and roots to the prisoners?" she asked him, looking humbly at the ground.

"What is it?" he asked indifferently. "Ah, yupon." He grinned at her. "Do they think they can make war in here?"

"No, no. It's for purification as you know." She heard insistency come into her voice, and she quieted herself. "Coosa-amathle asked for herbs."

"Oh, well, woman. He won't be around long to use them. They will send him to the fort in South Carolina soon."

She dared to give him a smile which suggested both intrigue and artless enthusiasm.

"You tell the white savages that these herbs will rid the warriors of angry thoughts."

He thought a moment, guffawed, took the bundle. "All right. I'll do it. But you come in too."

"I can't. I must go back and bring my sister and grandmother here. They wouldn't come till they knew it was safe."

He hesitated, still pondering. He looked at her signs of widowhood.

"My sister is single," she explained, "and I am a widow."

"Ah. Then she is not married."

"No. She soon will be, no doubt, for she is much more beautiful than I am."

He waved his hand, gave her lofty permission to leave, rose and went to the gate. She left quickly, looked back and saw he was looking back too. They waved, and now she was far enough away to dare to run. She felt sick at seeing so much evil in the eyes of a Yakitisee man.

She had done all she could. She had told her first lies, and she felt a little anxious about them.

They rode south to look for Apayaka's village.

During the first night on the journey, Eefe's low growl awoke See-ho-kee who instantly touched his nose to quiet him. She heard one of the horses snort in fear, knew that somebody or something was there, but she dared not go to look. She listened. There. A hoof crunched a shell. She heard a slap and a yell, "HAH-YAAA!" White man! Heard the horses run. Listened as silence filled in the space where the noise had been.

She lay awake a long time and finally slept, disturbed by evil dreams. She awoke once and was comforted by the knowledge that Eefe lay near, alert to the night sounds.

She had a new idea. Women did not possess weapons, and she had none, but she did have her mother's small sharp knife, with which she did many, many things from cutting meat to digging for roots.

The next morning she cut a green palm frond stem, heavy and well-balanced, and tied Pi-co-yee's knife to it. Her grandmother watched, her eyelids sloping to hide her approval or disapproval. She did not smile. See-ho-kee held up the lance and tested it for balance. She held it shoulder-high and pretended to throw it until she began to think that crude as it was, she could hurl it into a man's throat.

She felt nervous about the weapon, not that it wouldn't work but that it was inappropriate for a woman to use. Women did not use spears. Women didn't even use gigs for fish or frogs. But she must have *something* for their protection. She looked at her grandmother for confirmation.

"Try it," said her grandmother finally.

See-ho-kee tried it, threw it over and over, but it never went where she had sent it. Rather it took a new course and tumbled awkwardly. Nevertheless, she carried it along, feeling safer with it, feeling certain that anyone who attacked them would get a sharp blade in his belly before he saw his danger.

seventeen

The white man and the horses were gone. They began to walk. The weather was cool, but they were soon sweating.

In some places the white soldiers had widened the Indian trails into roads so that ammunition and food wagons could get through. The Yakitisee used these roads openly when there was peace following a council, for the roads were straight and easy to travel. See-ho-kee wished they could use the road south; her grandmother could not travel fast, because her eyes were weak, and she must watch closely to avoid entrapment by grasping grape tendrils. Some evil vines worked with the white men, See-ho-kee believed. They grew overnight across the Indian trails. It was very strange to her that vines would oppose her grandmother, who was so in tune with all living things, so careful never to injure except out of need, whereas the white soldiers killed a band of forest without compunction. She believed the evil spirits of dead whites lingered and influenced the spirits of the plants. No one had told her this; yet she believed it. Still, they must use the trails with no men to help defend them against attackers, with no weapons of their own.

They walked south. Anatho-yee slept against See-ho-kee's back, her small feet kicking softly with each step See-ho-kee took. Their grandmother never ceased talking; she talked about the days before the savages when they lived in a good log house, better than those built by white men, who had to be taught everything like children.

During the day they saw not another soul besides themselves. At night they slept in the woods without the comfort of the sacred fire and the protection of their men. See-ho-kee saw to it that they had food, edible if not palatable. It was cold. See-ho-kee made a bed of green palm fronds, cleared a circle around their sleeping place of undergrowth that might hide snakes. She took off her sheet and spread it over the three of them. They slept in a small tight huddle. She slept hard, woke briefly only once when she felt her grandmother tucking the sheet around her and Anatho-yee. She felt her heart move with love for the old woman.

In a few days they were out of food. Their walk, already slow and stumbling, became slower. See-ho-kee gave the last bits of food to Anatho-yee, tried to force some of it upon her grandmother, who closed her lips tightly and shook her head. She was not hungry, she said. See-ho-kee tried to think how to tell her grandmother of her soft feeling toward her, couldn't think how to say it, remained silent.

They went all one day without food, and at last, against her will, See-ho-kee began looking at Eefe who roved the fields and woods ahead of them, returning constantly to walk by her side. Grandmother did not say anything. Eefe was See-ho-kee's dog, her inheritance from her mother, along with a house in Ouithlacoochee, now burned to the ground by white soldiers. Their sleeping house had been burned for her mother's spirit.

All day long she looked at the dog and thought of meat. It would not be an evil thing to do. Many dogs had been eaten after the bad freeze; others had been eaten when Indians were running and could not stop to harvest their crops. It would not be evil.

But because of the flaw in her that let her become overtender, also inherited from Pi-co-yee who never gave up grieving for her dead baby, See-ho-kee could not bring herself to kill Eefe. He was an old dog; he had followed her for years, had lifted his ears in warning to anyone who approached her too closely.

She became aware of her grandmother's eyes, also following Eefe; yet the old woman said nothing, and See-ho-kee waited.

She had her mind made up when they rose on their third day without food. All night Anatho-yee had whimpered in her sleep, and this must stop; else they would be found and killed. Now Eefe became aware of her look, and he suddenly ran from them, disappeared like a shadow into the woods. One moment she saw him; the next, there seemed to be a space shaped like a shaggy dog, but he was gone. She sat on the ground, trying not to whimper like Anatho-yee.

Her grandmother stood over her, her face old and stern. "We will go now," she said.

See-ho-kee gritted her teeth in rage and fear, got up, put Anatho-yee on her back, and began walking. She watched all day for Eefe. She looked for food, and at last she found a few small roots which she roasted and mashed and divided among them. They were too weak to go on that day.

She gave up on Eefe. Even during the times he dashed away to hunt with her father and brothers, he had come back to her in a short time.

But he came. At dusk when incautious rabbits fed in the shadows, Eefe had made his strike, and now here he came with a dead rabbit, holding it high in the air. He had brought them a gift, she thought.

"Feed the fire, Grandmother," she said with thankfulness in her voice. "Eefe has brought us a gift."

It was not so. He had brought food for himself, and he tried to keep it with growls and feints, with angry slashing at her, his teeth snapping, close but never touching. "You old dog," she said. "You can't bite me, any more than I can eat you."

She cleaned the rabbit swiftly, cut it into four parts for speedy cooking, tossed Eefe his fourth and put the rest on the fire.

Anatho-yee slept without whimpers that night.

And now that they had been given some food, they found much more in a deserted village where a field of bright pumpkins beckoned. They roasted some, gorged, carried with them what they could, including the seeds.

About noon the following day, See-ho-kee finally saw a white man face-to-face and she immediately regretted her foolish wish to know what the white man looked like.

Eefe was scouting the country for rabbits and had not barked. She herself was not alert, never thinking there would be a white man here on this hard-to-walk trail, and besides she was concentrating on helping her grandmother over bad places, on carrying Anatho-yee on her back, on carrying her spear as a prod to warn away small lurkers.

Suddenly, with no warning, the white man stepped into the trail just behind her grandmother. She realized at once that he had seen the grandmother from the woods, that indeed he was as well-trained at hiding in the woods as were the Miccosukees.

She held as still as stone. Her grandmother went slowly ahead, unaware of the man, whose face See-ho-kee still could not see for it was turned toward her grandmother. See-ho-kee could hardly breathe. The man stood still too, looking ahead down the trail. The grandmother was old, had lived beyond the time most people lived, would not want See-ho-kee to help her by sacrificing herself and Anatho-yee. All these thoughts were in See-ho-kee's mind at once. You had to make cruel choices. She moved slightly off the path.

Now the man spoke in strange language. He held a hand toward her grandmother, who turned in terrified realization. He panted, spoke in a loud sorrowful voice. He approached the grandmother who held still and quiet. She gave no sign to indicate to him that See-ho-kee and Anatho-yee were behind him, but the wide, terrified eyes stared at him.

See-ho-kee turned her walking stick so that it became a spear.

The man was thin; she believed he was young. He wore ragged clothes, remnants of a soldier's uniform and a piece of an Indian robe. Now he bent over her grandmother who looked very small, and he begged her for something. He pleaded wildly. Was he sick-minded? What was it he wanted? He took her grandmother's hand and cried aloud. Was it food? No, for he had a gun and could certainly find game here.

She moved closer to him. He was indeed very young; his neck had the thin tender look of a boy-man; his hair curled below his collar; he wore no hat. Her grip on her lance was sure now. She fervently hoped Anatho-yee would stay quietly asleep.

He dropped her grandmother's hand, brought his gun around and lifted it. See-ho-kee's problem was solved; there was not a question of making a choice; her grandmother was in danger and she must do something. Her grandmother's life was as valuable as any other life, and she had the same right to live as Anatho-yee.

She made one swift, steady leap that put her by the man's side. His gun pointed at her grandmother who sank wordlessly down on the trail and waited. See-ho-kee yelled at him, "Hey, white man! Woman killer! Baby killer! Dog-flea! I'll kill you!"

He froze in astonishment, dropped back a step from the knife which approached his throat. She continued to scream every imprecation she could think of. She invented evil words. She ran the threatening lance back and forth through the air, ready for its mission, and now she stood between him and her grandmother.

He stared down at her, and for the first time she looked into a white person's eyes. The blue sky surrounded him as she looked up, and she faltered, for there seemed to be empty holes instead of eyes, all the way through his head and into the sky. She nearly spun to the ground from the horror of it, and only the thought of her grandmother huddling behind her and Anatho-yee on her back kept her from falling.

She screamed more epithets. "Man-who-has-no-eyes!" Man-who-kills-old-women!"

He held out a placating hand, said, "No. No. No." He stumbled backward, glanced down, looked back up at her. Now she saw that he *did* have eyes, for he was shaded now against the sun, and his eyes moved. They were a strange sky color, as she had heard of in the past, always without actually believing that such a thing could be possible and that the Breathmaker could have made such a peculiar error. They were eyes, real eyes. She lost her fear.

The man began weeping. He backed slowly away from them, talking, talking, talking in his language so filled with strange intonations. He cried and waved to the grandmother; he backed away, saying, "No, no, no."

She believed that he was a mad man, a lost mad white soldier.

His gun pointed downward, while her lance remained in position. She watched him leave the trail, listened till he was far away and they were safe.

Then she looked down at her grandmother and smiled, and the fear left the old woman's face. She reached up a hand, and See-ho-kee gave her a steady pull, and when she bounded up, See-ho-kee caught her to keep her from falling. Nothing had ever felt as good as the feel of this live, bony, little old woman.

"Would you have killed him?" her grandmother asked.

"Certainly," See-ho-kee said. She thought about it. "I don't know."

The next day they gathered some companions into their mission, a woman with two little boys, a dirty and sad-looking trio. See-ho-kee and her grandmother greeted them, tried to talk, discovered they spoke Creek. There was a nervous effort to communicate with simple language, and See-ho-kee finally asked her grandmother, who remembered the language from her girlhood, what she made of the woman's talk. "I think her people are scattered or killed, that she looks for someone to tell her where she must go to be with other Creeks. She wants to come with us."

It was the same interpretation See-ho-kee had made. She looked at the woman with a smile, gestured to herself. "Come with us," she said. "We can travel together till we find some of your people, or you may wish to stay with us from now on. We are Miccosukee."

The woman was impressed. "Oh, Miccosukee." She nodded, pleased at what appeared to be a welcome.

The six of them set out for the south. They had not gone far before they heard running feet to the north, and See-ho-kee cautioned for quiet, and all of them slipped silently off the trail into a heavy stand of tall ferns. There was not time to look for coral snakes, and See-ho-kee put the thought away. The runners came closer; she heard muttered oaths;

she recognized the language. Mikasuki! See-ho-kee thrust her head forward, enough to peer through the ferns. There were her brothers running like foxes, their faces intent and strange, their eyes glittering with excitement.

"Eemathle! Hitchiti-hajo!" She trilled the words in a small questioning voice. The men halted so fast that Eemathle crashed into Hitchiti-hajo. "Hitchiti-hajo! You clumsy white man!" the older brother hissed. The family snickered together the way they did as children.

"Watch your language, Eemathle," See-ho-kee said, still laughing with happiness and humor. "Grandmother is listening, and she will punish you." They laughed again, reached to pat Anatho-yee.

Now the alien woman came out, smiling hesitantly. See-ho-kee motioned her to come. "Here. Come here."

The woman came, keeping the two little boys behind her till she knew for certain that these were not wild men.

See-ho-kee tried to introduce her, saying, "She is *woman* or something like that."

Eemathle smiled. "That's white man's name for tayke. You also are *woman*." He looked at her with a concerned, questioning look. "You are faithful in your mourning?"

"Yes."

"I'll be supporting you when you're a hundred. You'll never get a husband."

Her brother would be silly in the very face of death.

"So? The work will be good for you. It will stir you out of bed once in a while."

Eemathle began a slow awkward speech to the woman. She brightened up at once and began to talk.

"Thla-noo-chee!" She thumped her chest.

"Ah, Thla-noo-chee. Little Mountain. She is named Thla-noo-chee."

"Where is she from?"

His Creek speech began again, slow and stumbling, and

immediately her speech burst forth.

"Thla-noo-che au-bau-lau. It means over-a-little-mountain."

"I have been there," their grandmother suddenly said. "Tell her my first husband came from E-chuse-is-li-gau, a nearby village named for a young child who was found there."

He spoke quickly. The woman's face lighted up, and she nodded to the grandmother. Then she looked sad. "The village is gone now," Eemathle translated. "All those towns are gone."

See-ho-kee's grandmother and Little Mountain looked at each other, with the grief raw on their faces. All those lost Creek villages. Little Mountain talked more. She had lived not far from Tus-ke-gee. She and her husband were peaceable people, who wanted to farm quietly. White men stole their slaves and killed their cattle, and she and her husband left rather than fight. Her people stayed to fight. But leaving didn't help her; they found a little glade nobody was using and planted corn and built a house, only the two of them with the little boys sleeping nearby. And white soldiers came and yelled at her husband and killed him and took her and her children to St. Augustine and made her live in the fort. She had the run of the fort, but a white soldier used her.

"She is afraid she is carrying a white baby," Eemathle said.

"What will she do if she is?"

He turned to her and questioned her again.

She answered matter-of-factly, no change of expression on her face.

"She will smother it," he said simply.

"Will she go with us now? Tell her we are fighters, that we will kill before we leave Florida, that we will run forever if we have to but that we'll not leave this land."

He talked for a long time, nodded at her response. "Ah. Yes. Good." He looked at See-ho-kee. "She will go with us."

"Tell me about our father," See-ho-kee said.

"He was still prisoner with the others when we left. We heard that he was working all the time to escape, that Coacoochee is in a mad fury, that they are all slim from drinking black drink."

She suddenly stared at Hitchiti-hajo. "Hitchiti-hajo! What are you doing here? You were running south when I last saw you."

"You are very slow in thought, little sister, but I knew you would think of that eventually." He accepted her cuff which was as swift and soft as a mother cat's punishing blow. "When I got back to St. Augustine, they were taking my brother and many other people to Tampa, and I followed. When we got to Picolata, I stepped out and yelled, made enough noise to frighten the soldiers, and my brother heard me and knew it was his chance. Some soldiers chased me, saw that I was crippled and thought they could catch me."

It was pleasant to hear her brothers laugh at exactly the same time she did.

"There came old Eemathle, quiet as a snake, running with his belly almost touching the ground, like a long wake in the grass. They saw him! He bolted off the other way, going like a deer this time, leaping high to top the bushes. Oh, it was a show. And the poor white soldiers were running hard." Hitchiti-hajo suddenly acted out the white men's part and panted like a dog. Eefe lifted his brows and wagged his tail. "And when I saw my brother was safely away, I left so fast the white men thought I had gone on a great wind into the sky." See-ho-kee frowned at this sacrilege.

Now Eemathle, who had been silent except for his bursts of laughter, said, "We went in two directions, and we had to bird-call all afternoon to find each other again.'' They laughed again.

''How did you find me?'' See-ho-kee asked.

''I came back up the same trail, and you weren't there. So I simply asked somebody.''

''Asked somebody? Why, there was not a soul on the trail.''

''Oh, yes, there was. A Uchee lay off the trail not two feet from you and you didn't see him. He told us where you were.''

It was frightening to think that she had been seen in spite of all her care.

She had a terrible thought. ''But what about our father? Will they hang him?''

The two men were silent for a moment. ''We don't know, See-ho-kee,'' Eemathle said. ''We don't think so. We hope he too will escape. In any case, he sent us word that no matter what happened to him, we must find you and reestablish the family farther south. And after all, I took Asi Yahola's summons to his family and they are on the way to join him. Surely the white men would not kill our taate, our daddy, when I have done what they asked. You did what you could by sending herbs.''

''And I told the ignorant woman what to pick,'' their grandmother said.

''That's right,'' See-ho-kee said. ''We have done all that we could. Now we must go on and hope for the best. If our father sends for us, then we'll go back to St. Augustine. But now let's join our great-uncle.''

''Yes, let's go,'' urged Hitchiti-hajo.

''Wait,'' said See-ho-kee. ''I will go no further without a gun.''

Her brothers turned startled faces toward her. ''Why?'' asked Eemathle. ''Aren't we here to protect you?''

''Yes. *Now* you are. But when I needed a gun, you were

not there, and all I had was this.'' She held up her lance.

The young men laughed and began to make jokes about her lance.

Their grandmother said sharply, ''Don't laugh.'' She told them about the lost white man. ''Give her a gun.''

The brothers became subdued, meekly consulted each other about which gun would best serve her, finally took a heavy handgun from Eemathle's bundle. He spent a while teaching her how to use it, forced her to shoot it once, smiled grimly at her wild leap back, forced her to shoot it again. He had her memorize and say back to him the exact way she would use the gun, and then he fastened it to her with a holster, worn like a belt over her mourning sheet. An atrocity, surely, but a necessary one.

She retrieved her mother's knife from the palm stem, noticing that her hand felt strangely empty when she threw away the lance.

Before they started the long walk, Eemathle spoke further to Little Mountain. Did she know about anything going on in the south? No. Had she heard of any battles they might chance upon? No. What could she tell them of happenings around St. Augustine which they hadn't heard in prison?

''Well, you surely heard of the Cheliklees?''

''Cherokees,'' said See-ho-kee, snatching at a familiar word.

Eemathle nodded and repeated, ''Cherokees.'' He listened to her, nodded again.

''The Cherokees are trying to persuade us to give up, to make peace. They ask us to come to council at Fort Mellon, to agree on a time and place where all Seminoles will meet and go to Arkansas.'' He shook his head and spat in vulgar imitation of a white man.

Did she know anything about the western part of Florida?

Yes. The corn fields were being readied for spring planting in a place called Wahoo Swamp.

See-ho-kee and her family were electrified by the news. Did their old neighbors consider it safe there now?

"Maybe we should go back," See-ho-kee said.

Her brothers hesitated. "What do you think, Grandmother?" Eemathle asked courteously.

"We must forget them and go south. The white soldiers may wear themselves out chasing Indians in the north and middle part of Florida. By the time they reach us, we may be strong enough."

It was wisdom. They shouldered their packs, Eemathle gave his instructions of caution, and they began a slow run to the south, the women and children in the middle of the line.

eighteen

The walking was hard and arduous. The grandmother suddenly could go no further, and she told them over and over in a thin high voice, "Go on, go on. Leave me till I rest. I'll be along later." She was petulant and unlike herself.

They consulted briefly, and Eemathle carried her first, the way you carry a long-legged child on your back, she hugging him. Her mind began to wander, and sometimes she sang war songs as if she had taken acee — the black drink — and herbs, and she cried out that she would do terrible things to the enemy till Eemathle was near to falling on the ground with laughter. The others chuckled with him. But then her mind cleared up, and she scolded him, said, "Eemathle, you fool, put me down. What are you doing, fool?"

And he soothed her and told her she was tired and he was only giving her a little rest, that was all, so enjoy it. She did for a while and then fussed again. "Put me down, you silly man."

The brothers took turns carrying her, so now there was one armed man in the front and one in the back with the old woman, and the rest of the group were in the middle. They were not close to enemy territory, they believed, and nobody worried too much about Eefe's joyful pursuit of game, nor about the grandmother's occasional singing. They moved along very fast, the three children running to keep up as long as they could after which See-ho-kee and Little Mountain carried the one falling back.

The men would not use their guns when they saw game, for the sound would be sure to bring soldiers if any were near, so they depended upon their bows and arrows, grunting with passion over their lack of skill, so accustomed to guns had they become. But occasionally they got a small animal, and sometimes they would go back off the trail to a hidden place and cook it at once, but more often they carried game with them till they found a place to camp at night.

Sometimes they met other red people on their way north to Fort Mellon for council. Eemathle tried to argue with them, told them what had happened when he and his father and brothers had gone under white flag for conference. Some of the men listened and were persuaded to turn back; others went doggedly on, saying they were sick of watching their women and children dying from running so much.

One day they had no food, and that night before they rested they found a palmetto full of ripe fruit, so heavy with sweetness they had to drive the bees away, apologizing all the while. They ate too much, savored the sweet, made wry faces over the bitter after-taste. Afterwards, See-ho-kee's stomach, unaccustomed to being full, heaved it all out again.

Her grandmother called out something to Little Mountain. "Coo-loo-me! Do you remember Coo-loo-me?"

Little Mountain turned back, smiling broadly and nodding. "Coo-loo-me!"

"Do you remember the wonderful melons they gave their visitors?" There was swift translation, and Little Mountain chattered with enthusiasm.

"There were never such melons anywhere else," the grandmother stated in a voice which refused another opinion. "Bring me a melon," she said to the group. "And the high mound covered with peach trees. Do you remember that?"

"Yes. Wonderful peaches."

"Bring me a peach." A gesture of command.

Little Mountain's eyes suddenly steamed. They went on.

They were getting close to Apayaka's camp. The trail showed signs of much traffic, and sometimes they heard people on nearby trails that cut across theirs.

One day they heard several runners coming with even strides, and all of their party slipped to cover. It was Coacoochee, followed by several of his warriors.

Eemathle stepped forward. "Hey, Coacoochee! You made it out of the fort!"

Coacoochee stopped, smiling, greeted all of them, halted his warriors for a little talk. They sat in a circle on the trail, giving Coacoochee the honor of facing east.

He told them of his escape from the fort, and it was a good story about a small high window through which they managed to get their heads and finally their bodies. They slipped down a rope the fifty feet to the ground, except for one who fell the whole way and had to be carried away. Coacoochee had made black drink for them, and all were thin and hungry.

He would have taken the day telling the tale, if her older brother had not interrupted with as much tact as possible to ask about their father. "Did he escape too? Tell us, sir. And why are you running so fast? Is something else wrong?"

Coacoochee eyed the rude young man with some distaste, but he finished his story in a few words and then said, "We are trying to head off Apayaka. He has been summoned to council at Fort Mellon, and he is going, we have been told. I will warn him of what happened to me and your father and Asi Yahola. If he goes, he will be betrayed and his people will be captured."

See-ho-kee and her brothers became as unmoving and hard as the coquina walls of Fort Marion, so great was their shock at this suggestion. Apayaka captured? He was their last resort, the only man they now felt would never surrender, never allow himself to be captured. Once they had absorbed the news, they burst into words, ideas, blurts of fanciful suggestions. It must not be. Their great-uncle must be stopped.

"Sir, if he is going to Fort Mellon, won't he take the trail just west of here?" Hitchiti-hajo cried. "Maybe you will miss him."

"Will you stay on this trail then and catch him if we go to the other?" Coacoochee asked Eemathle, as was proper, although Hitchiti had given the idea.

"Certainly," replied Eemathle.

"Where can we cross over easily?"

"Not far below here. A great oak is at the crossing and the scrub has been left to conceal the path to the west from the stupid white men, but you will see it easily. A small leap, and you are on your way to the other trail."

"Good. Then we'll go." Coacoochee got to his feet.

"Coacoochee, wait," said Hitchiti-hajo. "You haven't told us about our father."

See-ho-kee was near to fainting from hunger and excitement. The vision suddenly crept into her awareness: white soldiers marched into her mind, took over the jungle around them, flattened the trees, clouded the skies, obliterated her brothers, her little sister, the woman who traveled with them and the two thin boys she clasped, finally Eefe, who looked at her with puzzlement and whimpered. Now she heard only the sound of feet stamping together, felt only the quivering of the earth under the relentless march, saw only . . . Pi-co-yee's face.

"Mother!" she cried. She fell to the ground and lost all knowledge.

There was a time of haziness, and then she heard her grandmother speak in a quaver. "She is having her vision."

"Yes," said Hitchiti-hajo. His voice was low and troubled.

"Woman's vision," Coacoochee said with contempt.

Still unable to arise, See-ho-kee felt the sting of the words.

Eemathle said, "When she had her first visions, we didn't believe her either. But we have watched, and now we see that what she says is true. You would do well to listen."

She felt grateful to her brother, and she struggled hard to arise.

She began to think of stories she had heard about Coacoochee, tried to reconcile this contemptuous man to those stories: he loved to stay near the forts, using the white men's food and whiskey until they began thinking of capturing him, whereupon he always slipped away; he dressed himself with more elegance than any other chief, had adorned himself when he went to Fort Payton when he was captured, had carried a white plume for peaceful passage and a beautiful bead-pipe for General Hernandez from Asi Yahola; but he had often teased the white soldiers when he ran from them for he ran like a wild cat, and he would stop and jeer and beg them to run faster so that it would be more interesting for him. A strange, wild, comical man, a chief who was hard to know.

She was now fully awake, and she sat up and looked into Coacoochee's face, for he crouched in front of her and stared. She saw none of the rudeness she had heard in his speech.

Hitchiti now had his say, in stiff indignant language. "My sister and grandmother are the two who gathered the herbs and roots for your black drink, and my sister took them to the fort and left them."

Coacoochee was sober now. "I had not heard of a woman having a true vision before. I have visions myself. My dead twin sister, very beautiful and good, beckons me often, and I long to leave earth and go with her where we will be happy together forever. What is your vision?"

She told him, trying to make clear what terrified her. He listened with respect.

"And what are the white faces like?" he asked.

She tried to remember. "At first they are blank and pale, strange and threatening. But in the last part of the vision before I return, they are sad. Their faces are very sad."

Coacoochee was not a medicine man; yet he could understand her vision. "You see their cruelty at first; then you see their knowledge of guilt. This is a strong dream."

"And today I saw my mother. Her face smiled at me."

Now all were silent, thinking of this. Then he said, "You are like my twin sister. Beautiful."

It was a new thought to her.

"What about our father?" her older brother asked again.

"Oh, he is coming. He is two hours back."

There were exclamations and questions. How was he? Was he hurt? Why hadn't he come with Coacoochee? Was he on *this* trail?

Coacoochee said, "Yes, on this trail. Pardon me for not telling you this first." He now spoke directly to See-ho-kee.

"We must wait here for him," said Hitchiti-hajo.

"He is sick," Coacoochee said. "Hunger and black drink and a strange sickness. Yaha Chatee is taking care of him."

Yaha Chatee! It was the first word See-ho-kee had had of him for a long time.

"Yaha Chatee is looking for you," Coacoochee said, still speaking to See-ho-kee, "to see that all of you are safe and well."

He would not speak so frankly to her if he realized the scolding her brothers might feel obliged to give her when he was gone; she was, after all, still in mourning.

"His whole family is dead now. The second family he has lost."

"Nuff-kee? Nuff-kee is not dead!"

"Yes. And her child was stillborn. They sealed the baby into a hollow tree to prevent more famine and death. Nuff-kee was too starved to have the baby."

See-ho-kee thought of the life in Nuff-kee, the foolishness, the smiling way she talked and worked. She could not believe that Breathmaker would allow her to die.

As suddenly as it had begun, the meeting was over, and Coacoochee and his warriors loped away. Now the scolding would begin. But her brothers did not say a word.

They waited, spending the time looking for food for their father. At last he came. He shuffled slowly, leaning on Yaha Chatee on one side, a stick on the other. He was thin, sad, old. She saw clearly the shape of his skull and the look he would have when he was dead. She had a desperate feeling which swept away her senses for a moment, and then her grandmother touched her arm and whispered, "Food and rest. That's all he needs. He will be well." See-ho-kee felt comforted.

They decided to spend a night so he could sleep. See-ho-kee took quick looks at Yaha Chatee. He was older, sterner than she had remembered. She wished she could think of a delicate way to tell him what Coacoochee had said about her, but there was no way to do it. She moved away from him.

Finally they reached Apayaka, and Coacoochee was there, had caught the old man as he was leaving camp. See-ho-kee was amazed at the camp, for there were many Miccosukees, all working hard, not running like rabbits as her family had been doing, but working with purpose and assurance.

Apayaka greeted them. He was in a fury over the capture of Coacoochee and Blue Snake, as well as Asi Yahola and his people. "The white savages have no understanding of honor," he stormed. "You could as easily teach an alligator."

Nothing could stop her feeling of happiness. She swung Anatho-yee into her arms and hugged her. "You can feel peaceful now, little sister. We are at home, and we will live here forever."

But then she heard a question from Eemathle, "What are you doing, Uncle? What is all the excitement?"

"You didn't hear on the trail? We are getting ready for battle. They are coming now, Yakitisee warriors and white soldiers. They gather themselves and come from all directions. It will be the biggest battle we've fought. We will be ready this time, and we will kill all of them. There will be a dance around the scalp pole soon!"

But See-ho-kee could not exult with him. She saw smothering clouds of white birds which suddenly became people, in line after line after line, never wavering or falling, marching over the Yakitisee and killing them.

nineteen

See-ho-kee distrusted beautiful days, for it seemed to her that whenever a winter day, cool enough for pleasant working in the bright sun, came to cheer her, a bad thing happened. There would be a battle or the death of a close one. *Not Anatho-yee, not Yaha Chatee!* she begged her mother's spirit. On this day when they were gathering the last of the pumpkins and the few ears of hard corn still on the stalks, and when they considered whether they should be preparing the beds for new seeds to be planted in another month or two, on this gorgeous crisp day, the Cherokees came.

A runner came to announce them. They were on the way. Their chief was John Ross. John Ross wanted Apayaka to come to Fort Mellon for council. He would see to it that there was good straight talk and no lies. So the runner said.

See-ho-kee could not see that council had ever done anybody except the whites any good. Always, always, it ended up by sending more Indians off their land; more warriors were killed; more women died when they ran while carrying babies; more babies . . . . But she put her most awful thought away. Why was it always ready to come to her when there was something new, something about to be changed?

Some of the women hurried to sweep up the twigs from the square-ground. Others gathered refreshing foods and water for the visitors.

"No," said Apayaka, "don't bother to do that. We will meet in the field, not to give them a feeling of importance."

Sometimes now Apayaka's mind was out of pattern. She had always thought of him as the one steady indestructible person in her world, but sometimes he thought and spoke without sense. Not all the time. She wondered whether this was one of the times. He was still strong, he directed firmly, but he blundered in a peculiar way. He would ask a question, forget the answer and at once ask the question again. He had little tantrums over unimportant things he once would have laughed at. Most frightening was his idea that he was back at home with his family in his childhood, and sometimes he spoke to his parents. His *parents*, not their spirits.

Today he seemed fine, strong and unafraid, peaceful, not strange at all, except for his decision to meet the Cherokees in the field without even showing ordinary hospitality. There were times that he reminded her of her grandmother when they were on the long walk, but now her grandmother was well again, and as quick-witted as ever. The mind-strangeness had gone. Her father also had regained his strength and spirit from the sickness he had got in St. Augustine.

But why treat the Cherokees thus? They also were being

driven to Arkansas; they were enduring what the Miccosukees endured. And they were good men, who wished to bring peace between red and white men.

"Why is he so angry?" she asked Hitchiti-hajo.

He looked at her with wide indignant eyes. "And you're *not* angry?" he asked. "They should go and attend to their own affairs. They must think we are stupid and unable to decide what we will do."

The Cherokees came, and the Miccosukees met them in the field north of the village. They formed a square-ground, and Apayaka took his proper place, facing east. Without need for words, the rest took places appropriate to their ranks and clans. They took time for Otulkethlocko, the Owaale, to make medicine, and they were somber and passionate in response.

The Cherokees were polite and agreeable. One man spoke both Creek and Mikasuki, so the talk went freely. They observed the courtesies, taking their time. They came peacefully; they would smoke with their hosts; they wished not to rule the Miccosukees, merely to point out opportunities.

A tall young warrior looked at See-ho-kee and nodded. She sat to the side of him, in the back with the other women. "You are a woman of importance in your tribe, aren't you?" he said, glancing at her widow's dress.

She looked down soberly. "No." She slanted her eyes toward Yaha Chatee and was satisfied to see him as solemn and puffy as a mother toad. She let her eyes rove quickly over the others in the crowd and saw that the women had all witnessed this and were staring, that her father was alert to the man's attention, that Yaha Chatee looked down and refused to look up. The warrior hastily moved away.

The whole village was there, including the children, and the negotiators' voices were loud, for the effect upon the women, in hope they would persuade the men. But the

Cherokees understood that only the men would speak in the council.

"Many great chiefs are there already," the Cherokee interpreter said. "They are ready for their brothers to come to the square-ground to talk."

"Who is there?" asked Apayaka.

"Micanopy."

Apayaka had kept his smirk under control for the sake of politeness, but now he laughed.

"Micanopy," the interpreter repeated in a high voice to offset Apayaka's contempt. "Nocose Yahola, Tuskegee, Yaholoochee . . . "

"How many warriors?" asked Apayaka.

"Many. Eighty, I think."

"They will be captured and sent to Arkansas," Apayaka said with assurance.

"No. They are there under white flag and with our protection. We have been told by the white soldiers that they are there merely for talking. They can leave whenever they wish."

Now Apayaka began laughing, and others of the Miccosukees laughed. See-ho-kee smiled at her great-uncle. He threw back his head in a great guffaw, and his turban fell off and no wonder, for it was never properly arranged and sat on his head like an accident. His white hair stood up in a soft halo.

"You!" he said, still laughing, but angrily now. "You! Man-who-would-think-for-others! You are a fool." He went on laughing, and the laughter of the Miccosukees arose in angry challenge. "The white soldiers will keep them there."

The Cherokees were shocked and dazed over this reaction. "No. I tell you, they are under white flag."

"No matter," said Apayaka. "Let them be dressed in white flags, let them wear a white feather, let them carry the peace pipe, let them be blessed by the spirits of their ancestors, let them be protected by the horn fragments from the great serpent, let them deal in honor with the white men. None of that will matter. The white men will keep them and will not let them go.''

Apayaka looked with severe eyes at the Cherokees. ''This talk is over,'' he said.

There was consternation among the Cherokees who now were afraid they would be attacked. In stumbling words they asked Apayaka for safe passage from the village to the north.

''Certainly,'' he said. ''And for the rest of the way, if you wish it. We are angry, but we are honorable.''

The Cherokees left at once, accompanied by several Miccosukee warriors, including Eemathle.

Apayaka's high laughter started again. ''Good-bye,'' he called out. ''Good-bye, Man-who-would-think-for-others.''

The Cherokee chief turned, held up a hand in farewell, and went on.

See-ho-kee looked about her. It was still a day to enjoy. It was a *good* day.

When Eemathle and the other warriors returned, some weeks later, they reported that Coacoochee had also spurned the advice of the Cherokees. Their mission was a failure, and they had to tell this to General Jesup who went into a rage and ordered all the Indians who had come under the white flag to be imprisoned.

''We stayed a safe distance away,'' said Eemathle. ''We saw it, we saw the treachery. It was just as my great-uncle told us.'' He seemed very proud to say ''great-uncle.'' ''Over eighty men were put aboard a steamer and sent to St. Augustine. Micanopy was weeping.''

''And what of the Cherokees?'' Apayaka asked.

''Man-who-would-think-for-others was howling like a

wolf. He howled and screamed at General Jesup; he fell on the ground in a mad fit. But none of it did any good."

twenty

Apayaka directed all able-bodied men to prepare themselves for war by entering the sweathouse, where they purified themselves with black drink. On the fourth day they came out. Their war bundles contained pieces of leather to patch their moccasins in case they had to run a great distance in pursuit of the white men (or *from* the white men, a thought nobody would voice); their bundles also contained parched corn flour to make cakes on a hot stone; but most needful of all was the charm in their shot bags — the bones of the lion, a bit of horn from the snake — their protection, their war physic. These lion bones and these bits from the horned serpent had been kept for hundreds of years, and they were strength and energy during war. They were good medicine.

See-ho-kee, the other women and children, and the helpless old men were also ready for the impending battle. They had gathered food and reduced it to easy-to-carry portions, had hidden great caches of food to come back to, in case the white men managed to take over the camp. This was only a precaution, not a prediction, and everyone believed that this time they would have the victory they deserved.

Otulkethlocko, who was called Owaale, sang and danced, called incantations upon the spirits to protect them in the battle and to give courage to the warriors. All proper things were being done. No warrior had slept with his wife. See-ho-kee thought with something close to happiness that the white men had best beware; the white men who came would surely die. The war pole would be covered with their scalps.

Her brother Eemathle came in from scouting and reported that the white men would be at the Miccosukee camp by morning.

"White men are gathering and marching toward the Kissimmee River," Eemathle reported. "I saw the white soldiers burst into a small Seminole village. But I got there first, warned them, told them to send the soldiers this way to fight us. There were only a few Creeks, a few cattle farmers. An old man and four young men stayed and the women and children ran into the woods. I hid and listened. The old man told the white men that they were drying and jerking beef and that they were peaceful toward the white men. They *favored* the white way, they said. There were the Miccosukees, they said, pointing this way. Apayaka was their leader. The white men said, 'Aahh! Apayaka! Sam Jones! You are good friends to tell us.' And then the rascals told the old man that they were now captives, that they must go to Captain Munroe who waited at the Kissimmee."

Eemathle now grinned in delight. "You see, they could not bother with captives as they went into battle, and yet they were taking them, they thought. But, the old man asked them, 'What about the women and children, out free in the scrub? Wouldn't it be proper for me to go find them and then all would go together to Captain Munroe?' "

See-ho-kee worried about it. "But what about the villagers? What *will* happen to them?"

"Oh," said Eemathle blithely, "they hid out till the soldiers were gone, but by now they are probably back at work jerking beef."

He went on with the story, impatient to tell it. "The soldiers marched this way, heading for our trap. I trailed them awhile and then went ahead to get another person to show them the exact direction. So they came to a well-armed young man, and he acted for us too. He pointed to the encampment, told the white soldiers they would come to a heavily wooded hammock and a cypress swamp, that there Apayaka and Alligator and Coacoochee had their warriors. They were gleeful, thinking that they were about to catch us by surprise. So they halted their march and began making camp, only five miles from here. So I left them and ran home."

Eemathle turned to the attentive Apayaka and said eagerly, "When they are sleeping, we will go and kill them. Isn't that what we should do, Uncle?"

Apayaka frowned with distaste. "It would not be appropriate. We will follow our plans which all have agreed upon."

The next morning the white army passed through another camp; its residents left the cookfires burning and their half-eaten meat cast away and joined the watchers in the hammock. At this moment many Yakitisee were watching the progress of the white men.

Now it was Hitchiti-hajo's duty to go to point the way to them. He went out and stood guard over their several hundred head of cattle and their Indian ponies. He must let the whites surprise him and take him prisoner, and he too would point to the exact place where the Miccosukees waited.

He soon came home with his report. There were many soldiers, Hitchiti-hajo reported. *Many.* His report barely interrupted the furious pace of their work. Besides the preparations, Apayaka and Otulkethlocko, the Owaale, were now reminding the warriors of the fact that they were from great people, that their importance had not diminished, that they had come from the King of Mountains, the mountain that sang, where they had got their sacred fire and their sacred herbs, their laws, and their religion.

And the restless pole. "Remember the power of the restless pole," said Apayaka in a loud voice, so that See-ho-kee shivered at her work of cutting grass to make it easy for the white men to come into the prepared place. "The restless pole guided our fathers and mothers all the way from the King of Mountains to Georgia and then to Florida. The pole stood in each encampment, planted in the earth. The sacred bag containing charms was suspended from it. During the night the pole leaned in the direction they must go, and when at last it remained upright, they had come to Georgia, and there they lived for a long time till the white men came."

Even now the pole went with them into battle. The war pole.

"And think too of the Miccosukees," said Apayaka. "Remember that they fell from the sky at the lake called Miccosukee. Remember our greatness."

See-ho-kee cherished this story too. Sometimes she pondered about the two stories, how they did not seem to fit each other and she had finally decided that two branches of the family were involved. She was satisfied that both were true.

Ten warriors, disguised with trailing moss, climbed high

into the trees carrying their guns. They were to serve as lookers.

The leaders were ready. In the battle line Apayaka and Otulkethlocko, the Owaale, were near each other with their men, something that concerned See-ho-kee (who had no business being concerned, being only a woman). Neither man was a warrior. Her own father, Coosa-amathle would be a better defender, she thought, but power was not necessarily in experience or strength but rather in knowledge of sacred things, and she wished she could put away her fear. To mention her fear to anyone would be unthinkable; it would seem to be disloyal. Otulkethlocko's incantations and Apayaka's wisdom would surely make their section of the battle line very strong.

Over there was Coacoochee, savage and greedy for the killing; near him was Alligator, no longer joking. His unsmiling face turned him into a stranger.

The grass was cut; the entry was ready. If the white men did not take this way, despite the preparations, they would require days to get through the swamp and the high sawgrass that could cut shoes to ribbons and then begin on the feet and legs, inflicting wounds that might take years to heal. The white men knew this. They had lost many soldiers to sawgrass.

All was ready. Each warrior had chosen his own tree and had notched it to steady his rifle. If a man had two guns, he also had a woman or boy there to help him reload, but for the most part, the women and children were now at the rear. If there were a breakthrough into the hammock, then the women and children were to flee for their lives.

See-ho-kee was at the rear. Her father had instructed her explicitly; if the white men broke through, she was to take Anatho-yee all the way back to Okeechobee, Big Water, where there was a clear beach. "You run fast," Coosa-amathle said. "Go to the east. If you need to hide again, return to the woods, but when all is clear and you can run again, go east. We can find each other faster if all go east."

See-ho-kee was terrified. She realized from her father's speech that they were in a desperate situation. This gathering of Coacoochee, Alligator, and her great-uncle to defend themselves was a last great effort to keep from being pushed into the Everglades where living would be hard and uncertain, if not impossible.

Apayaka had also said a frightening thing: If it seemed you would be killed if you stayed there, then go. The idea was not to die but to live. It was the duty of the warriors to defend their people, and it was the duty of the women to save the children so that the Miccosukees would live, as the Breathmaker had intended.

Everywhere there was fear and solemn talk like this.

See-ho-kee thought with some relief that at least her grandmother was safe, for she had gone already and would wait in company with other old women, miles away to the east. Hitchiti-hajo had caught her another horse, and she had ridden away, waving and laughing, as if her mind were good as ever, as if she were still a girl. Eefe ran alongside the horse, as jaunty as she was.

The lookers in the trees called down softly that the white soldiers had arrived at the place readied for them. They had dismounted and led the horses back out of gunshot distance from the trees, just in case. A few men guarded the horses; a few reconnoitered the swamp.

"They don't see us yet," a looker whispered.

There was a breathlessness, a silence, a waiting in the hammock.

The white men soon saw that the clearing was the only way to cross, that the swamp would bog them down for hours or even days if they tried it. They hesitated, knowing their danger.

The white officers formed their men into lines, and the

entry began.

Immediately Apayaka's high, quavering war whoop trembled into the air, gathering volume. "Yo-ho-e-hee-eee! YO-HO-E-HEE-EEeee!" There was a single shot from near her, Apayaka's, she knew, the beginning of the battle. The other Indians began firing, and instantly every hushed bird set up a frightened complaint.

See-ho-kee stayed long enough to touch her father's arm, and he touched her and then waved her frantically away. She ran with Eefe and Anatho-yee and Little Mountain and the two little boys.

Her thoughts stayed with the men behind her. She knew what their order was. "Let us know when you shoot an officer." That was it. Coosa-amathle had told his sons over and over that the officer did not necessarily dress in a different way, but that they needed take only a moment to observe the actions of the men who always looked to the officer for instructions. See-ho-kee had listened, had wished she might stay and test her mind against a white officer who tried to conceal his rank.

Before she was out of hearing distance, the claims of hits were shouted out, each followed by a war whoop from Coacoochee or Alligator. Her uncle was now silent, having done what needed to be done to begin the fight. There were over three hundred Miccosukees fighting, she knew. How many of them would see her again?

She ran with Anatho-yee, cutting curves off the trail and coming back into it. So far it was easy; later would come the hard travel.

Behind them ran Little Mountain and her two stringy sons. All of them were ragged and dirty. See-ho-kee still wore a sheet made from feed-bags the white soldiers had tossed out at the fort. Moreover, she had often eaten bits of the grain the horses had missed, and she was no longer ashamed to do this. As soon as they reached the hidden place far back into the hammock, they stopped and gathered together in a tight little group. See-ho-kee saw that all of them were trembling, and she wished there were no need for quiet, so that she could tell them one of her grandmother's stories.

"Did you see? Did you see?" whispered Little Mountain in broken Mikasuki. "Your father shot the white chief. He fell, and the white men broke apart and ran back." She smiled, showing her broken teeth, and See-ho-kee smiled back, lifted in spirit at this news.

"Where were you that you could see them?" Little Mountain looked puzzled, and See-ho-kee repeated the question but in different words, as she often had to do with Little Mountain. She and the older woman never lost patience with each other in their efforts to talk.

"Oh. I was up in the tree," Little Mountain bent over and laughed silently, and her small sons grinned at her. "I was a bird." She flapped her arms lazily. "An eagle."

"You might have broken your bones getting down too."

"Oh, yes. I did break bones." She pulled her dress up, showed them a bruise on her shin, and laughed again. See-ho-kee was grateful to her for banishing the fright in the children's eyes. Her own trembling had stopped. She had great affection for Little Mountain, felt closer to her than to any woman except her grandmother since her mother died, perhaps even closer than to her grandmother whose mind was now absent much of the time, whose responsibilities had gradually fallen upon See-ho-kee. There were times when it felt to See-ho-kee as if keeping the children alive, teaching them what they must know to live, teaching them the stories of the old fathers and mothers had settled on her like a great burden. Often she tried to speak to Pi-co-yee's spirit and ask for help. There were many questions she had been too young and silly to ask, when her mother still lived. And now she could never ask them, unless her mother's spirit came. She knew Pi-co-yee had traveled with them, for her father had seen her, and indeed she herself had once seen her walking softly over a grassy place, looking radiant and alive. But her mother had not spoken.

So it was no wonder that Little Mountain was important to her, and she sometimes wondered whether her mother hadn't guided Little Mountain to her that day so many months ago. Her mother would understand that no woman could go on without at least one other woman for conversation — a mother, a sister, a friend like Nuff-kee, or a gaunt, broken-toothed Creek like Little Mountain. The two little boys were now like her own family too, were accustomed to working with the women and playing with the men, or dogging their steps when they hunted or fished. It had not been like this before the war, but now you did not question so much whether the Indians outside of your tribe should be welcomed like family. Now you needed each other.

They listened awhile to the shooting, fainter now but still vigorous. It seemed to See-ho-kee most of the shooting was now deeper into the hammock, not quite so far away. It could mean only one thing: They must be ready to run again. If the white soldiers had come blindly through the prepared place, they would use their big guns to kill. They would swarm over the Miccosukees.

"Do you hear any war whoops now?" she asked Little Mountain.

"No."

"Did you see Apayaka when you were in the tree?"

Little Mountain looked away, did not want to speak.

"Did you see my great-uncle?"

"Yes. His men were falling back. The white men were too many, the guns too strong."

She would not think about this yet. It was too terrible to think of. She must decide now whether they should run on to the lake and then east as her father told her, or whether to remain here where it was a hidden safe place. She and Little Mountain could hide the children and run to distract the white soldiers, as a mother bird would do.

A little distance away some forest clutter snapped under a foot. They were instantly motionless and silent. They listened for a long time, heard sounds of men coming, still far away, but nobody was near them, they believed.

"Find a place and dig a hole to hide the boys," she hissed at Little Mountain, who nodded, touched the two boys, put a finger to her lips, led them into the shadows.

She herself now found a safe place for her sister Anatho-yee. She whispered comforting words to the little girl, tucked food into her hand, said she must not answer if she heard strange language. She swiftly dug the hole, stopping in terror to listen as the sounds increased. At last she put the child down in. "You will be in a good place here, dear one. Be very still. Wait for me to come for you."

The great dark eyes followed her, but there was not a word of pleading. See-ho-kee covered the hole with palm fronds, arranging them to look as if they had tumbled together. She moved away quickly in case there were watching eyes, hid herself in a hollow among vines and ferns. From here she could see the fronds that covered Anatho-yee, and she could see the trail to the lake. She took out her gun and put a bullet in it, laid it on the ground in front of her.

They were in a bad situation because of her own stupidity, her desire to linger near her father. They should have gone straight through the hammock hours ago, should have followed her grandmother. Now she had to wait it out, not so hard for her, but an agonizing experience for the children, she knew. She listened, tried to hear Little Mountain at her preparations, but all was quiet except for the distant boom of guns and the shouts and high war whoops of men.

She should go now. It sounded as if the battle were moving this way, as if the whites had broken through, as if the white men's war would surround her and eat her in a few moments. It was too late to run. By the time she got Anatho-yee up and called Little Mountain to get the boys and join her in a quick run, the war would be there. She held absolutely still and thought with bitter regret that she had erred in staying so long.

The Indian warriors came. Only a few came at first, panting hard, tugging their guns through the brush, crashing with wild abandon. One flung himself behind a tree, and steadied his gun, saw nothing to shoot at, except his brothers. Ran on.

Now the main group came. She heard a rush of feet, a clanging of guns against each other, a grunt when somebody got a bullet, a scream, a slapping home of a new load, a gun firing very near her, a hoarse yell from the other side. She felt angry triumph. A white man had received a bullet too. She wanted to join this desperate retreat, but she stayed steady, *must* be steady, for Anatho-yee was her duty, her sister-daughter to protect, no matter what happened to father, brothers, herself. She peered through the ferns, watched and heard the agonizing flight, the attempts to reload and fire. There they were: her friends, her family, Creeks, Choctaws, Uchees, Shaw-a-nee, Miccosukees, crippled and bloody. All of Apayaka's warriors, even the old man himself, and Otulkethlocko, wild-eyed and unbelieving, ran past her, knowing to leap over the pit which hid Anatho-yee.

There were a few white men with the last of the Indians; now a swarm of them came. They stopped to aim and shoot. Somewhere a heavy gun boomed. See-ho-kee curled into a tight knot and closed her eyes, held very still. She hoped her heart which thrummed like a war drum could not be heard.

If I am this afraid, how does Anatho-yee feel, buried there, not knowing?

It seemed to last forever, the retreat, the pursuit, but finally all Indian warriors were gone, leaving their dead, and only white men remained, almost straggling now. It was still a very dangerous time for the hidden women and children. Twigs cracked under the careless feet of the white soldiers, and they muttered strange angry words when they stumbled.

She waited until there was not another man-sound anywhere. Stood up. Looked, looked, looked in quick animal jerks. Felt danger still lurking. Squatted again and waited. There was no sound except a piercingly beautiful question from a bird high in the trees.

She arose and started toward her sister. They must get past the white men somehow, must find Little Mountain and the boys, must go to the beach of Okeechobee and then to the east, in the path of the other Indians.

The very quiet was frightening. Again she crouched in the ferns. She felt herself in a state of scattering, as if pieces of her would seek places of safety: one bit to the haven of Pi-co-yee, one bit to home in Ouithlacoochee Cove, a bit to Wahoo Swamp, one to Apayaka's old village at Silver Springs, a bit to her father and brothers, to her grandmother — wherever they were. It occurred to her that this coming-apart sickness came from her having no center, no place of certain welcome.

Then, at last, when her need was so great, her mother's spirit visited her.

"See-ho-kee, be a woman. Don't look for a center. You *are* the center."

The voice was so clear, so steady and sure, she calmed at once and began thinking of herself as the middle of a revolving sphere, a person who could create stability.

Her resolve came back. Her mind gave herself quick commands. Get Anatho-yee, find Little Mountain and the boys, find a safe way to the lake shore and then to the east.

She tried to get up, and still she crouched like a little rabbit afraid of dogs. She clutched her gun, felt its strength. She scolded herself, and finally she stood.

At once, there was a tiny sound behind her, another in front. She tried to sort them out, held still and looked. Maybe her ears had fooled her, playing to her fear.

A white soldier stood not twenty feet away. His face was turned away and he could not see her where she stood in the shadow. She saw him with pure clarity; saw his dirty, elegant, blue uniform; saw his great leather cap up in a peak, giving him awesome height; saw a drop of sweat run down his flat cheek. She watched as he put his gun to his shoulder and fired into the underbrush.

The bullet barely left his gun when Little Mountain screamed, a high woman scream. See-ho-kee saw her stand erect clutching her throat to stop a geyser of blood, watched her raise a hand and point at the soldier, saw her bow and sink out of sight in the brush. The brush moved violently a moment.

It was the horror of Pi-co-yee's death over again. It was like losing her mother. The soldier was reloading, taking his time, unafraid. He concentrated, the way a person at work did. Was this the way Pi-co-yee's killer acted?

She lifted her gun, took aim as Eemathle had taught her, thought of her need for practice, wondered whether it would work. She was too far away. She went silently toward him, the gun pointing, both hands holding it up in position.

She contained her rage, kept it cold so that she could accomplish this without tremors. She thought to herself, *I am the center. I am the center.*

She checked her aim. She fired.

The sound made his arms fly out, made him leap into the air, made him say *Ooooffff,* made him fall. There was no other sound or movement.

She ran swiftly to Little Mountain to see whether she

could help her, knew it was useless. She touched her friend with love and grief.

She went back to the soldier who lay on his back. He was not quite dead, she saw; his eyes slitted and oozed tears. She looked at him with rage, not so cold and contained now. She thought about him, about what he had done. He had killed Little Mountain; he had killed Pi-co-yee; he had stolen their fields of pumpkin and corn; he had driven her family apart; he had driven them out of civilization into his own savage ways.

She took Pi-co-yee's knife and considered.

She hesitated.

She had a swift picture of the Ouithlacoochee where she had felt safe, with never a thought of spending her life running and running from his gun. He had done this. She gripped the knife.

She hesitated.

The man breathed unevenly.

She saw another picture. Her father helped Anatho-yee come from her mother's stricken body, held her up; she saw that last fragile breath, heard a tiny gasp as Anatho-yee received it.

Hesitated.

She saw Thlicklin's bent knee, saw him limping across a field. She saw her grandmother, old and puny, with no home to die in decently.

Hesitated.

She looked down at herself, at her filthy skinny hands, at her dirty coarse feed-sack sheet of mourning. Her rage exploded. She took off the soldier's hat and put it on herself, lifted the brown hair and began to cut. It was awkward, but she learned as she went, and when it was done, she tied the scalp to her sash and let the blood drip unheeded.

She went to Anatho-yee, tossed away the fronds, cooed reassurances, looked down and smiled. The terror slowly left the little girl's face, and she laughed silently at her hat. She reached up her hand. See-ho-kee gave her a steady pull, and when she came out, they held each other for a long moment.

They examined Little Mountain together; protecting Anatho-yee from the sight of death did not occur to See-ho-kee. She smoothed Little Mountain's hair and dress, straightened her limbs, stared with sorrow at the rough hand that clutched a piece of rotten wood.

"We must find the boys now," See-ho-kee said.

They began to search, looking for heaps of palm fronds that might hide their pit. The two walked about, Anatho-yee still only a toddler, and looked for a long time. The sun was going down; they *must* find them before dark. Night terror for the young was unbearable; she couldn't let them stay here all night.

At last she began to call them, softly at first. There was the answer of the wind in the trees. She began to think of the two boys staying in the hole forever, and she called in a loud, frightened voice, taking dangerous risk that another straggling soldier might hear her.

She called and called. Dark began to descend.

"*You* call them, Anatho-yee," she begged.

At once the voice piped out commands. What was she saying? Anatho-yee talked on and on in babyish, unintelligible shouts. *Creek!* See-ho-kee marveled. *She's speaking Creek!*

Her small helpless sister spoke two languages.

Now Anatho-yee quieted, and from near them, the boys answered.

The boys came out of their hiding place and were told what had happened. A woods spider, slow-moving from the cold, climbed across the older boy's leg, and with a quick reflex he slapped at it. See-ho-kee managed to grab his arm in time.

"Never kill a spider," she said, "or else your . . . " She couldn't go on. *His* mother was dead. Killing a spider couldn't kill her. But someone surely would die, maybe even herself, now the only mother he had.

The boy looked a question at her.

"It's very bad luck," she said. "You have much to learn."

Later, after the boys had knelt and touched their mother and cried and begged her to come with them, that all would be better in the next place, See-ho-kee stripped the soldier of all they could use, put his shirt on the oldest boy and his sash on the younger, took his coins to buy food, and quickly then led the children south to the lake.

The sun gave them two last flashing rays and showed them hundreds of footprints on the lake shore, prints of white feet and red feet.

See-ho-kee saw a steady trail of new prints left by a tiny field mouse. She considered the great importance of that mouse, for it still had breath, and Little Mountain had none.

twenty-one

See-ho-kee knew she would need all her strength to take the three children without assistance to the place, wherever it was, that Apayaka chose for the new village. She knew to go to the southeast; she knew to follow her tribe's footprints; she knew to avoid the white soldier's paths. That was all.

There were many problems. First and most frightening was their lack of food. She knew exactly where a good food cache was; she could find it easily, retrieve the food and bring it, give them all a good meal before beginning the long trip. But this meant leaving the children hidden for at least one day, a day lost in finding the other members of the tribe, making it almost impossible to catch them.

Remembering her terror when she couldn't find the little

boys, she decided against it. They must find food on the way. She sighed as she made her decision not go to back.

There was also the problem of coaxing the children — even Anatho-yee — to walk unreasonable distances, to eat strange foods, to be quiet hour after hour. She could do that; she would command; she would not give in to compassion. She would treat Anatho-yee like a child; she was not a baby.

Only at night, when they were ready to rest, would she love the children and tell them they were doing well.

Finally, there was a problem within her, a haunting thought that they had no certain place to go. Always before she had felt safe in knowing there was Ouithlacoochee Cove; if that were taken, they could go to Apayaka's village; if that were gone, there was Wahoo Swamp, all centers of security for her. Now she must find the people in a great wilderness. Now there was no center.

She could hardly believe the battle was over so fast, after their long preparation; the Yakitisee were gone; her family was gone; the white men were gone. She *hoped* the whites were gone, but she must keep constant watch.

On the first night when they stopped, she mixed the last of their cornmeal with water and fed it to the children, took a little herself, so that their complaining bellies would let them sleep. The children tumbled together and slept instantly. She could not sleep.

"Mother, I am too young. I am not strong enough to do this."

Instantly her mother was with her, and she made a quick gesture with her hand which said, *Of course, you are old enough. This is why Yaha Chatee looks at you with longing. And you are strong. You had my death and the long walk after for practice. Keep thinking of that.*

It was strange. Her mother's smiling face was still there when she closed her eyes. She felt better to have the spirit near.

"Mother, we have no central place to meet our family. There is no center any more. How can I make the trip without knowing where our center is?"

You are the center.

Her mother was gone.

What did it mean? She had taken comfort from her mother's pronouncement before, but she still wondered and worried about it. How could See-ho-kee be the center? She tried to go to sleep, could not for wondering what it meant.

It suddenly came to her. Apayaka was a center; with him straggled whoever was left, a few villagers, but *he* was the strong one, and wherever *he* walked, *they* went, clustering around him and using his strength.

Her mother was telling her she had strength, she must use it, she must take these children to a safe place. If Pi-co-yee thought she could do it, she *could.*

At last she was able to sleep. When she awoke in the morning, she discovered that Pi-co-yee had loaned her strength.

They left the shore of Okeechobee, moved through the hammocks toward the east. There were swamps and palmetto, hard to cross, very dangerous because of moccasins in the swamps, rattlesnakes in the palmetto. She must find the easiest way to walk. It would lengthen the trip but would make it safer. The smaller children, uncomplaining and obedient, took turns riding on her back, Anatho-yee having longer periods than the boy, for her walking was still babyish and uncertain. They walked in silence, stopped for rest often, and the three children lay immediately on the safe ground she chose; the three of them had the gift of quick sleeping. She propped herself against a tree or log where she could watch them. She stared at them, marvelled that they still were beautiful, despite their need for grooming and bathing, despite the weight they had lost.

By the second day their hunger had become painful, and Pi-co-yee sent them a turtle who marched as obstinately and slowly as a white man across a clearing. She killed the turtle with Pi-co-yee's knife, apologized to its spirit and thanked it. She had no way to cook it. They would eat it anyway. She handed a small piece of raw meat to each child who sat and stared at her in horror. "Eat!" she commanded gruffly. She looked, felt savage as she put a bloody bit into her own mouth and began to chew. The children took their own tiny bites, and all of them chewed and chewed, trying to make the meat become small enough to swallow. See-ho-kee observed that the more she chewed the larger the bite got, so she forced herself to swallow it. They swallowed, their big eyes watching her. This time she cut even smaller bites. "Don't chew much," she told them. "Only a little."

It took a long time for them to eat. She gave each a drink of water from her leather hat and they drank, and she patted them and told them they were good children.

There were no human tracks anywhere. Where had she lost all the footprints? Was she going *away* from her family. No, this is east. She was right.

They walked down a long open place with hammocks to the south. Behind them was swampland. To the north was open prairie. It was very beautiful in every direction, familiar in many ways although See-ho-kee had never seen this land before. They walked east for a long time, and she finally saw a break through the hammocks so that they could turn southward. Here suddenly she came across many tracks, made by both Indians and whites. The tracks, wind-softened for days, led through the clearing, and she followed with the children so that now at last they were east of the vast hammock land. Now they had a broad prairie to walk to the southeast, easy to walk, and See-ho-kee felt that it had been prepared for her to ease her labor of forcing the children ahead.

Yet it was not truly easy, for their fatigue was becoming so great that she knew that a rougher path would have stopped them forever; the buzzards would have gathered.

She needed to talk to her father and brothers. She wanted to see Yaha Chatee. She tried to persuade Pi-co-yee's spirit to visit; she wanted to ask how far it would be, how long it would take.

Her mother did not come.

They followed the clearing, looking for familiar tracks. Many Indians had been here in the last day or so, had left scattered bits of possessions they could no longer carry. There were a few things she wanted, could have used later, but she passed on to keep her arms free to give a child a rest. Her eyes moved from article to article, searching. No food had been abandoned. She began to throw away her own belongings, most of them. She saved her knife, the gun, her sash, two alligator-hide strips for shoes, whenever her own shoes were cut to pieces. She saved her medicine bag.

The prairie gradually became a marshland drained by a little creek which was filled with fish. She used her sheet as a net to move some agitated fish toward the bank, waited patiently for her chance, suddenly flipped a fish ashore.

The three children laughed softly, and the sound warmed her. They ate raw fish and liked it. She found a crane's nest, told the silly crane she had laid her eggs too early anyway, took the eggs, and they feasted till they couldn't swallow.

She gave each child two eggs to carry. They walked on.

The mornings were thick with mist, creating a curtain between them and the horizon and giving pleasure to the children who loved secret things. It amazed her to see their good spirits; for it had been a long walk for small children, a *long* walk. Today they were making good progress when she noticed that her sister's right shoe was coming apart, so she stopped at once for repair, thinking anxiously of the lost time. The older boy shyly showed his shoe to her, and half the sole was worn away so that his foot was criss-crossed with little cuts. She almost scolded him, almost said aloud, "You should have told me before it got so bad. You're a bad boy." But she knew he was trying hard to be a good warrior, brave and strong and unyielding to pain, so she patted him and went to work, refashioning all the shoes. She thanked her mother for this skill, and her mother smiled at her from the swamp. The sun suddenly touched her mother, and she shimmered with color like a drop of water and disappeared. See-ho-kee heard an echo of her mother's laughter.

A tremor began in her hands.

Now the older boy volunteered to carry Anatho-yee. She considered, nodded, told him to try it. He hoisted the little girl to his back, shifted and staggered, caught balance, tried to walk. His legs slowly spraddled and bent, and he fell to his knees. See-ho-kee caught her little sister before she could hit the ground.

See-ho-kee understood how painful his humiliation was, but she said nothing. In silence he led his little brother, and she lifted Anatho-yee to her back again. She looked back in a moment and saw that the boy was still suffering from shame. It would be a good time to stop and praise him for other things, she thought, but she also knew she must consider first her own strength. When she put time and thought into easing him, she stole strength from all. She went on in silence.

Enormous flocks of birds flew over them constantly, called to each other with noisy abandon. The wonderful loud insistent cries distracted her all at once and made her happy for the life above her. She thought of the Breathmaker with gratitude. This was the way it used to be for the Indians, she thought; the world was filled with them as the sky with birds. Now she remembered her vision of the white men coming like waves of birds, and she grimly came back to her ordeal of rescuing three children. Still she was touched by the teeming life, and she began to feel the life in herself; she saw life in the green world around her; she felt life in the sand she walked on, now warmed by the sun, and the sand responded to her with mute acceptance.

That night the moon came out and watched her, and she studied it, trying to see the man and dog that inhabited it. Soon she slept as hard as the children.

A sudden loud snort awoke her at dawn. She and the children looked with fright at a huge hog grazing for acorns. He snorted again, and she arose quickly and lifted the children into the low branches of an oak, climbed up with them, lifted each higher, pulled herself up out of the hog's reach. He ignored them, went on searching for acorns. She saw he was not a threat, and when he came directly under her, she dropped a twig on his back and shouted, "Go out of our woods, white man. Graze in your own fields." She clapped her hands, and the hog squealed and ran into the scrub. The two boys laughed until she feared they would fall, and Anatho-yee smiled.

They went on, but she was left with the thought that there may have been a way to corner the pig and shoot it for food. Foolish as it was, she entertained the thought during an hour of hard walking before fatigue finally drove it away.

I have lost count of the days, she realized. She tried to figure it out. There must have been four at least. She asked the older boy, and he responded with a vague look. It was important to know this, she felt. They would ask her how many days it took, when she found Apayaka's village. She would not allow herself to doubt that she would find it. She picked up a small stick and made four careful cuts on it, half-sure she had not made enough, and she stuck the stick into her sash which was laden with many things.

Again they walked east. There was wet prairie to the

south of them, swamp to the north, and still their clearing held. She had no desire to shorten the trip by cutting across the wet prairie, lovely as it was, for the children would not be able to move fast.

They came to a ruined village, each house burned, and she had a vision of the oily palm fronds burning like torches. The frame of a house leaned into itself like a pitiful dying creature. She felt sick seeing it, and quickly she looked for white men's tracks. There were none; indeed there were no human tracks, and she soon knew that the village had been destroyed a long time ago, perhaps by the Indians themselves as they retreated south. She and the solemn children sat in the middle of the square-ground for a rest, and she felt the village spirits touch her; she felt their questions, but she could not see them, nor understand what they wanted to know.

She drew the children close to her, let them rest longer than usual, for this place had a feeling of home about it, and they could almost hear friendly talk and village sounds.

A brisk scuffling sound came from the woods. She and the children froze and her eyes began a practiced search for escape routes. Two dogs thrust into the open, stared at them, wagging with good intentions. See-ho-kee relaxed and laughed softly. The dogs were still civilized. "Don't talk to them," she cautioned the children. "They might go with us; they might bark at a rabbit and bring the white soldiers."

They went on, all looking wistfully back. After they were far away, it occurred to See-ho-kee that she should have caught the smaller dog and killed it. Apayaka would have done that; he would have acted with instinct to get food for his people. How could her mother's spirit believe she was the center? It had been a long time since they ate.

The endless walk had become torture for the children, and the small boy's eyes constantly ran tears although he never let out a sound of weeping. See-ho-kee's head floated sometimes from fatigue and worry.

She began to think of the two white men she had met. They were human after all. She told herself this: White people are human. It was a great discovery, for she had thought since she was small that only beasts could pursue the Indians with such ferocity; only beasts could put her and the three children into such trouble. But the whites were human although they had no understanding.

In her mind she tried to speak to the first white soldier, the mad man with blue eyes, for she yearned to give him the gift of understanding. *You are here fighting for the land,* she said. *You don't know the land. You have no understanding of the land. You can't own the land; it owns you. The land lets you rise; then it claims you.*

She felt guilty thinking these thoughts, for she secretly believed the white man could have been taught civility if only they could speak together. But Apayaka had talked to many white men until at length he lost all patience and said, "No more talk! Any Miccosukee who talks to the white man is our enemy!" And surely he knew best.

But her mind persisted in trying to speak to the mad white soldier. *We will fight you all our lives for the right to live here. We will scatter and hide like field birds, and we will never give in.*

Sometimes she felt her face become hot with anger, a quick flush of rage and it was gone; anger was not truly a part of her nature. It used to be that she was peaceful, even afraid, not angry as her father and her great-uncle were.

She had a sharp focused picture of the strange blue eyes, and with the picture she suddenly smelled burning gun powder. An ugly sight, an ugly smell. The battle at Okeechobee came back to her although she closed her eyes and ears against it. Screams and moans and crackling fire. The stir and lift of an injured man, his brown arm thrusting up and falling. All of it came back to her, now seen in cruel detail.

She turned in desperation to the children to dispel the vision, and right at her face was the small boy she carried. His eyes were swollen from weeping. He touched her face, and she came back to the long open field through which they walked.

The next morning she noticed the stick, thought about it, felt uncertain, believed she had missed recording a day or perhaps two. The walk had now stretched out into an eternity.

They came to a little rise in pineland, near the ocean, See-ho-kee felt sure, for many seabirds wheeled above her, screaming their dissatisfaction, and returning east to the salt water. There was excitement in the air, a different feeling. She looked at the sick bright eyes of the children and tried to believe that the fevered look was excitement over nearing the rest of the tribe. She knew it was not so, realized that her own eyes probably glittered the way the Owaale's did when he was preparing the young men for battle. She must redouble her efforts, must maintain caution, must not be carried away by false excitement.

She shot her gun into a flight of birds and brought down an egret. The meat was stringy, but they ate ravenously.

At this place there were no more footprints. They had disappeared into the swamp. But See-ho-kee and the children must stay on dry land for she could not get them across swampland and the buzzards would surely get them there. It was a lonely frightening decision to go through the trackless pine woods, but she decided; they started; they walked on without looking back. The pines led south.

At least there was no fear now of meeting white men. She began telling stories to the children. "You listen to this, and you remember," she told them. It was essential to have their attention, no matter how demanding their stomachs were for food, no matter how much their legs ached. They had to hear these stories and pass them on to their children; else her grandmother's years of tale-telling would be lost.

Her grandmother was dead! She suddenly knew this. No old woman could survive this trip, even with a horse to ride. She tried to see her spirit but could not.

In her grandmother's honor, to preserve her work of tale-telling, See-ho-kee talked above her hard breathing, told tale after tale elaborating on the old tales so that they would seem more immediate to the children. She spoke in Mikasuki, but she frequently doubled back and added a Creek word or two to make it easier for the boys. When the younger boy questioned and puzzled over a word, Anatho-yee translated easily.

When your belly hurts from hunger, her grandmother used to tell her (in the days when they were not hungry), *you can only ache. You cannot see anything that is beautiful.*

See-ho-kee had often observed this truth for herself since then, but now they skirted several small salt lakes which were covered with enormous flocks of roseate spoonbills, cranes, egrets — all together. She saw their beauty; she became a part of them.

They passed cypress swamps where giant trees lived. At night they heard alligators splashing. In the daytime she listened to the screams of the parakeets; she saw flocks of turkeys, admired them though she had no wish for one to eat. She especially loved the flocks of parakeets, watched them flash through the woods in a single sweeping movement.

She caught a catfish and they ate it.

She had learned to love the fog that fell over them in the morning, like a blanket to hide them from danger. The high ground they now followed had scrub pines, and she missed the taller pines she used to know. The walking would have been pleasant except for their pain and fatigue and hunger. Nothing she could find for food satisfied the hunger any more.

They took hope. They came to two trails, one leading to the northeast, the other to the southeast, and there were many footprints on each. She searched for white men's tracks, saw that they went to the north, and so she took the trail to the southeast. See-ho-kee pointed out footprints. Everywhere she looked for horses' hoof prints, thinking of her grandmother. There were none. This reminded her: *My grandmother is dead.*

She studied a narrow footprint. "That could be Apayaka," she said. "We must go faster now; we will catch them soon." They tried to. Their leaden legs would not hurry.

She no longer felt quite so safe from the white men, for she had no doubt the northeast trail led to their coastal fort. Fort Lauderdale. An ugly frightening sound. But surely they were close to their family now. It amazed her that she had seen no one since they lost the others.

Again they walked due south, parallel to a great swamp. There were now great flocks of curlews flying overhead, so many the sky was filled with wings. From here she could look west and see islands in the swamp, either hammocks or mounds left by the old people who lived here before. Could people be living there now? It seemed possible. It would be hard for the white men to get there, loaded down with goods as they always were when they traveled.

When they were becoming careless from numb fatigue, they at last heard voices, and the four of them ran to hide like young quail, scattering and going under shelter, as they had been taught. See-ho-kee listened. They were Indians. Creeks!

She ran out, called a greeting, called the boys to talk for her. There were several people staring from the field at her and the children; there was the semblance of a village, roughly constructed, three shelters. No fire burned. She saw an old woman and two young women not much older than herself, a crippled man who hopped on one leg to stare at her. His face had frozen into a permanent wince. They talked quickly, she tried to understand and respond. They had the remnants of a garden; one place had been a pumpkin garden, but the pumpkins were gone. Did they have food? she asked.

The older boy translated. They had very little food, he told her. They had fled here, but if the white soldiers came again, this time they would surrender.

The old woman brought out four small pieces of jerked beef and gave one to each, and they chewed it eagerly. See-ho-kee had forgotten how good it was. It was gone very quickly, and she wondered whether it was all, whether the people here had nothing for themselves to eat, whether they could not share more with her.

The two little boys talked at furious speed to their new friends, pointing eagerly to her and Anatho-yee. She grasped the meaning of what they said, if not the words, for they gestured and stamped the ground in their excitement like little men. She heard them say "Miccosukee," and she watched the others carefully to see how they reacted. The Creek man smiled and said, "Oh? Miccosukee! Your people are down there." He pointed to the south, but his thumb wavered as if it weren't sure where to point.

Now the man questioned the older boy about his own family. "Creek?" he asked, pointing to the boy's chest. And he talked more, saying that now the boys should live with *them,* here in this village. They would build it up to be a big village, and the boys would have a house here until they married and moved away to their wives' villages.

See-ho-kee's heart began a slow painful beat while she waited for the boy to think. She suddenly knew that he was as dear to her as a brother. As her own child.

The boy shook his head. "No. No." He took the small boy's hand and moved over to See-ho-kee. "We are Miccosukee now. She needs us. We need her."

The smaller boy put his arm around her possessively, and the Creeks laughed. They nodded and smiled at See-ho-kee, and the old woman brought out pieces of roasted pumpkin, chewy and sweet from hours by a slow fire. She talked to the boys, gestured to the shelter.

The older boy looked doubtful. "She says we may stay here to rest."

See-ho-kee shook her head. "No, we must go on now. It is still early in the day."

The boy translated, and there was a clamor of protest from the Creeks. "No. No. Stay and rest a day. Sleep here tonight. Look at the children. You will kill them if you force them on."

She felt languor overtake her, even before she agreed, and when at last she nodded agreement, her eyes wanted to close.

"Here," they said. "Come here and sleep in this shelter. Nobody will bother you."

They slept together all day into the late evening, and when See-ho-kee awoke, she found pumpkin and water near them. They ate and slept again. She awoke before daybreak and marveled that the night noises seemed so much tamer, so friendly. She felt stronger. She tested her hands, saw that she still had the tremor she had noticed days back, but it seemed not as bad now. She lay awake till dawn, enjoying her ease, comfortable with her lack of responsibility.

When the others awoke, there was more conversation about what she should do.

"Do you seek your Miccosukee family?" the crippled man asked her.

"We are looking for Apayaka," she said.

His face lighted up. "Oh. Apayaka!" He laughed with admiration. "Sam-Jones-be-damned! The white man's torment! Isn't it true?"

She smiled with pride. "Yes."

"Very brave man. Well, woman, you still have far to walk."

"How many days?"

He countered by asking, "Where were you when you started walking, and how many days has it been?"

"I was at the northeast shore of the big lake after the battle, and I lost my family. We could not keep up." Now she held up the stick. "It could be two days more, maybe three. Sometimes my mind was too tired to think well."

The villagers looked at the stick and the children, finally at her. Their eyes were sad; one woman had tears. "I know that it is a long walk. My husband died there, and they could not go back to tend his body. It was too far away."

"Two more days," the man said, after studying her stick, the children, the sky, her trembling hands. "You need two full days."

It sounded easy. They could do that; she knew they could.

The villagers accompanied them to the edge of camp, and here the crippled man gave good directions. He pointed. "Go to the south for two days. Then get on high ground, perhaps in a tree, and look to the west. You will see a group of little islands holding their heads above the swamp. Perhaps they are still a little to the south of you; if so, you need to walk again. When they are finally west of you and you can get a good line on them, you will see Sam Jones' Islands, seven of them."

"And that's where they are?"

"That's where they are. Get there as soon as you can, for the white men want him above all others. He may have to move again, and you will never find your family."

She was tempted to leave at once, without time for manners or further directions, but she waited.

"What is the walk like?"

"Easy walk. Very easy walk. Not like some you've seen the last few days."

"Is there a swamp where we can hide if the white soldiers come?"

"Yes. There is swamp to the west. All the way you have swamp. But don't be afraid of white men. There are none here now."

He had told the truth. The first day of walking was easier, now that they had rested and eaten, now that the ground was level and dry. Again they watched wild animals and birds; once they saw two cows who looked up at them without stopping their perpetual chewing. Whose cows were they? she wondered. Were their owners hereabouts or were they dead? She watched hopefully for red people, but despite the dim path through the grass, there were no people anywhere except themselves.

By the second day their exhaustion and hunger were back, and again the tears rolled from the small boy's eyes. She stopped and put Anatho-yee down for the big boy to lead and took up the small boy. She wiped his tears and patted his behind and smiled at him to give him courage. He gave her a half-smile and leaned against her throat and went instantly to sleep.

At the end of the second day, she stopped to look for the islands. They went to the nearest high place, and she climbed a tree. It was nearly dark.

Seven islands. There they were. Seven islands touched by the sun, off to the southwest. Her constant trembling made it hard to cling to the tree as she came down. The islands were very far away. The crippled man had told her the walk to this place would be easy, and it was, but he had not told her the islands were so very far from here.

"Did you see them? Are they there?" the children asked.

"They are there. I saw them with the sun on them."

She went to her knees so that she could hold the children

to her. *I am the center,* she thought.

They found a place to sleep and went to bed early, but See-ho-kee awoke often in painful excitement.

In the morning they looked along the edge of the swamp for a boat. There was none. She went out into the water several times, looking for the safest, most shallow way. The water was deeper than she expected, too deep for the two smaller children. She went out farther, and now the water was waist deep. Beyond, it appeared drier, but the sawgrass rippled like water under the wind. The islands were far away, too far for her to leave the children and go for help. What else could she do? Maybe it would be safe to scream for help. Her mind dismissed this as insane. White soldiers were looking for Apayaka now. Why point the way to them? It was too far away; a scream could not be heard from this distance.

A cool wind came from the northeast, setting miles of sawgrass into motion, a giant wave that seemed to follow a giant hand. It reminded her of the waves she had often observed on bayshores where millions of tiny crabs covered the ground, and when her foot stepped near, panic in the nearest crab went in an instant to the next crab and the next and the next until their swift retreat turned the whole beach into a giant wave.

She believed the wind was a warning to the grass. Maybe to her and the children too. She needed medicine to ward off evil, to strengthen her for this last great walk. But there was no proper medicine for this.

She couldn't trust even the older boy to walk there. The grass would cut him to pieces. She knew what she must do. She had known from the beginning she must take Anathoyee and go on. If Apayaka were there, if *any* of her clan were there, they would send for the boys.

As soon as the thought became solid in her mind, two things happened: The older boy jerked his head around and looked at her in terror, as if her thought had reached him. The second thing that happened was that Little Mountain suddenly sat between her two boys. She looked just as she had before she died, unkempt, worried but unsurrendering. See-ho-kee looked at the children, but they had not noticed Little Mountain.

I give you my sons, said Little Mountain. *They are yours.*

See-ho-kee marveled that she could now understand Little Mountain perfectly without translation. She nodded. "It is a great gift. You see, Little Mountain, I cannot carry all three children there." She waved to the distant unseen islands.

They are your sons. Little Mountain's smile showed the gap in her teeth. She seemed not to understand that See-ho-kee had done the best she could, that now she had more to do than was possible. Little Mountain nodded encouragingly.

"How will I do it?"

But Little Mountain had given her gift and departed. See-ho-kee looked at the older boy. He stood very close to her, put his hand in hers.

"I will walk the whole way, Waache," he said. Waache. Mother.

He had never called her that before. She had become his Miccosukee mother.

She must carry them. How could she do it? Her mind set itself to the problem, and Little Mountain's voice came once or twice to help. She stripped the children's clothes off, looked regretfully at the worn cloth, doubled the material over thin spots, began to make two slings, one for the small boy to hold him safely on her back, one for Anatho-yee who would ride in the front, her legs curved around See-ho-kee's waist. Anatho-yee would make the whole trip facing backward and must realize right away that she could not swing around to see what was next. See-ho-kee would carry the older boy in her left arm, so that whenever they came to a dry place, she could let him down to walk. Once the smaller children were in place though, she would not let them down till she reached the first island. She had seen a large island to the north away from the seven and she could use it to help her find the others.

She sewed with swift long stitches, resewed for strength. She explained to the children, gave them warnings about how hard it would be, how they must be brave, and at last they were in place and she walked toward the swamp. The total weight was staggering. She could not believe that three small thin children could hang upon her with such weight. She argued with Little Mountain as she went. "You will kill all of us with your insistence. Thank you for your sons. I accept them. But Anatho-yee is my sister-daughter. I helped her come from my mother as she was dying. You wouldn't expect me to leave *her*."

Little Mountain remained silent though See-ho-kee knew very well she hovered nearby, ready to help.

She kept remembering the long, long wave of sawgrass and the dark stretches of swamp water. They started. She carried a strong stick, to lean on or to hit with.

Slowly, carefully, she walked toward the islands, invisible from here. She fixed the sun's position in her mind, considered how it would cross the northern sky, how it would be at her back from the right, then on her right arm, finally would touch Anatho-yee's left cheek. She could not get lost with this guardian.

Very soon she walked in water to her knees. She came to the deep place and struggled through it, came to the first thickets of sawgrass. It grew in patches, not everywhere as it had appeared from the tree. She let the big boy down, put him directly behind her, so that she and her stick could clear a safe way. They walked faster than they had on dry land, dodging the deadly sawgrass, slogging up out of the sucking peat. Her left moccasin came off and was lost at once; then her right one went; she believed the boy's moccasins had gone too. She walked the day away.

She had never before been so deeply into a swamp where there were no trails. She realized that all sounds were different here. There were no dogs barking, no people talking, no sound of chipping out a cypress canoe, no hogs rooting, no horses. There was only the sound of the seagulls calling with harsh insistence, the way the white men did. A sick chill went over her when she thought about the gulls. They might be watching her for the white men; they might be spirits of the dead white people.

"Mother, help me," she said. "Little Mountain, they are my sons, but you gave birth to them. Help me."

The gulls turned in a great circle and flew away to the east. She stood and watched them with wonder, amazed at the power she had over them. Or could it be that it was getting late and they were going home?

The sun touched Anatho-yee's cheek! They still had far to go, and soon it would be dark.

"Watch for a good wide place without grass, without water," she told the older boy.

Now he chattered with importance and eagerness to stop and rest. "Here is one. What do you think of this?" he asked.

"Do you want to lie in water all night?"

"No." Then in a moment, "This one then. This one is good, isn't it?"

She realized the sawgrass was closing in on them, that the bare spots between came fewer now. They must stop now, whether it was good or not. Painfully she put the children down, sat a moment, and hoped the trembling would go out of her body, but when it continued, she got up and cleared away a circle of the grass, thrashing at it with her stick, cutting some of the stalks with her mother's knife. She must establish a space which would frighten animals away. A pang of homesickness stirred her when she thought of the sacred fire and the safe space it made. When the circle was cleared, she took her stick and struck the grass all around the edge of the circle to frighten away the lurkers. She marked a cross in the circle pointing east, west, north, south. Long before they were asleep, the cold, wet swamp had soaked them. See-ho-kee's mind was troubled about it, and she woke up often and tried to think of a way to dry the children. But there was no way.

The second day in the sawgrass See-ho-kee felt her mind wandering, and she tried to think of only one thing, where the sun must touch her, where it must touch Anatho-yee. Here, where no landmarks of any sort helped her, she had only the sun, and she couldn't think for a moment what to do when the sky turned winter gray and hid the sun. She went on for a few minutes, realized the terrible danger, stopped for a rest. If the sun came out, they would go on; if it hid itself, they would wait. In a few minutes it showed itself dimly behind sky haze, and she took the children up again and went on.

During the afternoon of the second day she tried to carry the older boy as well as the other two children, for his feet were bleeding, and she was afraid the water they now walked in would make the small wounds into large sores. All of them now had many sawgrass cuts, and See-ho-kee noticed that they didn't hurt at first, that it took a while for the body to notice what had happened. Her tremors forced her to put the big boy down.

She walked on, holding herself up with the stick. She had come to regard it as a close friend, and sometimes she talked to it and to the spirit of the tree it had come from.

She gave up looking ahead, watched the ground all the time except when she was checking their progress as indicated by the sun's rays. And so it was a surprise when she felt herself coming out of the water, moving up. She noticed the pull first, the effort of going uphill; then she saw the grass thin out very fast, and she knew they were coming up on one of the islands. Her feet were swollen and shapeless. She walked around an alligator wallow, then a small pond of cattails. And suddenly she stood on dry land. There were trees ahead. She needed to climb one to see whether they had made it to the seven islands or whether she had wandered to another place, but her trembling was much worse and she sank to her knees before she could loosen the slings from the children. At last they all lay together. She was afraid she would sleep and they would be discovered by white men. Or else, they would be eaten by alligators.

She saw her mother's glowing face, her bright smile.

"Mother, help us! Tell us where to go next."

Rest, See-ho-kee. You have done very well. She saw Little Mountain's broken smile, saw her nod. *Apayaka is coming,* said her mother.

She went to sleep, holding the children, feeling their bodies warm as the sun dried them.

She woke in a fright, heard sounds, trembled uncontrollably. Stood up, her gun making great wobbly circles. Toed the children awake so they could run and hide. Heard a wild snort, a moan, and there was Eefe leaping with fierce joy upon her. She fell. "See-ho-kee! *SEE-HO-KEE!*" Eefe licked her face.

There they were, her Miccosukee family. Apayaka stared at her and the children, the tears streaming from his eyes, and he was speechless. There, her father, thin and old. She must have been away from him for years, he was so changed. There her brother Hitchiti-hajo (Oh, Thlicklin), his mouth hung open. He pulled her up to him.

There! The flash of a beautiful shirt, the one she had made for Yaha Chatee. Yaha Chatee.

The women. All stared at her and the children as if they

had returned from the dead.

"Where is Eemathle?"

"He is searching for you. He will be home soon to see whether we have heard any news of you. Hitchiti-hajo searched for several days."

"And my grandmother? Did she die easily?"

Her father laughed. "Not yet. There she is."

See-ho-kee turned, saw the beloved old woman, they stood close to each other, the two of them half-laughing.

But the other Miccosukee children? Her look flashed desperately about her. Finally she was able to ask, "Where are the children?"

Apayaka said, "They are here. They hid when we knew someone had come. Children! Yaatooche! Come out. It is safe."

They came out, the smallest in the arms of a little girl, and See-ho-kee counted.

"These are *all*?" she asked.

There were solemn nods, but no one spoke.

Her trembling wouldn't cease, had become a part of her.

"Well, I have three," she said. "These are my children." She said this as much to Yaha Chatee as to anyone else, and she saw him nod and accept them.

Everywhere she looked there was love and welcome. Each of her children was lifted by a different person and carried to the village.

Yaha Chatee carried her. He felt strong and loving. She allowed herself to be weak and babyish. She allowed herself to cry. He spoke no word to her. Her mourning period had not ended, though now she could picture only a pair of spectacles when she remembered her husband. Spectacles and glinting teeth.

twenty-two

During the healing days that followed, See-ho-kee's visions disappeared, and her mother and Little Mountain never came, leaving her with no sense of loss, however, for the memory of the visions held the same clarity with which she had first seen the spirits. At any time she chose, she would retrace those experiences and tell others about them.

She became a highly respected member of her clan; she had had a journey in the wilderness that would equal any brave's ordeal at puberty. She was brave, they declared. She tried to tell them that it was not so, that she was the very opposite of brave, that she had been more terrified than the weakest member of the clan. But they wouldn't have it, and to her great happiness people began bringing her gifts. One came without words from Yaha: a pair of alligator shoes which would protect her feet from the sharp coral on the edges of the village. The medicine man had nearly healed her feet; the cuts were now slim, tender scars, and the swelling from the thongs had gone. She and the children were now well-fed, and food came steadily from other families to boost the supply in her grandmother's cheke.

Still, she worried about the food. There were no crops; there was only game, and much of the time the men were out and away, trying to find out what the white men planned to do next. So, game meat came in slowly. It would be time soon to plant if they were allowed to, but the crops would not come for a long time.

A marvelous thing happened to help them. A neighboring Miccosukee came with the good news. A ship, carrying rice had wrecked at Coonte Hatchee, called New River by the white men, an odd name, for it was known by the Indians to be a very old river. They had long valued it for the thick beds of coonte on its banks. They must get there very quickly before the rice was gone, before soldiers came to protect it. Already Indians from other villages were harvesting this unexpected crop, unexpected at least by See-ho-kee and her people who had not had a part in wrecking the ship.

Now came an opportunity for the Chakaika Indian who was visiting them. He had a Miccosukee ancestor whose kinship he valued, and each year he came to stay awhile, no matter where the White Man's War had sent them. See-ho-kee had always enjoyed seeing him, for he loved to tease the women, to tell them how beautiful they were, to suggest they put their husbands away and accept him instead. All the women recognized this teasing as half-serious. His language was understandable but strangely accented, a pleasing sound to See-ho-kee. This visit had been different. He concentrated his sly attention on her and she was half-pleased at the effect on Yaha Chatee and half-embarrassed, for the Chakaika — twice her age — invited swift, deadly punishment for courting a mourning widow. She ignored him.

But now the Chakaika was very valuable to the clan. The Chakaikas were Spanish Indians, well-taught in the art of sailing, and Apayaka had asked him to use his time with them in teaching any idle young man to sail. They now had three dugouts fitted with masts and great triangular sails. These boats could sail into the wind, once the Miccosukee men had pushed them to Coonte Hatchee, and indeed, to help them along, they had dug a shallow ditch to portage the boats to the river. The ditches were well hidden by grass and willow and had never been discovered by the soldiers. The Miccosukees were now adept at using the boats, and Yaha Chatee had once invited See-ho-kee and her grandmother and children for a sail after a winter squall had lifted the Everglades waters almost to their chekes. The sail had been delightful, and See-ho-kee had determined that she would sail again. Today she announced that she would go; and Apayaka agreed that she could go and also that two older women could go to help carry the rice. See-ho-kee felt honored to be needed.

On this day the ditches held only mud with occasional pools of water, which made the portage hard, but they used the sails right away and the winds helped with the pushing. It didn't take long to reach Coonte Hatchee, and then they went with the speed of the wind.

"I would carry rice many times for a good ride like this," someone said. It was pleasant and happy. Everyone joked and laughed in low voices.

It was not long till they approached the beach and they had to use paddles to control the power of the wind and water, but they wished to come out with much speed and vigor, knowing how impressive it was to see three great dugouts moving like seabirds.

Ah, there was the wrecked ship, not hurt too much, it

seemed, for she stood high on the beach except for her back part which trailed like an otter's tail in the water. People were gathered about the ship like bees on a cluster of ripe palmetto berries. They stopped their work to stare in amazement at the three great birds approaching them. The Miccosukee sailors laughed with pleasure. See-ho-kee bent forward with laughter, sat back and met the Chakaika's smile. She glimpsed a frown crossing Yaha Chatee's face. Hitchiti-hajo caught the whole interaction and stared at See-ho-kee who bent forward again, unable to keep her laughter inside where it would not offend Yaha Chatee.

The foolishness stopped as soon as they had given hurried greetings to other Indians and had begun loading the dugouts. It would be tricky to load as much rice as possible without making the boats founder. They would not sink, but the wet rice might be lost before they could get it dried out. They took care not to be too greedy on this trip.

While the women worked at loading the rice, most of the Seminole men drifted together at the boats and listened to Chakaika-the-man-with-many-dimes as he described the art of sailing. He would help them, he said. He would teach them. This conversation went on for a long time, endangering the whole endeavor, because no one knew when the white soldiers would come. See-ho-kee straightened up in disgust.

"Will three women have to do the work for a whole village?" she called, knowing it was a rude thing to do and saying it anyway.

The men all turned to look at her and then back to their talk for a few minutes more to show she could not tell them what to do. As they returned to their work, her father came and scolded her till she smarted. But the work went forward swiftly.

It was an adventure, something she had never had a part in before. It was as if spirits looking over the Miccosukees favored them now. She felt such hope over this great gift of food that she began believing that her vision of wave after wave of white people had lessened in power, that perhaps the white people were stopped at last. It was peaceful, happy, warm. People laughed and worked hard.

When the dugouts were loaded, Chakaika-dime-man led them up the Coonte Hatchee again to the nearest place to their village, and there they stopped and unloaded and cached the rice. They went back for more. There would be need for much help from the other villagers to get the rice home.

As soon as See-ho-kee got home, she put on a kettle of rice. Her children and grandmother hovered near, willing to taste its doneness, hardly able to wait.

It had been a very hard day, an interesting and exciting day, and See-ho-kee didn't feel lost or afraid. She was still a center.

twenty-three

The weather lightened; the last northern birds went home.

New people began joining forces with Apayaka as they lost their villages to the white soldiers. The villagers had eaten their rice, but they still had coonte, still had wild meat.

The news kept them tense. Scouts came to report that many Indians had given up. Most Negro warriors had surrendered after General Jesup promised to free them. Nobody at Apayaka's village accepted this for the truth; it was more of the white man's trickery, they believed. But other Indians did believe it, and this eliminated the reason for fighting for all those warriors who had gone to war primarily to protect their black friends and secondarily to keep their lands. Even the free Negroes had been their dependents against white slave-traders who were not as particular about their legal status as about their skin color. As the blacks left, so did many Yakitisee who were sick of the horrors and suffering of their flight about the peninsula.

Apayaka and a few others stood firm in their refusal to leave.

Holatoochee had been captured with forty warriors and now was combing the swamps with Abraham to find others who would surrender. They persuaded Alligator, who had already begun to believe that further bloodshed was useless, to come in with eighty-eight Seminoles and twenty-seven Negroes.

When this news came, the villagers nervously watched Apayaka. He seemed smaller these days, See-ho-kee thought. His eyes darted about when he heard the news, as if he were looking somewhere for help. But in a moment he settled down. "We will not surrender," he said. See-ho-kee returned thankfully to her work, and she saw the relief on other faces. They would be steady.

But now the whole pursuit would be toward Apayaka, the white man's hated Sam-Jones-be-damned. See-ho-kee looked at the little old man and tried to see in him what the white man saw. Why were they so afraid? He had given up fighting them now, unless they attacked first. He led his people to safety; that was all. What terrified the whites when they heard his name? She looked at her beloved great-uncle with pride and tenderness and she was as firm in her determination to stay in Florida as he was.

From their lookouts on Pine Island the men saw white soldiers coming, still very far from the village; the white soldiers pushed boats filled with muskets through the mud. The scouts whooped the word back to the hidden people, one man passing his shout to the next and he to the next. Colonel Bankhead and all the white soldiers turned and listened, and Bankhead lifted a white flag and called for council. "It is for your sake we offer talk instead of war," he shouted. "Most of your brothers are now in the forts, safe and well-fed."

The scout took careful aim; his bullet splintered the flag pole. He came quickly down from his perch and ran to join his people while the white soldiers took up their guns and the pursuit.

It didn't amount to much. The white soldiers were too tired, too confused. When they saw they couldn't find the Miccosukees, they gave up and retreated, not knowing that with one more day of pursuit they would have cornered the villagers and finished Sam-Jones-be-damned.

"Don't trust it," Apayaka told his clan. "Another leader will take it up. Another group will come. We must move to the south."

There was much argument. Hadn't they repulsed the whites? The land to the south was hard to live in, had bad coral jutting up like knives in the pineland. Better to stay and fight to the death than to run like animals.

Apayaka kept his patience with them. "We must move," he said. "We must prepare for war and we must move."

But, until the news of the next white leader came, the Miccosukees resisted the idea.

The villagers soon learned they were still in danger. Colonel Harney took up the task of catching — or killing — Apayaka. The news came that Harney was looking for them, and they understood the danger. Still they argued. Surely here, guarded by sawgrass, hidden by hundreds of miles of desolate swamps, surely they were safe from the soldiers. After all, Colonel Bankhead hadn't found them.

Colonel Harney had only fifty men, they heard, and relief went through the village, followed by laughter. Then they learned that the fifty men had new guns that would shoot without reloading, so that each man was like ten. Colt's rifles, they were named. They tried to picture such a gun, and the fear spread.

The village grew in strength as angry Creek warriors brought their families to what seemed to be the last safe stronghold in Florida. Apayaka and his people welcomed them. These days See-ho-kee heard as much Creek spoken as Miccosukee, and her two little boys brightened and chattered to the new children and glowed with pleasure when they were able to translate for adults. Fear grew less as the people came in, one or two families at a time. Apayaka became jaunty and happy, like his former self in the days before the white men set him to running. They now had seventy-five warriors. True, they hadn't many guns or much ammunition, but every warrior worked constantly to add to the supply of bows and arrows.

Many tongues were spoken here, and See-ho-kee often heard her grandmother greet someone with delight, and she would introduce the newcomer to See-ho-kee by saying, "This is your sister whose father lived in an old town near mine. She is from O-che-au-po-fau where General McGillivray had apple trees. Oh, those good apples."

See-ho-kee's mouth watered for an apple, for she had eaten one when she was small, and she remembered it well.

Always, always they prepared for war, even with the hope that Colonel Harney and his men would never find them.

See-ho-kee wanted to forget Colonel Harney; he was a nightmare to her; her mind wavered on the edge of a vision about Colonel Harney and his terrible repeating rifle that spoke again and again before he reloaded. The Miccosukees thought of the gun as a strong evil and they tried to make medicine strong enough to defeat it.

At last they knew they must go. Many Indians who had been captured had been forced to point to their hiding place, and it was only a matter of time till Colonel Harney with his men and their evil guns came. For a week they prepared food to carry, made alligator shoes to protect their feet in the coral land in the south, slaughtered and skinned the rest of their cattle, jerked the beef, loaded their boats and headed south through the sawgrass. They moved swiftly, and See-ho-kee marveled at the speed with which they covered the ground that had clung to her so that she could barely move. Then she carried three children; now she carried only Anatho-yee, and sometimes the little girl ran beside her. Now, everybody helped when there was a need; no job belonged to one person only. A long trail, slashed through the grass by young men, welcomed them. There was not time enough to make a run without a trail, however much it terrified them to help the white men find the way.

The grandmother walked ahead of See-ho-kee, using two poles for steadiness. See-ho-kee wished there were a horse for her. "Grandmother, why do we go through the grass when we could go east to the high land and then walk easily to the south?"

The second she let the words out she realized her stupidity.

"The white man can do that too," her grandmother said. "And while we are walking this short way, the white man will have to come west through many miles of mangrove which were placed there for our protection. And if he comes through the mangrove, then his leather shoes will be cut off his feet and he will be cut to the bone with coral. The coral too, was placed there to protect us. The white man doesn't understand that the alligator was put here for our food and for shoes tougher than coral."

"Where are we going?"

"We will go as far as we must. If we have to go out to the ocean islands, we will."

See-ho-kee saw an unexpected sight; three turtles, all of a kind, faced each other, apparently conversing among themselves. She turned her face away and walked on. In a moment she said to her grandmother, "I saw three turtles. Do you think it was a town?"

"Yes," said her grandmother. "Undoubtedly. And if you had looked about you, you would have seen their square-ground and their sacred fire and maybe even their spirits."

"I know," said See-ho-kee. "That's why I looked away."

Her grandmother nodded with understanding. It was not good to spy on animal towns.

There was no shade; the sun was burning them; there was no water, and the earth itself looked dead and cracked. They went on, finally coming to scrub pine and at last to some woods. They sighed with relief when Apayaka said they would stay here to rest. This meant one night, perhaps two. They settled together in families, each with a cooking fire where stew with frybread was begun. In the last of the daylight the girls went out for coonte, which was abundant, and the boys went for a deer. Hides — bear, cattle, deer — were spread for beds for the very young and the old; it was still very cold at night. They slept hard; they felt safe, for what white man could come to this place over coral stone? Apayaka set two men as guards, one to the east, one to the north, and this increased their feeling of safety. Colonel Harney began to seem like a bad dream that had passed.

See-ho-kee shivered in the morning air as she prepared food. She glanced with some envy at the girls going out for coonte, a job she used to do lightheartedly with Nuff-kee, digging without fear that she would be seen and shot by a white soldier. She looked around the camp. There were twenty-seven fires with many people grouped around each, and with enough food for all, though it was wild food and not as good as corn and pumpkin and beans. She didn't worry about the flavor of food any more; she worried only about having enough. She liked this place; she could visualize houses, a square-ground, a roundhouse, games, Busk. Above all, Busk.

They spent the morning working, gathering food, readying themselves for the next long walk. Still Apayaka had not spoken about leaving, and she knew he was reluctant to go until they had rested. The old man was tough as his own shoes; he needed no more rest than the youngest warrior there, but he also knew most of the old were having trouble keeping up.

The sun passed its high point, and still they hadn't moved. See-ho-kee threw venison into the pot, glad that they would have another night here. She wished they could stay.

And then he came. Colonel Harney came.

A great whoop from the east warned them, a series of whoops over and over, a tremor of terror in the shrill calls, which meant that the white soldiers were already upon them. There was no need or time for talk; the women grabbed what they could and tied food, utensils, clothing in bundles. They swept up babies, cuffed tots into action, ran from the camp as the soldiers came in. Three groups of soldiers came, firing their terrible guns.

The warriors took shelter, each to a tree and fired until their ammunition ran low, retreated to a tree behind, fired and screamed to make it sound like many more men than were actually there. At last they retreated and screamed only, for there were no more balls to fire. In this way they held the soldiers for a while so that the women and children got away.

See-ho-kee had become used to running, to grabbing up necessities and running. The only thing that was different now was that *first* she stuck her gun in her sash, hoping she would have a chance to use it, and *then* she saw to the food. On the flight she thought bitterly of her coonte grater lying on the ground, lost forever; she noticed then that she felt no terror as she used to but only a sullen heavy rage and a wish to kill again. She cast glances again and again at her children who ran with sober concentration.

She fantasized as she ran. A soldier would come, and she would shoot him in the stomach so that the ants would have time to help him to his death. She would not be satisfied with killing quickly again.

She left this camp with the same sense of heartpulling that she had felt when they left Ouithlacoochee Cove, and she thought now of the peace of having twenty-seven fires cooking food around them, of having a good place to sleep, enough coonte for tomorrow, enough alligator-leather for shoes, good water, the holy ground under her feet. It was too much to bear, losing this, and still she bore it.

She took up her old argument with the white-haired mad soldier. *You can drive me away from the land, but the land is not yours. The land is mine. It is part of me; I am part of it. The land is mine!*

When all were together again, miles away, the last warrior to rejoin them said that Harney and his men had halted, too exhausted to pursue the Indians. "They're in *our* camp, eating our food," the warrior said angrily.

The Miccosukees were heartsick; yet they gathered for council, as if everything were the same. They expressed sorrow over the one dead warrior and one captured woman, two people lost to them. They discussed what to do next, listening to each other. The grandmother was called upon to offer her wisdom.

"We must consider Busk," she said.

See-ho-kee was humbled before her grandmother's strength. They had lost two of their people; they had lost their homes again; they had lost all they had. And yet the old woman said, "We must consider Busk." The Green Corn Dance. The old life was still in existence. It was still in their hearts. Busk was a time of renewal, a time of cleansing, a time of punishing wrong-doers. See-ho-kee prayed that the thought would be considered and taken up at once. Maybe she and Yaha Chatee would be pledged to each other, for her mourning had only one year to go. Maybe all of them would be stronger after the Green Corn Dance.

All agreed with the grandmother. They would look for a safe place and plan it; they would have Busk as if all were well.

And so their wandering began again.

twenty-four

The Green Corn Dance was poor, and nothing was done to arrange See-ho-kee's marriage, for the most urgent matters must be attended to. Yaha Chatee had said nothing to any of her relatives about a wedding, and she suffered some hurt from this, although she knew very well it would have been a serious breach of manners, and even morals, for him to suggest marriage before her mourning was finished.

In the spring of the following year she took matters into her own hands. She was nineteen, much too old to be unmarried, and she had three children to feed. Her home situation had become intolerable. Her father had taken a new wife, chosen appropriately from her mother's clan, a good young woman not much older than See-ho-kee. At first she was happy to have Coosa-amathle's bride as a new friend, but the household became tense as the young wife made suggestions to herself and her grandmother. She suggested ways to make the children better-behaved, the grossest insult in blunt words. When the grandmother, properly the head of the house, suggested something to *her*, she shrugged as if the grandmother's mind were becoming feeble.

See-ho-kee decided to establish her own household and move into it with the children and her grandmother, who was willing enough, if they could find someone strong enough to add building a cheke to his work. Coosa-amathle and his sons were certainly not available for this work, for their scouting and hunting kept them occupied much of the time. Also Coosa-amathle was much in love with his new wife and spent his time at home swaggering about her till See-ho-kee turned away in disgust.

What loomed in her mind above all else though was the fact that she had only ten days left of her mourning period. For the past four years she had gone to her grandmother for her monthly hair-combing, an occasion of great pleasure and relief to her, and today she had her last one. Neither she nor her grandmother had said a word about it, but they giggled and talked about hair-styles, pretending that the talk had nothing to do with them, that they were above all that sort of thing. See-ho-kee knew exactly how she would look on that first day of freedom. She would bathe herself vigorously, using whatever plants she could find. She would crumple sweet-smelling leaves and rub them on her arms and legs. She would wash her hair and comb it while it was wet so that it would obey her when she lifted and curved it into a magnificent crown that flowed a little to one side.

Then she would put on the dress she had secretly worked on for months, whenever there was a chance. A dress full of color and life, a dress that dismissed all idea of death.

She would be beautiful. Yaha Chatee would adore her so much he would not be able to resist her, not a moment.

Yet, there was a troublesome thought that came to her mind so often she could no longer dismiss it. Who was the real See-ho-kee, this ugly sad widow with hair falling untidily over her face or the glowing woman she pictured? And if she were *this* woman, would Yaha Chatee love only the second woman? It suddenly became important to her to have Yaha Chatee love her for the way she was, no matter whether she were young and beautiful or old and wrinkled. He must love the real See-ho-kee.

Why had the man not spoken to her yet? Was he sullen? Or could it be that he had no intention of *ever* marrying her? He knew very well that her mourning period was nearly up; in fact, some people had even suggested to her that she dispense with the rest of her grief ordeal, that there were no relatives of Fixonechee left to protest it, that these were unusual times. She resisted these ideas. She was sure though that everybody would have forgiven them if they had talked to each other, even if they had slept together.

He made no move toward her. What was the matter with the man? Some people even wondered whether he preferred men to women. She knew better. She remembered too well the day their childish sex play suddenly became something hot and urgent, so that his eyes took on a bright ardor, so that she had to give and give, had to take and take, so that a pleasure scream tore away from her with no warning. And everybody heard and smiled. And from then on he could call forth that scream from her whenever they met in the oak glade, in the pines, on the seashore. For she had no resistance to him, nor he to her. What a stupid girl she had been in those days! She should have refused Fixonechee's courtship. Nothing he had was important to her. Not his maturity, not his riches. Not his assurance. Nothing.

But Yaha Chatee's friendly soft talk stayed with her through all the wars, all the flights from the white soldiers. The memory of their love-making still had power over her body. She wanted him. She *wanted* him.

Now, at last, she understood the way *he* felt. She had turned him sour and half-angry. Somehow, young and ignorant as she had been, she should have realized he was her true husband, and she should have resisted all pressures to marry Fixonechee. Yaha Chatee would not court her now, feeling the way he did; his Indian pride had been hurt; the male Miccosukees were, after all, accustomed to being courted, both for their gallantry and for their beauty. She must go and court him.

She approached him at last. Her love and physical ache for him were tempered by a cruelty, a sharp thought she honed. She *must* have a husband. She would threaten him with the Chakaika-dime-man, if he withdrew, and it would be no idle threat. She had to think of the children, and she was prepared for sharp bargaining.

See-ho-kee whispered to him about a meeting, and she went to the place, not sure at all whether he would come. He came, his face foreign and sharp, his eyes suspicious as a wild bird's. They talked together in the deep, dark hammock, where suddenly the interlacing of trees, the clinging moss, the thousands of nodding yellow orchids transported her into wordless joy. All was quiet; no children were here to listen. She was eager to get it over with and settled; he was embarrassed and uneasy, fearful that she took him aside for lover's play.

"I see what you are thinking, Yaha Chatee. But calm yourself. I want to talk to you, that's all."

He was still wary. She talked of ordinary things for a moment or so: the state of their village, a new baby, the cruelty of the white men. To each remark he nodded and kept his stern profile toward her.

"You are still worried about coming here. When I go back to the house, I will be as clean and unrumpled as when I left, and there will be no rolling in the leaves with you," she suddenly blurted.

For the first time he looked at her, startled at her vehemence. "Good. I was afraid you would tempt me to help you break your mourning."

"Not at all. Though in nine days it will be my right to go to any man I wish."

"Chakaika-dime-man, I suppose!" He was angry again.

It was her place to be humble. She said nothing. She gave him a new turban with a four-corners design in the colors that would invoke the blessings of the winds. He examined it and nodded his acceptance, but he didn't put it on. She stepped back a little distance to talk.

The words wouldn't come. It took more courage than she had expected. After all, this was her old playmate with whom she had always felt comfortable and chatty, but now he seemed so adult and remote that the words choked her.

I am the center, she thought. *The center has the right to speak and lead.*

Her voice came back. "I wish you to call me *my wife,*" she said. "I wish to call you *my husband.* If you agree to this, we will tell my grandmother and my father, and we will sleep together."

Yaha Chatee did not respond for a long time. She waited, tremulous and hopeful.

At last, he shook his head. "How can I be sure you really want me? I was ready once before."

"You didn't speak," she said in a loud angry voice. "Why didn't you speak? Why didn't you have someone speak for me?"

"There wasn't a proper person to do it. I was adopted, remember. Who was the person to speak? I didn't know how to go about it. And I thought you surely knew I wanted you; you must have known. Your marriage was suddenly arranged, and I had lost you before I knew it was happening."

She grimly withheld her tears. They stood in silence, their heads lowered. The courting must continue. She would tell him the truth.

"I was a young fool. I didn't know what I was doing. Now all I can remember about Fixonechee is that he wore a white man's glasses, but I can remember everything about you, even the times we played as children, the times we swam together, the times I always won in games I knew you could have won, the words you spoke to me, your way of smiling, your mouth, your eyes. I remember your beauty and your honor in fighting. I remember that you stayed away from me, even when you wanted me, for it was proper. I remember your dancing, better than anyone else's. I remember all things about you, what foods you favor, what colors, what patterns. I remember little gifts. I remember the good smell of your body. I remember our love-making, and I dream about it at night when I am helpless, and I awake needing you."

Her voice was breaking; she must be quiet and let him think. She waited.

Oh. He was weeping.

Finally he said, "It would be wrong to promise ourselves in this way. I want to be your husband, but I can't think how to arrange it; after all, your mourning goes for nine more days, and even then there is no one to speak for me. It would not be right. The old ways are proper, and this would be improper."

I want to be your husband . . . I want to be your husband . . . I want to be your husband.

See-ho-kee's heart raced; she felt limp with happiness.

"I don't know," said Yaha Chatee. "The spirits may not look kindly on this."

See-ho-kee thought of her mother's spirit and knew there would be approval and love for her, no matter how she managed to get the marriage arranged. But if Yaha Chatee felt so unsure, she must think of the way.

Still, she had to have reassurance. "If we can arrange this in an acceptable way, do you truly want to be my husband?" She must know whether he wanted her, now, the way she looked now, wearing these ugly clothes.

His smile left her no doubt, and he quickly stepped forward to hold her, caught himself and resisted the sin. They stood close so that their hands nearly touched, so that she could feel the heat from his body, so that her breathing lost its rhythm and became gusty. His eyes were hot and bright; his twisted smile reflected his need for her. They stepped apart. Yaha Chatee put his turban on, and they went back to the village, where everybody smiled and pretended not to see.

twenty-five

After a time of wandering through the swamps southwest of Lake Okeechobee, Apayaka's people settled on new islands, not far from Hospetarke and his clan, not far from powerful Owaale (whom the white men persisted in calling Prophet), not far from the Spanish Chakaikas, where See-ho-kee's old friend Chakaika-dime-man lived, when he wasn't visiting the rest of the peninsula. At the coldest time of the past winter, plans had been made to hold the Green Corn Dance at a great central council-ground, and foot-paths began to cross each other to the four camps and to the council-ground, although no paths were allowed to form outside of the swamps, where the enemy might be led to them.

It would be the best celebration of Busk in living memory, they had promised each other. It would be a time for regaining the power the White Man's War had leached from them.

See-ho-kee looked forward to Busk for another reason; her determination on marriage at that time would admit to no problems, no barriers. It had only to be arranged. She spoke to her grandmother about it, asked help for arrangements. To her astonishment, her grandmother said she would gladly help if Yaha Chatee came to her for help; else how could she be sure this was not just a girl's dream in See-ho-kee's head?

She talked again with Yaha, told him her grandmother was ready to help. Would he speak to her? Yaha pondered, tried to decide whether it was appropriate. They parted and she continued to wait.

Suddenly, even before Busk, a hopeful thing happened. General Macomb replaced General Taylor in the White Man's War, with orders to *end* the war and to protect the citizens. The news overyjoyed the Miccosukees deep in the Everglades. General Macomb was different from the other white soldiers they had known; his mind was clear. He saw at once the injustices that had been perpetrated against the Yakitisee. He allowed General Taylor to continue his game of squares by which he divided Florida into great square-grounds, each to be searched for Indians, one at a time. He had some difficulty with the Indians who refused to stay in the squares and be caught. But General Macomb released many prisoners and sent them back to their people in the southern swamps. Then he called for a great council at Fort King. It would be the most dramatic, most colorful council ever held. He would even build a huge council house to hold the meeting. They would see; just come and bring their warriors, they were told. It would not be like the other times when the Yakitisee had gone to meetings under a white flag and then been betrayed. They would see.

The men argued in Apayaka's camp. *Remember all those times?* angry voices asked.

Yes, others responded, also with angry voices. *But isn't it true that Macomb has actually sent prisoners back? You can see he is a man of substance. He is truthful.*

Ah, said the first group. *No white man is truthful. Will you continue to fall for that old trick?*

Yet they wanted — desperately craved — peace, and they listened when Yaha Chatee spoke, while (See-o-kee shivered with pride.

"Nobody knows for certain that all white men are liars," Yaha Chatee said. "Every person here knows at least one Indian who is a liar, so we also are imperfect." There were nods of agreement; there was care not to look at any person who could be called a liar. "And since all of us know at least one liar, it is possible that there is one white man who is *not* a liar. Isn't that so? Why don't we give this white man Macomb some trust to do what he says he will do?"

In the end they decided to go to council. See-ho-kee was fiercely proud of Yaha Chatee. *My husband,* her mind spoke. *My husband.*

Not long before Busk, Chitto Tustenuggee, who would speak for Apayaka, led one hundred men from the village, and they met the other Yakitisee at Fort King. General Macomb gave them all the pomp and pageantry he had promised, and he proclaimed that the war was ended.

The war was ended.

The Indians smoked their pipes in silence and listened, knowing that terms would be stated, also knowing it could not be this simple.

On the islands in the Everglades, life continued in age-old patterns. The women began preparing for Busk: cleaning and raking the square-ground, making bright new clothes and gathering old things to be burned, cleaning every house of all impurities, clearing the paths again, readying them for white sand.

See-ho-kee's time for mourning was three days past, and she had yet to change into her new clothes. This was the time to do it, she realized. It was her right to put away the frayed sheet, to bathe as often as she wished, to comb her hair till it was itself again, to put on her new dress, modest as it was. She would do this and let Yaha see her as soon as he returned.

She dressed herself, laughed at the women who began to tease her openly, expressing pity for Yaha Chatee when he saw her. "The poor man," a friend said. "His eyes will start from his head, and he will tremble, and he will try to rush you to the woods, as he did when you were children."

See-ho-kee laughed and said, "I hope so."

There was a good deal of giggling and chatter all that day, and even the grandmother enjoyed making fun at See-ho-kee's expense.

Chitto Tustenuggee signed for Apayaka and came back to report, his warriors exhilarated to bring home the news. See-ho-kee was excited almost beyond endurance, knowing that she had never been this beautiful before, not even when she first reached puberty; all the women at the village told her so; even old Apayaka told her so, his pleasure at seeing her like this showing up in a multitude of laugh wrinkles. That day, the old man's mind was clear, and she accepted this fact like a gift from the Breathmaker.

She watched Yaha Chatee when he came in with the other fighters. She smothered her giggle when she saw him look quickly over all the other women for her, a quick glance, a puzzlement on his face. Where was she? His eyes passed lightly over her and continued the search.

He saw her. He saw her! And the women had spoken truly, for See-ho-kee, looking at him with full-face boldness, saw his eyes grow big, saw his mouth drop open, saw him tremble. He looked down hastily, to hide his emotion, but from then on, she watched and caught him looking at her again and again, and each time she let her eyes welcome him.

Chitto Tustenuggee reported to the villagers that the Indians must withdraw to the part of Florida south of Pease Creek, that they must stay there under the protection of the United States, until other arrangements were made. Chitto believed it was a good agreement.

The villagers accepted the terms. The war was over; they were already living in the truce area, and they could stay here, protected by white soldiers, a very good change in their lives, although it was strange and would be hard to get used to.

Apayaka said that it was good, and he encouraged his people to abide by the agreement. There was a quick release of tension: relief, sighs, adjustment to the new spirit of friendship and peace.

Immediately they continued planning and working toward the Green Corn Dance; Miccosukees celebrated earlier than other Yakitisee. See-ho-kee felt joyful, for she fully intended to see that Yaha Chatee and she would be married at the festival.

As work proceeded, Yaha stood near her and muttered, "Come with me." She followed, obedient as a wife, and he walked ahead of her into the woods, where she found he had placed a blanket. "We no longer have to wait," he said. "You are free." And, although he didn't ask her whether she was willing, she heard the uncertainty in his voice, and she dropped to her knees and lay back on the blanket.

She remembered that their youthful lovemaking had much touching and fondling, but this time Yaha Chatee merely pushed her dress back and unbound his robe so that they could lie, skin to skin, feeling the wonder of it. *I will not scream this time,* she told herself. *No use to make all of them laugh at us, if they hear me.*

He entered her body, and she controlled the small moan. Their hunger made the lovemaking convulsive and quick, and she only moaned, and they lay back for a small nap. He awoke her with his hands which touched every part of her, till she could endure it no longer. She forced him down upon her, and this time the moan was harder to contain. They stayed a long time, talking and fondling. On the third time her legs took a life of their own and reached up to hug him; her mouth had its own mind and bit his shoulder; her body decided and forced the moan into a scream. She hugged him, arms and legs, and rocked, while Yaha chuckled with pleasure, the way he used to do.

As they walked back home, she wondered whether he had given her a child. She doubted it. She had not even thought of a child while they made love. She had thought only of Yaha. Yaha. Yaha Chatee.

Plans for the Green Corn Dance rituals were made in utmost secrecy, and the Miccosukees informed the most trusted Indians and no white people except the half-whites who had grown up with them. Peace didn't bring enough trust to endanger sacred things.

It was just as well, for the peace was quickly seen as tenuous. The printed papers of the white people blasted out their fury about the giveaway of Florida to Indian savages. *Next thing,* the papers said, *Whites will be killed in their beds. The Seminoles must be sent away where they can do no more hurt.* Newspaper stories came back to the four groups of armed warriors in the swamps, and nerves began to tighten up again among the Yakitisee.

The first small stream of angry white Floridians poured across the state, the most frightening and dangerous of whom were called the Crackers. They were ragged, dirty, bearded men who wore white hats, who rode horses with flowing tails, who carried ready rifles, whose eyes were bleak, whose only emotion was anger. They considered it a patriotic duty to *kill* the Yakitisee or at least to send them back where they came from. In this way they would protect themselves, their country, their way of life. These angry men moved into South Florida.

The Miccosukees began to ask, *Where is our protection?*

Busk work continued. In the evenings before the celebration the grandmother explained to the people, "This is the way Busk was, and this is the way it will be in the future when all of our wars are past." She described the whole ceremony, all the dances, including the turkey dance the women had danced once when she was small, though none of the other women remembered it. Apayaka himself helped her to demonstrate the dances and to tell the old stories, for they were being lost just as the dances were, a terrifying thing indeed, for what would happen to them if they didn't know the tales of their ancestors and the proper way to act? And both the old people spoke of old times and old towns. "I have eaten fish from the Chat-to-ho-che River," Apayaka told them.

"So have I!" said the grandmother. "They are better than the fish we have here." And nobody smiled, although everybody noticed these days that whatever the grandmother had had in her young days was always better than what she had now.

At last, Yaha Chatee took See-ho-kee to talk to her grandmother, and he asked for permission to marry.

"She is nineteen years old, entering middle age," he said bravely. "She needs me. She has three children to raise, and she needs a man to build her a house and bring meat to her, but how can we arrange it? I have no mother or sister or aunt to speak for me, nor does See-ho-kee, so what can we do?"

He said all this in front of See-ho-kee, who kept silent, though her heart's wild leaping seemed noisy to her.

"We wish only to do the proper thing," he said. "We

wish to do everything the old way, but times are different now, and we want to know how to live in these circumstances. Can you help us?''

The grandmother's laughter burst forth. She said, ''Yes, that is very good. You wish to be married merely for establishing a home for See-ho-kee's children and also to bring meat to her. This is the reason you'll marry her?''

See-ho-kee could never resist her grandmother's laughter, and she laughed too, and Yaha Chatee's face became deep red. He ground out, ''Yes, there is another reason. I have a strong need to be with See-ho-kee; I wish always to have her face before me. I need to see her face. We have already lain together, and I want the right to kill any man who tries to lie with her again. I wish to live with her in a proper manner.'' His forthright answer stopped their laughter.

See-ho-kee thought about this. He needed to be with her and see her face!

''Grandmother, we have lain together once. . . .'' she began. Her voice failed.

''Oh, I know that,'' her grandmother said. ''All of us know that.''

''But now, Grandmother, all he will do is follow me around and gawk at me to be sure another man doesn't catch me. He has no time to lie with me! I want it settled.''

The two women laughed again, but tenderly this time and not in a jeering way. Yaha, seeing that the old woman was sympathetic and would help, began to smile.

The grandmother also believed in the old ways, although she had not always followed them herself, and she wished to do things right as much as Yaha Chatee did. ''I will help you,'' she said.

She quickly persuaded women to serve as aunts and intermediaries. They spoke to Coosa-amathle and Apayaka who agreed that the marriage must occur at the Green Corn Dance. It turned out that the Green Corn Dance was sad in a way, but it was the celebration See-ho-kee would remember best, for it was the dearest one she ever knew.

Many Indians from the Ten Thousand Islands came to the Green Corn Dance; the camp was clean; old fires were covered with white sand, and new ones were built. There was forgiveness. The spirits of the old ones ruled the Miccosukees and the other Indians who had joined them, and they felt strengthened by the ritual, though food and drink were scarce.

Next year, Busk would be even greater, they said. Next year, peace would be everywhere.

But on the days when the men met on the council ground, with their friends from other clans, there was still some angry talk. Apayaka was there; Chitto Tustenuggee, Billy Bowlegs, and Halleck Tustenugee were there, along with many warriors. Yaha was honored to sit near Apayaka. Chakaika-dime-man was there, very angry, very raw over See-ho-kee's marriage plans, angry too (as were all the Chakaika warriors) because the white men were preparing to build a trading post near the Caloosahatchie. It would be the same old thing: The white men would rob the Indians; more white men would come; soon the Indians would be pushed into the sea.

"No," said Apayaka. "I do not believe this. The trading post was agreed to in our end-of-the-wars pact at Fort King. The post will give us a place to sell our goods so that we can buy what we need."

But the Chakaikas, who had managed to this day to stay out of the wars, were irritable and fearful of seeing more angry-eyed Crackers moving into their domain.

The Chakaikas' anger cast a shadow over the ceremony, and finally Otulkethlocko, the Owaale, spoke for them, for he saw the same dangers they saw.

"I will tell you the story of Secretary Poinsett," the Owaale said. His voice carried to the edge of the men's meeting ground to the women, and See-ho-kee came out of her dream of marriage, and she shuddered at the warning in the Owaale's voice. "Listen to me about Secretary Poinsett. He wrote a letter which said that forcing the Yakitisee to stay in one place would make it easier to remove us from Florida. That very letter was in the newspaper, for all to see, and it was read to me by a white soldier who agreed with me that it was an evil letter."

Anger burned like a white light over the meeting. Still, Apayaka and Chitto Tustenuggee and Billy Bowlegs called for peace and conjured the warriors to obey the agreement.

The next day the angry council halted for a while, and dancing and feasting began.

See-ho-kee and Yaha Chatee were married so quickly that she nearly fell down from the relief of not having to brace herself against a refusal. The tribal council still had this right. The grandmother told the fathers and mothers of the gifts Yaha Chatee had brought to her and to Anatho-yee, told them about the house Yaha and his friends had built for See-ho-kee.

See-ho-kee wanted to add that he had worked himself nearly sick, bargaining for a new blanket and for pots, cutting trees for the posts to hold up their roof. She wanted to boast.

And very quickly it was agreed that she was now bound to him. He owned her. She had not thought of it in just that way before, but it gave her more pleasure than worry.

When the Green Corn Dance was over, they slept together in their new cheke, leaving the grandmother and the three children in the old lodge for a few days until See-ho-kee could get used to the pleasures of marriage. She discovered it was good to sleep with him, and she was pleased to see that she could turn him from an urgent frowning man to a peaceful smiling boy, any time she wished. She liked that, and she realized she owned him as much as he did her. But when weeks had passed, and Yaha was able to draw little screams from her often, she quit worrying about who owned whom.

twenty-six

After the story-telling was finished one night, the grandmother couldn't stop talking. Even after they had lain down and Yaha Chatee and the children were already asleep, she talked on as if she must tell all in a hurry.

"Did I tell you about my sabia stone?" asked the grandmother. "I got it in Au-be-coo-che."

See-ho-kee needed sleep herself, but she listened, knowing the value of what her grandmother had to tell. She was not one of those old women who told the same tale over and over except for their legends; she brought out stories as bright and magic as the sabia stone she kept in a deerskin pouch, always away from the house because its power was so great.

"Did I tell you about the town of Au-be-coo-chee?" the

grandmother asked the dark. "When I was a girl I went there with my parents to a celebration, and a handsome boy watched me all day and danced near me at night but without talking, and the next day he told me he would show me a beautiful cave. Did I tell you about that cave?"

See-ho-kee didn't need to answer. The story went ahead.

"He took a pine torch there to show me, and it was a magnificent cave; I nearly wept with excitement. The light showed us the great clusters of stone flowers growing up to the ceiling, and there was a spring and he held me so I could drink from it but not fall in. I had never had a man touch me as he did. And pretty soon he found a smooth place to lie, and we lay together and he was slow and gentle, but still I didn't like it much. He was my first one."

She became quiet, and See-ho-kee, now wide-awake, was afraid she wouldn't finish the story.

"He was your first one," she prompted.

"Oh, yes, the first one," her grandmother went on. "I thought I wouldn't do that again, but then during the night I thought about it and it seemed better than I remembered.

"The next day I stood near him until he suddenly took me by the hand and led me to the cave. We saw the cave every day. By the end of the visit *I* took *him* by the hand and led him. He was my first one."

Again a long silence. "He was your first one," See-ho-kee repeated.

"Yes. On my last day there, he gave me the sabia. He told me that a blue sabia was no good for a man, that it belonged to a woman. And he told me how to control it, that if it were kept too close it would charm you into sexual need." The grandmother laughed. "And he was right." She sighed. "He was my first one, and I often thought that I should have married him."

See-ho-kee waited, wondering whether there were more to the tale.

"The sabia is now yours," her grandmother suddenly said. Then they went to sleep, for See-ho-kee knew the old woman needed her rest. Tomorrow would be soon enough to learn about the proper control of the sabia, if the grandmother really intended it for her.

But her grandmother didn't wake up the next morning.

They tended to her burial; they honored her; they grieved.

For four days they did no business, no trading, nothing that could be skipped, and they mourned. But nothing seemed to See-ho-kee to be enough to do to express her grief. She felt angry that nobody else in the village seemed to see how great their loss was, for nobody else had listened to the old stories as much as she had.

At last, she took her grandmother's buckskin sack down from the tree where it had always hung, and she took out the sabia and held it in the sun. Its life glowed and rolled and turned, but she was not afraid of it. Rather, she was comforted. Later she would study it and learn its power.

twenty-seven

The Chakaikas went away, full of anger that the white men were still coming down from the north and crowding them. There would be a trading post near them, a control over the Indians, the Chakaikas believed. The Chakaikas had not fought alongside the Indians during the White Man's War, had enjoyed a remoteness until now. They had not yet suffered as the Miccosukees had, and now that their lives were disrupted, they had no patience with the Indians who wanted peace. The Chakaikas had promised nothing, had agreed to nothing, would never limit themselves to living in the southern part of the peninsula even if they considered their islands home.

Their hunting land was being crowded by other Indians, but the Chakaikas did not blame them. They blamed the white men.

Yet, life went on. Anatho-yee lost a tooth, and she managed to throw it all the way over the cheke. See-ho-kee cheered, and they were happy, because now they were assured that another tooth could grow. Suddenly the tooth came whizzing back over the cheke, and the woman and girl stared at each other fearfully. Had a bad spirit tossed it back?

They tiptoed around the house, found Little Mountain's sons sitting and giggling helplessly. See-ho-kee walked away and let Anatho-yee pummel the laughing boys.

A month after See-ho-kee celebrated the Green Corn Dance and her marriage, two weeks after she lost her grandmother, Chakaika-dime-man came with news of their first attack against the whites. He was angry and boastful, but his flirting glance roamed about, as he talked, touched See-ho-kee, passed on, to light finally on a woman who had been rejected by her husband. She painted her face in a peculiar way to invite men, and now she and Chakaika-dime-man exchanged looks and struck a silent bargain. The comfort of her food and her body for his dimes and the meat he would bring, so long as he chose to stay. It would not be their first time together.

But when he talked, he seemed to talk to everybody except the woman. "The Chakaikas are greater warriors than you have realized," he said. "Our chief led us to attack the camp where the soldiers lived. They were building a fort and a store. We killed many of them, and we captured some, and we took much silver."

Here he glanced at the painted woman and gave her another silent promise. She smiled to herself, looked about her, fingered the dimes she already wore. "And Hospetarke's people took the store. We are all very rich now; we have many good things; we have Colt's rifles; we have cloth. I will sell you some things if you wish."

The listeners watched old Apayaka to try to guess what he thought, but the old face settled into expressionless mystery. "Was Hospetarke there himself?" Apayaka asked.

"Yes. He took the first shot. Passacka was his chief, and he led after that."

Apayaka shook his head in a troubled way. Hospetarke was a very old man too, and the two of them had enjoyed long talks during the Green Corn Dance, two old men sitting on animal skins in the sun, bending and laughing together.

They waited to see what Apayaka would say; they gave him time to sort his thoughts. At last he said, "It will commence again. The white man never understood that we are all different, from different tribes, clans, villages. The white man will blame all of us."

"We have Colt's rifles," Chakaika-dime-man said again, defensively this time. The eyes of the listening warriors gleamed.

"You attacked Harney?" Apayaka asked.

"Yes." The Chakaika snorted with mirth. "He was out hunting hogs. He has plenty of food, but he hunted anyway. We didn't catch him."

"Harney is a big man," said Apayaka. "This will hurt his feelings. He will become enraged. Tell Passacka and Hospetarke to get ready for him. He will come for revenge."

Chakaika-dime-man maintained his courteous look, but See-ho-kee felt that he would toss his head if a younger man had said this. He arose now and went toward the cheke of the painted woman, and she followed.

Apayaka was right. A few days later they heard that forty-six Indians visiting Fort Mellon for provisions were taken by surprise and shipped off to jail in Charleston. From there they would go to the West.

The white men blamed the Creeks and the Miccosukees who had met at Fort King and agreed to stay south of Pease

River. More forts began to spring up. The war was renewed.

Indian shelters were burned. Fifteen hundred acres of corn and pumpkins were destroyed.

Indians and whites attacked each other wherever they met. Now the whites brought bloodhounds to track the Indians, but it didn't work. The bloodhounds refused to track.

Busk was barely over, and again they were fighting for their lives.

See-ho-kee labored hard to care for her family, but she did not worry about the war. She couldn't. Her mind and heart hurt from the absence of her grandmother.

twenty-eight

See-ho-kee had heard that the white men were now celebrating the end of their year 1840 and the beginning of their next year. It was a curious custom of theirs, but not surprising; they didn't know the value of celebrating Busk.

The days had turned very cold. Life was harder accordingly, for crops didn't grow, and food was limited to fish and game, which set up a perpetual hunger for civilized foods: pumpkin bread, warm sofkee, beans. No one complained, not even the children.

The White Man's War went on and on. Often the warriors were away for long periods so that even wild meat became scarce, and See-ho-kee sometimes took her gun out to look for game. She sometimes thought bitterly of her lack of training in this great art, remembered the days her brothers had spent in the fields with men in the tribe, learning to track and shoot. It wasn't something you could know suddenly. So more often than not, she came back with a land turtle or a fish rather than something she needed to shoot. They were getting by, but they lived in fear and hunger.

There was continuous communication with the men who were out; often runners came with news and warnings and orders to move within two days of a battle or confrontation or change in the white man's thinking.

There were fights in the north part of Florida again, near St. Augustine, where Coosa Tustenuggee and Halleck Tustenuggee fell upon any group of whites who allowed themselves to be separated from the main body of whites. There was no longer any hesitation about killing women. The whites called this depredation; the Indians called it protection of their lands and people. If a white woman were brought to an Indian woman's place to live, the Indian lost her home.

There was more feeling of security here in the grassy waters than there was in the north however, for all travel here meant boats, which Indians had in plenty. There was seldom a daylight hour when no one was working at a cypress log, and old men who could do nothing else still worked at this. It was hard, exacting work, yet the skinny old men had not lost the power to do it, though not as quickly as they once could. But white men were as helpless with boats as they were with language, could never get the hang of either. They muttered in Mikasuki in short harsh monosyllables; they hacked at cypress logs till they ruined the line of the boat so that it was hard to steer.

So, it was with great astonishment that See-ho-kee heard one morning that many, many boats, filled with white soldiers, were approaching. There would not be a fight, the Miccosukees would run if they needed to, for there were only Apayaka and three older men and two younger men, so dreadfully wounded they could not fight, so exhausted they lay in their chekes all day trying to regain their strength. See-ho-kee talked to her great-uncle, explained to him that the boats were coming, that someone needed to go out and see what the wild white men were doing, whether they sought battle.

Apayaka had the pitiful look of confusion he so often had now. He tried to listen, but his eyes roved about vaguely, and he appeared to listen to spirits rather than to See-ho-kee.

"I think I had better go and look, Uncle," she said. "I had better take two others with me, so that at least one can come back with a warning, if it comes to that."

"Good. Go and watch them, son," Apayaka said. "Tell them I will come and kill them if they want to fight."

She felt sorrowful for the old man, for she realized he couldn't bear to think of a woman going out to do a dangerous task like this, and his wavering mind had decided she was a man.

"Hurry," he suddenly said in a sharp anxious tone. "We must not let them attack us by surprise. There is danger that we would have to abandon the sick and the children."

She stared at him, realizing his mind had cleared, and she turned to enlist two other women for her mission.

Only the painted-face-woman was willing to go, for the others were already gathering essential items to carry with them if the white men came.

They went quickly to the edge of the island and saw the boats coming. *Many* boats, *Indian* boats, bought by the soldiers from Indians who had given up and gone to the West, she supposed, or perhaps stolen from Indians. The line of dugouts came with good speed toward the island, curved around it in the deep water. She was amazed to see that the soldiers had great dexterity in poling the dugouts, and the painted-face-woman turned a startled look to meet her own. "They are sailors," whispered the woman. "Do you see that their uniforms are different?"

It was true. So these were water soldiers who could use boats as well as the men of her own clan. They were different in another way. They were wary in case of attack, but they seemed to have no interest in searching the island for people despite the telltale smoke rising from the cook fires. The third dugout carried a black man, their interpreter, she assumed. She stared at him. Julius! It was Julius, once a slave of her father's, captured by the first white soldiers to come into the Ouithlacoochee Cove. He had been her family's friend whose slavery meant simply that he gave them vegetables and they gave him meat, that he reported what he had heard to them, that they protected him (if they could) against the whites. She had a strange feeling seeing Julius, now better fed and clothed than she, now heavy and healthy, yet more slavish than he had been with her clan. She saw him nod and agree when someone spoke to him. She watched his agreeable smile.

She stood boldly up and moved forward, leaving the painted-face-woman in hiding so that she may still run back with a warning.

"Julius! You are alive! We thought you had died or been given back to Georgia slave-owners."

He stared at her, shading his eyes against the sun, and the white men now watched her and the shore with attention, though no gun was lifted.

"Do I know you?" asked Julius.

"See-ho-kee."

He seemed to ponder back across the years, unable to believe she was there. "See-ho-kee! See-ho-kee!" he said to the nearest sailor. "See-ho-kee!" to the other sailors who turned to look, as if her name would tell them everything.

Quickly they had a brisk talk in Mikasuki, she telling him about her mother, about her grandmother, about Apayaka.

She was careful not to say Sam Jones, and so was he, for the peaceful tour might end in a chase and death.

"There's no need to fear, See-ho-kee. These men are not looking for a fight. We are led by John McLaughlin."

He pointed to a man in the second canoe, and she looked at the peaceful face of the leader. It was still very strange to look at a white person, and she had turbulent spasms in her stomach as she stared.

The canoes were moving westward, and she suddenly realized her duty was to find out why. Where were they going? Whom did they plan to attack? She must get all possible information to take back to Apayaka, because to the west were many other groups including the Prophet's village and Hospetarke's people.

"Who is it they look for? Whom do they wish to fight?" she called.

The white men still looked at her with smiling interested faces, with no belligerence.

"They are not fighting," said Julius. His Mikasuki was clumsy now, hard to follow. She ran alongside the dugout now, hoping to get information.

"John McLaughlin," she said. "It is a strange name, a softer name than most white names. What does it mean?"

Julius roared out a question to John McLaughlin, who turned and smiled. He answered. "He says Lake Man or one from the lake," Julius told her.

"Oh. But they don't want to fight?"

"No."

"But what is it they want to do?"

Julius smiled. "John McLaughlin wants to be the first man to cross the Everglades, east to west, by boat."

She hadn't time to consider this strange wish properly, for the boats were pulling away.

"Is your leader a mad man? Doesn't he know all of us have done this, down to the smallest child?"

"He probably knows you have done it, but he will be the first *white* man to do it. And he is not mad."

"If he is not mad, does he do this because he is a lake man, compelled to travel in watery places?"

"I don't know. He is a white man who must be the first to do it."

It was something See-ho-kee could not understand. John McLaughlin's need to win, his competitive spirit against other white men was incomprehensible.

"He has a private demon?" She was talking in a loud voice now that the boats were farther away.

"I think so," Julius called back. "All of them have demons of some kind." He grinned at her, and she laughed. But still she liked John McLaughlin, for he turned occasionally toward her and smiled, and he didn't appear to be pressed by a demon.

"His demon is worse than most, because he must cross water all his life. He is Lake Man. You remember who I am, See-ho-kee? I am King's Gift."

She nodded, and both of them laughed.

Now Julius waved a friendly farewell and began poling again. See-ho-kee watched till they left. John McLaughlin. A name almost as musical as a Mikasuki word, with only a hiccup of the white man's abrupt speech in it.

She understood John McLaughlin, not why he was in a hurry but because he was the only white man who had undertaken something big for the pleasure of it, without destroying a thing. Other white men would have built a road.

When she and the painted-face-woman went back, she told them, "There was a good man named John McLaughlin, who does not want to kill, who is a man driven by a demon that forces him across the waters from east to west."

They thought about this for a while, and all agreed that they felt sorry for John McLaughlin.

twenty-nine

Early the next morning Chakaika-dime-man came, whistling a warning so that they would not shoot him, and everyone gathered about him in the dim winter light. His arm hung at an odd, twisted angle, so sorely wounded that See-ho-kee knew at once that no medicine could ever make his hand of any use again.

"Harney came with his men," Chakaika-dime-man said in his peculiar accent, so charming before, so touched with horror now that See-ho-kee hated to listen, yet *had* to listen. "They came in many boats; they took revenge. Harney has killed us; he has captured us; he has scattered us to the four winds."

She suddenly comprehended the terrible meaning of John McLaughlin's mad mission. Now white men could roam the swamps as easily as red men.

"They came in boats. *They dressed like Indians.* We were ready to welcome them until we saw them at the last minute. It was a great surprise. Their faces were stained with hickory hulls or perhaps with white magic. Until they were upon us, we didn't see their blue eyes."

See-ho-kee felt sick, remembering the blue holes in a soldier's face, and that horror returned to her, added to her sick fear that it was the end; the end of her family had at last begun. *You have thought this before,* she told herself. *You thought this when Pi-co-yee died, when Hitchiti-hajo was wounded, when Nuff-kee died, when you had to bring the children across the swamp. And still we go on.* The sick terror slowly faded.

"Harney captured some men, killed some. He let the women and children live. Chakaika saw at the beginning he was captured, and he smiled and held out his hand in friendship and surrendered to a soldier. The soldier shot him down. They captured some warriors. They *hanged* them. Then they hanged Chakaika's body alongside the others, where his mother, his wife, his sister could see him swinging in the moonlight. They shot me, thought I was dead, and I rolled away into the shadow, hid under an old canoe hull till they left with their prisoners. I hear Chakaika's mother now, crying in a small voice to his spirit. I see his huge body hanging like a slaughtered animal and I hear her cry. His wife and his sister made no sound. They stared at him and then they stared at Harney, thinking evil of him."

As Chakaika-dime-man told his story, he nursed his dangling arm, tried to support it so it would hurt less, but his good hand quickly moved away each time. He began looking pitifully to each face. *Who will take me to her cookfire?* his expression said. *I am a man who can bring no meat. Who will take me to her cheke? I am a man without dimes.*

For things were different now. In recent times a strange Indian would have been welcomed like a brother, if he were not from an enemy tribe, but now the struggle to live had become so desperate that Chakaika-dime-man's presence might make a child go hungry. Eyes looked away. They listened with courtesy; a woman handed him a cup of sofkee; another eased him down to a feed sack she had spread on the ground as a bed. When he turned his anguished face toward each one though, the eyes looked away.

See-ho-kee felt a warning from a spirit hovering near, whose spirit she couldn't sense. She looked quickly around, settled her glance on Apayaka. She was horrified to see her uncle's face. His eyes stood out; the muscles in his face lay like ropes under the skin.

He gave a high-pitched yelp, like a battle cry, began screaming shrill and loud, over and over, scream, scream, scream, *scream.* He began stamping his feet; he shook his fists over his head; he screamed. She recognized it as a fit of fury like those that used to terrify the white men.

"I will *kill* them, I will *kill* them," he shrilled. "They hanged our brothers." His speech became incoherent, his yelps softer, and suddenly he went down in a faint. He lay still for a moment while See-ho-kee knelt anxiously over him.

He came to with a gasp, as if he had stopped breathing for a while. Calm now, sensible, he sat up and looked at Chakaika-dime-man. "How did our brothers act in the face of death?" he asked.

"They faced the white men. They would not beg. They would not agree to go for other Indians. They looked their hatred without words. They died without sound. Nor did the women cry, except for the small cries from the old mother. The women watched without words."

"Good," said Apayaka. "The white men didn't get satisfaction in killing them."

He was calm now. There were no more cries about killing, for he knew he could not kill them now, with the few warriors left to him.

The talk went on for a short time, but Chakaika-dime-man sent more and more pleading looks about him, and the women were slipping away, one at a time, to return to their cook fires, to cook whatever they had. See-ho-kee stood in painful thought, thinking of what would happen to Yaha Chatee if he were hurt and in another village where hunger also stalked the weak. But if she did welcome the dime-man, what if she had only food enough for her two boys and for Anatho-yee to eat? She must be free enough to go get food too, and she would be tied to her cheke to nurse him back to strength. And even then, what good would he be? She must not be ruled by foolish compassion.

While she agonized over the plight of Chakaika-dime-man, the painted-face-woman, who had waited modestly outside the circle, now nudged her way in. She looked down at Chakaika-dime-man who had come and gone from her cheke like an arrogant chief for many years. Now he was useless to her, a burden to anyone who took him.

"Come," she said, holding out her hand. He looked up, his face less anguished, and he rolled over on his good arm and tried to rise. Helping hands reached down.

The villagers watched as the two walked to her cheke, she with a supporting arm around his waist.

"Well, I *couldn't* take him," a plaintive voice said. "I have my mother to care for and two children."

There was a rush of explanations, voices interrupting other voices, in the rude way white people talked.

"And what about *her*?" See-ho-kee asked. "Her living comes from men who come to visit, and now that will not happen."

They were silent as they thought of it.

"She is a better woman than we are," See-ho-kee said.

In a moment they nodded their agreement. It was a new thought.

thirty

Halleck Tustenuggee, cunning and swift, punished the soldiers and white settlers wherever he could find them. These actions had a great effect on Hitchiti-hajo, who had become a sober, quiet man, moved by hatred and desire for revenge. When he and the other men of the clan came into camp at night, worn out and haggard with the constant running, the others ate and slept. Hitchiti-hajo hunched over the fire and thought. One night when everyone in camp except Hitchiti slept, his voice woke See-ho-kee. He was still at the fire and he sang an old song softly. She listened, her spirit straining in the direction of her brother who lately had become so remote that even when they talked, she felt he was elsewhere.

She sat up and looked around at her sleeping family.

Yaha Chatee slept with his arm covering his face as if he didn't want to look for the dangers the night hid. Nobody stirred. All slept on as if the great war song were a chant to calm a baby. Only her brother sang, yet she heard a chorus of voices; she heard a drum; she heard the anguished shouts of the leaders; she heard the singing of a thousand warriors; she felt the beat of their feet hitting the earth; she smelled the smells of hate and fear; she felt the heat of bodies. All this from a soft, slow song from her brother. She arose and searched for the shoes she had made him, had planned to give him tomorrow, found them, went to the fire and squatted by his side.

She waited till he finished the song, waited till he wished to speak. At last he said, "My sister can't sleep tonight?"

"I am worried for my brother," she said, equally gentle and formal. "My brother has a sickness he has not described to me."

He smiled at her; she had caught him the way she used to do when they were children and he tried to have a secret. He nodded. "I am like a turtle. I have no enemy until one attacks me; *then* I bite him to death. But I want to be a mountain lion. I want to *attack.* I want to spend my life seeking and killing the white men. This is what sickens me, seeing my family running in the swamps like frightened deer, seeing you trying to care for your children without a proper place to live. I cannot laugh any more. I cannot think of marriage, and now the woman I had thought to marry has married another man."

Oh. Here was the added hurt. She knew the woman, a friend of her family, in Halleck Tustenuggee's clan, a good woman, lost now to her brother.

"I am sorry for your hurts."

"And I am sorry for yours, Little Sister."

They were quiet as they thought of the evil shadows cast over their family by the white seekers of all the land.

She gave him his new shoes, and his face lightened for a moment. "These shoes will help me to catch the enemy. He will not escape me now."

"I hope so, Brother."

At last he was ready to tell her what he planned. "Tomorrow I will go to join Halleck Tustenuggee. There are still enough warriors with him that he can attack and win, and he doesn't wait for the white man to come. He seeks him out."

She wanted to argue. *Halleck Tustenuggee cannot look at the bitter truth. The white men are over us like clouds of birds, and we must hide to live.* That is what she wanted to say. *You will see, Brother, Halleck seeks capture; Halleck seeks death.*

But she kept quiet. He must follow his vision as she followed hers.

"After all," Hitchiti-hajo said, "Coosa Tustenuggee and Halleck Tustenuggee are also Miccosukees. I see it as my duty to go where I can do most to defeat the whites. With them I will see a lot of action. And what is happening here? Warriors are drifting away. Now there are more women and children with Apayaka than fighting men."

She couldn't keep quiet. "Apayaka has been right every time, and he is right now. He will fight if he must, but now is the time to stay alive, lest all Miccosukees left in Florida be lost and forgotten, so that the white man will find our bones and look at them and say, 'Whose bones are these? Who were these people?' "

Hitchiti shook his head. "If we fight only when we're cornered, then we fight the way the white man plans, not the way *we* wish. This way they will kill us all. Or worse, we will be captured and sent to the West."

"Will you speak to Apayaka?"

"No. We have thought it out, and we go in the morning, Eemathle and I." Both her brothers!

She felt mourning take over her spirit, heard mourning cries in her thoughts as if Hitchiti-hajo had died. She could not speak to him of this, and again they sat in silence, each free to pursue thoughts without interruption by the other, a strong feeling to have between brother and sister.

Then her mother's spirit came and told her, "Look hard at your brother."

See-ho-kee stared at him, saw his spirit rise and go west, hovering over the swamp. "Thlicklin," she called. Immediately his body and spirit became one again, and she saw him look at her strangely.

She arose, reached a hand to his shoulder. "I will miss my brother."

"And I will miss my sister."

In the morning he and Eemathle were gone, and she told the family where they were. There was much head-shaking and some anger, but for See-ho-kee and her children there was only sadness. Yaha Chatee's wistful look told her that he wished he might have gone too.

In the next few days See-ho-kee lived in torment, waiting to hear that Hitchiti-hajo had either been captured and sent to the West or had been killed, and that his spirit traveled now with the dead on the great road westward. However, news came in every few days, and no such thing occurred. Gradually she relaxed and paid more attention to her work.

The first news that came said that Halleck Tustenuggee's plan to plant crops last winter had succeeded. It was safe to plant, he had told his villagers and other Indians; as long as they kept south of Pease Creek, they would not be molested. Now those great gardens with an incredible amount of food were nearly ready, and harvest would begin soon.

Joy spread through Apayaka's family when they heard this. In a few more days Hitchiti-hajo came, ready to barter food for guns, for Halleck Tustenuggee planned to attack and attack, as soon as the crops were safely in. "We want muskets,'' Hitchiti said. ''A Colt's rifle exploded and killed a man and crippled another. But we'll take Colt's rifles if you won't sell muskets.'' See-ho-kee took comfort in seeing her brother, trading goods with them for another group of Miccosukees. It was so normal and real, her fears dissipated. They had a small feast in celebration, and Hitchiti-hajo went back, his horse pulling a stretcher loaded with guns. He would transfer these weapons to a boat and take them to Halleck. ''I promise you,'' Hitchiti told them, ''many boatloads of food will come to you soon. As soon as the crops are ready, we will pick your part first, even before our own.''

The tension between See-ho-kee's shoulders let go when she heard these words, for she knew that now there would be food for the children. There also would be food enough so that her own health might return. She was deeply embarrassed that she had not yet become pregnant. Her monthly period had ceased to come long ago, even before her grandmother died, and her grandmother had comforted her by saying it was merely the lack of adequate food. ''It will come back,'' her grandmother told her, ''and you will have your babies.''

But it had not happened. Each month she lived a lie for three days, withdrawing from her neighbors, eating alone from separate dishes, living out the age-old ritual of menstruation as if it were really happening. Nobody besides herself knew the truth. Sometimes she wondered whether other half-starved women acted out the same guilty lie, but she dared not ask anyone.

thirty-one

A bad thing happened. The white general sent his promise to all the free Indians that he would reward them with much money for coming in, for surrendering and agreeing to go to the West. There was immediate consternation in Apayaka's village, for they knew very well that the hungry ones, the wandering homeless ones, had little resistance; they would soon give in to this lure. Coosa Tustenuggee had gone already, had accepted five thousand dollars for bringing his sixty warriors, who received their share of the money.

The swamps were becoming more lonely, more threatening, as their brothers took money and disappeared. Some surrendered. Some tried to negotiate. Coacoochee went to Fort Cummings, dressed in the costume he had stolen from a troupe of Shakespearean actors near St. Augustine. He had saved the costumes for a time worthy of such elegance, and his men were also beautifully dressed in costumes.

This was the prank that Coacoochee loved best, to come to the enemy fort, dressed beautifully, strident in his demands for food and liquor, quick in his promises to do whatever they wished. He loved watching the white soldiers seethe at his insults, helpless to do anything to him for fear of bringing the other Indians down upon them.

Fort Cummings had a surprise for Coacoochee though, for here he found his captive daughter, whom he had believed dead, and she ran to him with her hands full of bullets and powder she had found and hidden for him. His arrogant face crumpled, and he wept.

The white general sent out more money to persuade the Indians to come in. Many Indians came to beg food and liquor, intending to get by for a while without giving in. This tactic was despised by Apayaka who declared to See-ho-kee that he would starve in the swamps before he would do that. She didn't feel so sure. If they did actually run out of food, and if her three children were near to death, she didn't know what she would do, but secretly she feared she would surrender. These days her fear loomed almost as large as her hatred of the white soldiers.

She suggested this to Apayaka, and he shook his head sternly. "It is better to kill a white man for food than to beg him for it. Your spirit sickens when you beg. You bow to him; you try to please him. You swallow your hatred, and it eats out your guts."

She knew he was right, and she tried to put her fear away.

Meanwhile Coacoochee and fifteen of his best men went from fort to fort and lived on good food and liquor under pretense that they would eventually bring in all their people.

At last, in the spring of 1841, when Coacoochee and his men had thirty days to bring in his people, the white major captured them, though the thirty days had not yet passed, and then a new white chief, Colonel Worth, came to give Coacoochee warning. "I give you friendly greeting," Colonel Worth said, according to a messenger from Coacoochee's village. "I welcome you and your fifteen men here. But you must send for your people, and if they do not come, we will hang all of you by the neck."

The messenger wept as he told them what Coacoochee said about the white man. "Coacoochee said that the white men had pretended to be friends, but then he had tortured the Indian women and children, had indeed tortured all Yakitisee people by forcing them off their land. The white man offered his hand, and the Indian took it, but the white man was full of trickery and deceit. His good words were lies. When Coacoochee asked for only a little land down south to care for his family and for burial, the white man refused him and jailed him. He escaped and they caught him again. He told the white man his heart felt as if he had irons caught in it, but the white man didn't care."

Then the runner said that Coacoochee would not go out on the sad mission to get his people; preferred to remain a prisoner. Instead he sent pleas to his people to come to the white side, to give in, to prepare to go west. In his message he told his people that he was heartsick. He advised his old comrades to build a fire, to dance around it in the moonlight, to listen just before the break of day to the spirits of their dead, and there they would find courage to surrender.

It was terrifying to Apayaka's people to consider the effect that Coacoochee's messages to the other Indians would have. If the others broke and ran, this small group would be pursued like rabbits before dogs, and they would die, separate from each other, lonely and afraid. Coacoochee's messengers must not be allowed to come.

As was their custom, the Miccosukees considered their responses a long time before speaking. Apayaka spoke first. "When they come to ask us to surrender, we will kill them. Go back and tell them that when Indians come to ask, guns will tell them hello."

The war became even more dreadful, as brothers warned brothers to stay away.

The villagers agreed to Apayaka's thought. They were surprised when the news bearer told them that Halleck, Tigertail, Octiarche and others were planning a meeting near Fort King to consider exactly what they had agreed upon.

"When you see them," said Apayaka, "tell them that messengers from Coacoochee will die here. Tell them they must do the same thing."

The man left, and soon the news came back that the meeting near Fort King ended with the same decision, but that when it came right down to it, they were unable to kill a messenger and sent him away with a strong scolding.

By August almost all of Coacoochee's people had surrendered.

Worse, Coacoochee persuaded old, tremulous Hospetarke to come in for council, and again Colonel Worth betrayed a trust. They imprisoned Hospetarke and his fifteen warriors. See-ho-kee heard that the sick and tired old man seemed almost glad to give up, the struggle had been so long and hard. Again she marveled at her great-uncle, who was even older, whose battles had been just as hard, whose walks as long.

The next news runner told them that Ouithlacoochee Cove, their old home which so often appeared in See-ho-kee's dreams, was under attack again. Many Yakitisee who had gone to the Everglades in their retreat after the Okeechobee fight had given up ever finding peace and safety and had returned to the cove. It was as if the war had never happened, as if the first time at the cove were a dream of what was actually happening now. See-ho-kee tried not to think of what was happening there lest it weaken her for her struggle here. It was better to remember Ouithlacoochee, to remember the real house made of logs as Indians used to build them, to remember the comfort and safety, to remember laughter that was boisterous and happy rather than subdued and wry.

Coacoochee was out of prison now, the messenger said. He was looking for all old friends, now that his own people were in. "He will know not to come here," Apayaka said grimly. He did know, and he never came.

In the fall of 1841 all the people Coacoochee had lured to Fort Brooke left by boat. It was the end of them so far as See-ho-kee and her family were concerned.

A week later several chiefs, led by Alligator, and their people left the same way.

Now Halleck Tustenuggee and Apayaka were left.

thirty-two

Halleck's food didn't come, for his warriors now ran for their lives.

Apayaka's people wandered, then settled, and wandered again. For a year they did this, always drifting downward to the earth, living like animals, sometimes forgetting who they were, who their beloved men had been, what their legends consisted of. The Breathmaker guarded them against madness. See-ho-kee's mother was often with her now, and sometimes her grandmother's spirit appeared briefly and pointed at something to help her focus her attention on what must be done to save the children. This was the thought that kept her strong: *I am the center. I will save the children.* When things were most desperate, she belabored Yaha Chatee out of his exhaustion to go find food. She nagged at him mercilessly when he was tempted to join the languid men who spent the day at the square, trying to talk through their plight. She saw clearly that talk didn't help like action. And when Yaha Chatee came back with fish or game, she praised the quality of the meat, for he needed this to restore his spirit.

The thin bodies of the three children kept her spirit strong.

Wherever they wandered, Hitchiti-hajo found them. Sometimes he came with two or three friends, and they bragged of their exploits till See-ho-kee feared Yaha Chatee would join them. The white soldiers searched everywhere for Halleck, Hitchiti told them. This lifted the pressure on Apayaka's people. See-ho-kee had a sudden appreciation for Halleck's warriors.

On a bright spring day in 1842 See-ho-kee watched the last birds gather to fly north, and she welcomed the coming summer. She planted pumpkin seeds in a field which was only roughly worked, and she asked the medicine man to use his power to let the seeds survive, to let them work till the pumpkins were yellow. She was satisfied after his incantations and use of treasures from the medicine bag that it would work, that they would have pumpkin bread next fall. She looked up and saw a runner, an older man who steadily jogged across the high land. He returned her wave with a nod and headed directly for the square. She dropped her planting stick and ran to hear the news, eager for good news, fearful of bad.

The runner had a strong sense of what was proper, and he waited till the men were seated in their place, till the women and children huddled on the split-log benches where they were allowed to sit if there were no fast. It was good, See-ho-kee thought, that at least the war had brought this, the women's privilege of listening.

"Halleck Tustenuggee has been attacked by the white

soldiers," the runner told them. "They are scattered like deer and now they run through the swamps, wild and confused. The attack took place in that beautiful hammock southeast of Peliklakaha."

There were nods from many of the listeners, for all remembered the hammock and the times they had stopped there to rest during their wandering.

"How did they find our brothers?" asked Apayaka grimly.

"There were Indians friendly to the whites and there were Negroes who wanted white friendship, and those men led them into the dark hidden places in the jungle. Do not forgive them for this treachery."

Howls of anger interrupted the speaker and quickly died away so the rest of the news might be told.

"I was near Halleck himself," said the runner, his eyes glistening with emotion. "Halleck screamed his rage, just as you have done. He screamed an order to us. 'Kill them *first,*' he said. And we did. The Indian and Negro traitors went down in the first barrage of shots. This gave the white soldiers a moment to shoot at us without return fire, and many of our people were hurt.

"Then we turned our guns on the soldiers. But they are much more skillful than they used to be; they use the trees for protection as we have taught them. And they had many men, at least four hundred. No matter how many whites we kill, more come to fight us."

This was not surprising to See-ho-kee. Years ago her vision had shown her this.

"While we fought toward the front, some white soldiers went to our rear and attacked, and our forces scattered; our resistance was broken. Still, we managed to escape, but now we have nothing. We are broken in spirit and body. I am the only one strong enough to come here without food or rest."

"Where are the others?" asked Apayaka.

"Halleck is at Fort King having council with the white colonel. Colonel Worth. This is a white man's name that means *of great value.*" His grin was wry, and the ghost of it touched the other faces. "Halleck is trying to bargain for food and liquor."

See-ho-kee sighed. When they came to bargaining for liquor, it was the end.

"Do you know Hitchiti-hajo?" See-ho-kee called, no longer able to wait for one of the men to ask. Nobody frowned at her, for all wanted to know this.

"Yes. He is not hurt. He is like the others — hungry and tired. We lost our camp; we lost all our goods; we lost many weapons."

It was a double hurt, for the white men no doubt had destroyed all the vegetables in their path.

But her brother was not wounded. What more could See-ho-kee ask for in such times as these?

thirty-three

Hitchiti-hajo did not come to them, as they hoped he would. Rather, he and a few others of Halleck's men looked for small groups of whites to attack, for small settlements to raid, for abandoned forts, for whatever had been discarded. They acted out of desperate bravado, aware that whatever they did now was useless, but they were unwilling to surrender to the white savages. Apayaka now sent his own runners out for news, for Halleck could no longer keep communications open.

Halleck still talked to Colonel Worth, still bargained for food for his wives and children. This worked for a few days.

Their runner came in and told the Miccosukees all this. "There is even bigger news," he said, pleased to be able to tell it. "Halleck's people have all been invited in for drinking and feasting, for considering the best way to work out our problems.''

Apayaka stepped out in the square, his small frail figure unimpressive, his face wild. ''Go back now. Go and tell them not to do this. This is a white man's treachery.''

The runner looked chastened. ''It is too late, Beloved Man. They have already gone. When I left there, they were gathering for their journey to Fort King.'' Apayaka wept quietly.

The runner rested one day and started back to see what had happened, but another runner had to replace him for the return trip, so exhausted had he become.

Again, Apayaka was right.

The feasting, drinking, and dancing at Fort King had lasted only a little while when Colonel Worth's soldiers surrounded them and took them prisoner.

Halleck raged helplessly and fainted from strong emotion.

As usual, See-ho-kee listened with deep anxiety about Hitchiti-hajo. Had he escaped? No, the runner told them. He also had been captured. All Apayaka's efforts had been in vain; the advice he and See-ho-kee had given Hitchiti, cautioning him not to go to a white man's council, ever again, had been ignored. ''Why did he do this?'' several people asked at once.

He believed Halleck had a plan, that Halleck wanted them there to fight, wanted them to get white men's food. He is a Halleck man now.''

''And Eemathle?''

''He, too, was captured.''

In this way she lost her brothers.

Apayaka became almost demented. For the next two months she stayed close to him, cared for the old man tenderly, angrily fended off those of the clan who remarked about the confusion in his thinking. Once she even quarreled with her husband, beloved as he was. Yaha Chatee suggested in a soft tentative voice that it was time for Apayaka to sit as retired chief, ready to help in councils of course, but with less authority. See-ho-kee blazed her wrath at him.

"No, my husband, you will not say this to the others; you will not prepare my uncle for death."

"But they suggested it to *me*," he protested, his voice still soft, his face anxious for her understanding.

"Then ignore them for the rabbits they are. They are fools. Let them talk. Remind them who led us out of danger many times. Remind them that my brother Hitchiti-hajo would be here *now* if he had listened to our uncle."

"This is true, my wife. But it is also true that he is more confused than he used to be, and often he seems as mad as a dog with summer disease."

She sighed, searched for words to show him a greater truth. "He is thinking of Hitchiti, just as I am. He is seeing what will happen soon. He is seeing Hitchiti and Eemathle on their way to Tampa, then on the ship, then on the long walk. He sees Hitchiti crying for us; he feels his heart pulled with pain of leaving. He sees him eating bad food and sickening. He sees him dying. I too see all this, but I am strong enough to stand more than he can. You will see. Apayaka's mind will come back, then leave, according to the sorrow he must suffer. Now it is bad. Next week it will be better. In the meantime, we must trust him and care for him."

After this talk Yaha Chatee watched the old man, forgave him when he forgot something he had just said with great oratory and passion, defended him against the complainers. See-ho-kee drew close to her husband in love. She could no longer have good talks with her father who was busy with his second family, but she knew he suffered too.

It came true, as she had pictured it to Yaha Chatee. Halleck Tustenuggee, with forty men and eighty women, was sent to Tampa. The runner who told them the sad news also told them there would be a great council at Cedar Key; the whites and reds would end their war.

"We will not go," said Apayaka. A few people complained, for they hated to miss the free food and liquor, and then too, they said, maybe the old man's mind was too weak now to make a good decision.

Yaha Chatee stood in council and said he would kill the first man to start for council against Apayaka's command. They heard him silently and went about their work.

This was in July, 1842; there were no crops. See-ho-kee was twenty-one and still childless. She was middle-aged now, for most women lived to forty-two or -three.

thirty-four

A young boy came in the middle of summer, 1842, to tell that Halleck Tustenuggee had been sent with his forty warriors and eighty women to New Orleans.

Sadness spread across the camp like fog, and See-ho-kee knew that it was as she had expected. Thlicklin was gone from her forever, unless she too would be captured and taken to Arkansas. She did not believe this would happen, for the white soldiers apparently had given up their pursuit of Apayaka and seemed willing for him to live on in the swamps.

Billy Bowlegs, now chief of the Yakitisee, was on his way to Cedar Key for council with Tiger Tail and Octiarche and the white Colonel Worth. Again Apayaka had advised against it. Never try to deal with the white men. That was his creed. But Billy Bowlegs, after listening with careful respect to the old man, had told him he must go; somebody needed to make Colonel Worth understand that they wanted only a little land in the glades, that they didn't wish to fight any longer, that they *would* fight if they were forced to the West. The young messenger told Apayaka of meeting Billy Bowlegs on the way to the council.

"We don't wish to hear of that," said the old man. "Tell us about Halleck. How did his people act in front of the captors?" Apayaka trembled all the time now; his mind was often cluttered with things over and done with; his hands fumbled at whatever work he tried. But today his eyes were bright and piercing, his manner certain. He ignored his trembling hands. "Were they brave?"

"They were brave. Most of them said not a word; most of them turned away from the white men in embarrassment over their wounds and their capture."

"How did Halleck Tustenuggee act?"

"He was very angry. Colonel Worth had promised him a letter which was to say that he was a brave warrior, that he had done all he could do in defending his homeland, a good letter about his courage. When the letter didn't come, he screamed and cursed the soldiers and tried to reach them. Halleck said, 'I have been hunted like a wolf, and now I am to be sent away like a dog.' The soldiers grabbed him and held him. Then one read him a paper; it was the letter he had asked for. He was a brave man who loved his people and his land, and he had fought till the last moment. That's what the letter said. He heard the letter and wept."

There was silence while the small group of people around Apayaka and See-ho-kee thought about Halleck, their own eyes also wet with tears, for it was painful to think of the tall, thin, smiling man in such a state.

"And Hitchiti-hajo?" See-ho-kee had to know the last information she could get about her brother.

"He behaved well. He refused to speak. He would not look at the white soldiers. He walked past them as if he were circling rattlesnakes, and he did not say a word while I was near him."

"Did he look sad?"

The boy considered. "No. He looked angry and unforgiving. Eemathle was the same."

"Good," grunted Apayaka.

Then the war ended.

A month from the time Hitchiti left for the West, Colonel Worth announced the end of the war. Those Indians who agreed to live in the southern part of Florida would be allowed to stay. Billy Bowlegs was jubilant. He had bargained hard for this, and now at last they settled and began building houses and planting gardens. "You will see," Billy Bowlegs said. "A white messenger will come to tell us."

Apayaka said stoutly that he would do nothing to undermine the treaty, but that his people should be wary of white men's promises. He himself did not believe the war was over.

"We must send out messengers to all Indians that we will live with the agreement and that we want them to do the same," Billy Bowlegs said. Apayaka agreed they must make this effort.

"We will try," he said. "We have tried before though, and the white men have always held a snake in their hands when we shook hands."

See-ho-kee wanted to believe it was really over; she worked harder than anybody else in camp to begin their new life. But in her heart she knew her great-uncle was right.

Two months later Colonel Worth captured Tiger Tail by treachery. In the winter Tiger Tail died on the way to Arkansas. There was no retaliation.

It took them many tense months to realize that the war had actually ended.

thirty-five

Before the first subtle signs of fall came to south Florida, a white man arrived with an announcement from Colonel Worth.

"We will not meet him," Apayaka said.

Billy Bowlegs, the new chief of all the Yakitisee, came; he was soft and persuasive. "We *must* meet him, Beloved Man. He will tell us where our lands are, where we may hunt in safety, where we may live under their protection."

The old man resisted stubbornly, and finally they compromised, for even with his confusion Apayaka could see that these ten broken men could no longer resist. They would listen from the hammock. They would not meet the white man face to face; they would never meet the white man face to face again if Apayaka had his way.

And so they sat, listening behind the trees, taking their proper places as if they were on the square-ground. The white man spoke; the translator roared. Hostilities had ceased, they heard. The Indians may live in this land: south of the line from the mouth of Tallockchopco, up the left bank to the fork of the southern branch, and following that stream to the northern edge of Lake Istokpoga, down the east side of the lake to the creek emptying into the Kissimmee River, down the left bank of the Kissimmee to Lake Okeechobee, south through the lake and Everglades to Shark River, to the Gulf.

Each part of the line was described until it was clear to everyone there, and there was acknowledgment that it must be this way. Nobody argued or talked back, and only Apayaka shook his head with rage when the translator told them that these lands were assigned for hunting and planting temporarily. *Temporarily.* When she heard this, See-ho-kee knew the uncertainties that would follow her the rest of her life.

She looked at the people, so few of them now: gaunt, dirty, skeletal, silent people, who spoke only when it was necessary.

It became a problem to her to see her family like this, not healthy and brave as they had been when she was a child. She tried to think what could be done about it. Now, the meeting over, they still sat, unable to overcome their lethargy.

The problem was not lack of food, though there still was a constant struggle to have enough. The whole group worked at this job. The problem was a malaise, a drooping of spirit, a lack of caring. Even Yaha Chatee was cursed with the sickness. *All* the adults had the sickness, she realized, after she had studied them and thought about it. No longer did Apayaka's medicine put fire and life into them. "I will tell them," she thought. She tried once or twice to tell the people about it, tried to help them to rouse themselves, to begin their lives again, to prepare their children for a better way to live. They stared at her dully and couldn't think of a response.

She knew they would live, if they could cure themselves of their hopelessness. All was not lost. Here, after all, was Anatho-yee, who was thin but healthy and strong, her short legs muscled from long walks. And here were Little Mountain's two boys, now her own sons, the older one of whom was this minute protecting Anatho-yee from a hornet.

And here in her belly she carried her first child.

The future was no grimmer than the past; the future was guaranteed in these children.

She wandered away from them, stayed by herself in the swamp, watched the turtle, watched the alligator, watched the fish. Took no food, no water. Sat on the damp earth in the sultry heat and waited. Listened and watched for good or bad signs.

When it was nearly dark, when the danger of being attacked by an alligator or bitten by a snake was greatest, her mother came. "Tell the children your grandparents' names," her mother said. Her mother had taken on the beauty of her younger self, her face full, her eyes bright and happy. She left at once, though See-ho-kee felt her protection as she made her way through the dark swamp, for no wild animal came near.

She gathered all the children at once, took them to the only fire in the village, told them to listen to her as they used to do in the old times. She looked with some nervousness at the older women, for she was doing a grandmother's work now. No one objected, and one or two women looked at her with dull interest.

"My mother's name was Pi-co-yee," See-ho-kee said. "That was before her first son was born. Then she was called Hopoy's mother, but her first name stayed within her breast to help her remember the times when she was a girl. My father's name is Coosa-amathle, a name given him after he took his first scalp, long ago in the north part of Florida. In that place the white man Andrew Jackson burned the homes of Indian family groups, and later my father killed a white man in retaliation."

She paused. She did not want to think of or talk about the wars. She wanted them only to know about where they had come from, so their spirit would come back to them.

"My grandmother's name was . . . " she paused and stared into the dark, past the fire. "My grandmother's name before she had her first child was . . . . "

She didn't know the name. Yet she must have heard it at some time or other. The name was lost. She bowed her head to hide the panic on her face, tried to think of other names of the old people, could not. The names were lost.

The villages. She would tell the villages' names.

"In the old times before our fathers and mothers came to Florida, they lived on the Chat-to-ho-che River. The river fed their land. Say that name: CHAT-TO-HO-CHE."

"Chat-to-ho-che."

The word came in a whisper, like a bit of wind on a dry leaf.

"No," she said. "Don't be afraid. We will say these names in a big voice. We will even *sing* the names of the villages where they lived."

She chanted, "Cow-e-tugh." She paused. "Now say that name."

"Cow-e-tugh." The little dry whisper again, but caught in the same rhythm she had given them.

"These are the old villages of the Yakitisee," she said, "villages of the Miccosukees, the Uchees . . . " She saw a small boy lift his head in sudden interest, for his father was Uchee. " . . . the Tallahassees, the Alachuas, the Choctaws, the Chickasaws, the Muscogees. All those people and more too. These are the village names. Say them in a singing voice."

"COW-E-TUH-TAL-LAU-HAS-SEE!"

The whispered echo followed.

"No," said See-ho-kee. "It is safe now to sing in a loud voice. The white man is not here. Do it right. I will see your arms scratched if you don't do it right."

"CUS-SE-TUH!" she sang.

The children whispered in concert, their eyes watching her with terror. Now she realized that the children had been hushed too many years on pain of death. They could not sing.

"It is all right," she said. "I will sing; you will whisper."

Her chant went on, "U-chee, Oo-se-oo-chee, Che-au-hau, Hitch-e-tee, Pa-la-chooc-la, O-co-nee, Sau-woog-e-lo, Sau-woog-e-loo-che, Eu-fau-lau. Say O-CO-NEE. Many of our fathers and mothers came from there. O-CO-NEE!"

The whispers followed.

I am the center. I will lead these children out of their sorrow.

"These were the Indian towns in the northwestern part of Florida," she said. "Sing them. Sim-e-no-le-tal-lau-ha-see, Au-lot-che-wau, Oc-le-wau-hau thluc-co, Mic-co-sooc-e . . ."

Suddenly every child smiled, and she felt great happiness within her. "Good," she said after their whisper. "Mic-co-sooc-e." This time they chanted very softly.

She now saw that the rest of the village had gathered around them. "Tomorrow night I will tell you the stories my grandmother told me about that town," a woman volunteered.

"We will listen gladly," See-ho-kee said.

She went on with the names, listed all as she had learned them from her grandmother, and she listened with satisfaction when the dry little whispers became a song.

"We-cho-took-me.

"Tal-lau-gue chapco-pop-cau.

"Cull-oo-sau hatche."

Then she tried to name the Creek towns on the Coo-sau and Tal-la-poo-sa Rivers, and she could not remember all of them.

"Talle-see.

"Foosce-hat-che." She could not think.

"E-cun-hut-kee," chanted a man.

"Sau-va-no-gee," sang a woman. There were pauses, but the singing and whispering went on and on into the night, until at last the children fell asleep.

She began remembering the rest. They sang themselves into her mind; she knew what to say to them tomorrow. "Sing these names. Remember them, for our people lived there."

"Mook-lau-sau.

"O-che-au-po-fau.

"Ki-a-li-jee.

"Coo-sau.

"Tus-ke-gee.

"Took-au-bat-che.

"Coo-sau-dee. Nau-chee.

"Eu-fau-lau-hat-che.

"Hill-au-bee. Aut-tos-see.

"Hoith-le Waulee. Coo-loome.

"We-wo-cau. Woo-co-coie."

Say these names. Say them in a singing voice. Remember them.

"Puc-cun-tal-lau-has-see. Hook-choie.

"Eu-fau-lau. Hook-choie-oo-che.

"Au-be-coo-chee."

And when they had finished saying the names of the old towns, she would have them to learn the villages *she* had known. Pa-lat-ka. We-tump-ka. Peli-kla-ka-ha. O-ki-humky. Pico-la-ta. Ok-hol-wa-kee. Ouithla-coo-chee. A-lachua. Mic-co-sukee.

For these villages were all dead now. It was no longer dangerous to say the names.

She heard the names. She heard the children's whispers. The whispers.

The whispers.

(Remember Them)

AFTERWORD

At the end of the Second Seminole War, thirty-three Miccosukee warriors remained in Florida. There were about three hundred Seminoles left, including women and children. Many had died; many had been removed to the West. The Indians withdrew into the Everglades and lived in small family groups, separate from the rest of the tribe.

They began rebuilding their lives and families. Gradually they came back together, and the Miccosukees separated from the Seminoles and became themselves again.

Now there are about seven hundred and fifty Miccosukees in Florida, still struggling to live and to preserve their culture. They are sustained by their history of courage.

Names of People and Places in Say These Names (Remember Them)

In some cases, early spellings are used in the belief they were written with attention to phonetic differences. Words with this mark (*) are names of actual people.

*Abraham — important black interpreter from Peli-kla-ka-ha
Alachua — village during Seminole Wars
Anatho-yee — See-ho-kee's small sister
*Apayaka (also Arpeika, Sam Jones, Sam-Jones-Be-Damned, Arpieka, Aripeka, etc.) — Miccosukee chief from Okihumky
*Asi Yahola — Osceola, famous Seminole warrior
*Charley Amathla of We-tump-ka
*Bankhead, Lt. Col. James
*Billy Bowlegs — chief of Florida Seminoles at end of Second Seminole War
*Blue Snake
*John Caesar — important black leader
*Chakaika — chief of the Spanish Indians
Chakaika-dime-man
Che-au-hau — old Creek town
*Chitto Tustenuggee
*Clinch, General Duncan L.
*Coacoochee — (Wildcat) a hot-blooded and contemptuous warrior with Alachua and Miccosukee ancestry; son of Philip
*Coa Hadjo
Coo-loo-me — old Creek town
Coosa-amathle — See-ho-kee's father
*Coosa Tustenuggee
Cow-e-tugh — old Creek town
Cow-e-tuh Tal-lau-has-see — old Creek town
Cus-se-tuh — old Creek town
*Dade, Major Francis L. — leader of white soldiers at Dade Massacre. He died in the first volley from the Indians.
E-chuse-is-li-gau — old Creek town

Eemathle — See-ho-kee's brother
*Emathla — King Philip, Coacoochee's father
*Fixonechee — one of the first Indians to die in the Second Seminole War
*Gardiner, Captain George Washington
*Halleck Tustenuggee
*Halpatter-Tustenuggee — Alligator
*Harney, Lt. Col. William S. — officer who annihilated the Chakaika warriors
*Hernandez, Brig. Gen. Joseph M.
Hit-che-tee — old Creek town
Hitchiti-hajo — See-ho-kee's brother
*Holata Mico
*Holatoochee
*Hospetarke
Hopoy — boy-name of Eemathle, See-ho-kee's brother
*Illis-higher-Hadjo — medicine man
*Jesup, Major General Thomas S.
Julius
*Lechotichee
*Macomb, Major General Alexander
Marcy
*McLaughlin, Lt. John T. — first white man to lead a detachment of men across Big Cypress Swamp and the Everglades by boat
*Micanopy — a chief; village during Seminole Wars
Miccosukee — a tribe of Florida Indians, a lake, a new town in Florida
Mic-co-sooc-e — old village in Georgia; also old town in Florida
Mikasuki — language of the Miccosukees
*Captain Munroe
*Nocose Yahola
Ok-hol-wa-kee — Indian village during Seminole Wars
Okihumky — Indian village during Seminole Wars
Oose-oo-chee — old Creek town
*Octiarche

*Ote Emathla — Jumper
*Otulkethlocko — medicine man called Prophet by white people
Ouithla-coo-chee — Indian village during Seminole Wars
Ouithlacoochee Cove — now Withlacoochee Cove, in West Florida
Pa-lat-ka — Indian village during Seminole Wars
*Passacka
Peli-kla-ka-ha — village during Seminole Wars
*John Philip — Emathla's slave
Pico-la-ta — village during Seminole Wars
Pi-co-yee — See-ho-kee's mother
*Erastus Rogers
*John Ross
See-ho-kee
Thla-noo-chee — Little Mountain
Thla-noo-che au-bau-lau — old Creek town
Thlicklin — boy-name of Hitchiti-hajo, See-ho-kee's brother
*Thlocklo Tustenuggee — Tiger Tail
*Thompson, Wiley — an agent who tried to remove Florida Indians to the West. He insulted Asi Yahola, who subsequently killed him.
*Tomoka John
*Tuckose Emathla — John Hicks
Tus-ke-gee — old Creek town
U-chee — old Creek town
We-tump-ka (Wetumpkey, Wetumpky, Witamky) — village during Seminole Wars
Wetumpka Hammock, southeast of Fort Drane
*Worth, Col. William Jenkins
Yaha Chatee
*Yaholoochee
Yakitisee — Indian people
*Yuchi Billy

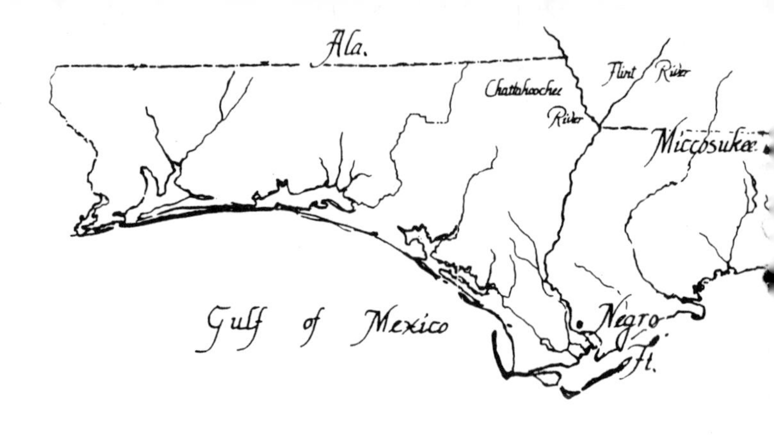

LEGEND

⊙ Beginning of Story

1. See-ho-kee's family walks to Ft. King for council. Chapter Two.
2. They move to Big Swamp and retreat to Ouithlacoochee Cove. Chapter Seven.
3. A victory is celebrated in Wahoo Swamp. Chapter Eight.
4. Second battle at Ouithlacoochee Cove. Chapter Ten.
5. They go for food at the hammock near Ft. Drane and again flee to the cove. They return to Wahoo Swamp. Chapters Eleven and Twelve.
6. Family wanders, following their warriors. Chapter Sixteen.
7. See-ho-kee takes herbs to Fort Marion at St. Augustine. Chapter Sixteen.
8. See-ho-kee and her grandmother ride south to find Apayaka. Chapters Sixteen and Seventeen.
9. They meet her brothers. Chapter Seventeen.
10. They meet Coacoochee and continue to Apayaka's camp. Chapter Eighteen.
11. See-ho-kee's walk with the children. Chapter Twenty-one.
12. Indians flee from Harney. Chapter Twenty-three.
13. They wander aimlessly. Chapters Twenty-three to Twenty-five.
14. Chakaika Battle. Chapter Twenty-nine.
15. The war ends. Chapter Thirty-five.